Are You Afraid of the Dark?

Seth C. Adams

OneMoreChapter

One More Chapter an imprint of
HarperCollins*Publishers*
The News Building
1 London Bridge Street
London SE1 9GF

www.harpercollins.co.uk

This paperback edition 2019

First published in Great Britain in ebook format
by HarperCollins*Publishers* 2019

A catalogue record for this book
is available from the British Library

ISBN: 978-0-00-834768-0

This novel is entirely a work of fiction.
The names, characters and incidents portrayed in it are
the work of the author's imagination. Any resemblance to
actual persons, living or dead, events or localities is
entirely coincidental.

Set in Minion by
Palimpsest Book Production Limited, Falkirk, Stirlingshire

Printed and bound in the UK by CPI Group (UK) Ltd,
Croydon CR0 4YY

For Mom and Dad. Always. None of this would be happening if not for your unwavering love and support.

Chapter One

1.

The whisper-rustle of the grass and trees preceded him, like the conspiratorial murmurings of a gathering mob. Then the bloodied man appeared through the low-hanging branches and thick shrubbery, as if birthed from the trembling foliage.

He stopped when he saw Reggie. His hands pressed to his stomach where the blood soaked through. The scarlet blotch, thick and wet, made Reggie think of an ink stain spreading through the fabric of a nice starched dress shirt.

The man's face was sweaty and pale. His breath was laboured, but he seemed otherwise calm and serene. Not as if he were bleeding to death, but rather as if he'd just entered a room at a party where he was a distinguished guest.

The man tried a smile; grimaced, stumbled.

Reggie set down the stick he'd been carrying and

dropped the rock he'd been launching at wasp nests like a missile. He jogged over to the tall man.

The bloodied man staggered against a stout pine, leaned against it, slid down to a sitting position like a morning runner taking a break on a park bench. Reggie knelt down to offer the man what help he could. It was what you did when someone was in trouble and needed help.

The man stopped him with an upraised hand.

'*No ambulance ...*' he coughed. '*No police ...*'

He reached into his jacket for something. The effort was too great. He toppled over on his side; rolled over on his back. Looked up into the sky. Blinking, staring up as if at something grand and imposing.

The dusk-red sun shone off the blood in bright daggers of light, so that it seemed almost an astronomical phenomenon. Something caught by Hubble for science textbooks.

Then the man's eyes closed slowly, like window shutters pulled shut, and his breathing slowed also, the chest moving up and down steadily like a billows coming to rest. It was then it dawned on Reggie that this was serious shit.

He leaned over to pull the man's jacket open. Saw the bundle of money his hand was resting near in one pocket. As well as the shoulder holster strapped to the man's side, and the obsidian-black surface of the pistol there.

Reggie wondered which of the two – money or gun – the man had intended to grab.

He took the money, pocketed it, looked around him.

The trees, tall and silent. Summer birds twitting and fluttering from perch to perch. No others watching, only the quiet earth.

He ran home as fast as his legs had ever carried him.

2.

He charged into the house, passing the kitchen in a blur where his mom stood over the sink, the water running and dishes clinking together.

'*What're you up to?*' her voice bellowed after him as he ran down the hall to the bathroom. The cupboard doors under the sink opened on squeaky hinges, making him wince.

'*Just playing!*' he yelled back at her.

The water continued to run in the kitchen. He was safe for the moment and let his breath out. He grabbed the hydrogen peroxide, sterile pads, aspirin, and gauze from the First Aid kit and shut the cupboard again.

He flashed by the kitchen as fast as the first time, back to the front door and out.

'*Be back for dinner!*' she called after him.

'*Okay!*' he hollered back, already dashing across the yard towards the garage.

Inside he found the old sled leaning against one wall, unused for years, still where his dad had last put it. Reggie found a length of rope also, knotted it around the steering grips of the sled, looped the other end around his shoulder, and hefted the sled across his back.

Peroxide, pads, aspirin bottle, and gauze bundled and rolled in the hem of his shirt, sled over his shoulder, he started back down the dirt road towards the near and yet oh-so-distant woods and the gut shot man awaiting him.

3.

The man had awakened while he'd been gone, and pulled his gun on Reggie as Reggie skid to a halt a couple yards away. The man had crawled a good ways from where Reggie had left him, speckled blood trail dotting the leaves and dirt behind him like a snail's slime tracks.

He stared at Reggie uncomprehendingly, like he was seeing an alien creature. The hand holding the pistol trembled slightly, weak, but also uncertainly, like an epileptic appendage.

'I didn't call the police,' Reggie said, wondering why he hadn't as he stood there looking into the barrel of the gun. It seemed deep and wide. A chasm of endless depth.

Calling the police was what you did when you saw someone with a gun. Calling an ambulance was what you did when you came across someone injured. He'd done neither.

Reggie thought of his dad sprawled in similar fashion, pressing his hands against a similar wound, and almost turned back then and there. It was a short run to the house, and he could be on the phone in minutes, the police and ambulance here almost as fast.

Then Reggie thought of the man's admonition, and the gun aimed at his face. Even injured, squinting and gasping through the pain, the man's face was intense. Focused. His eyes a bright arctic blue.

The man fell back again, looking up, his gun arm flopping to the ground like a reeled-in fish flopping its last breaths.

'I brought First Aid stuff,' Reggie said, stepping tentatively closer to the man.

Flapping fish-arm coming back to life, the man waved him over. Reggie didn't like it when the pistol briefly pointed his way again with the waving. He thought of the gun going off, accidentally or otherwise, and blood coming out of him like it was from the man.

Or maybe getting hit in the face by the bullet and his head exploding.

Would he feel it? he wondered. Would he feel himself die?

He knelt again by the man, unrolling his shirt like a strip of carpet and the peroxide, sterile pads, gauze, and aspirin fell out in a clutter. The man rolled over, groaning, to stare at the stuff. Then he looked up at Reggie; blinked slowly again like a man in deep, leisurely thought.

'*I'll need ... your help ...*' the man said, whispering.

Reggie nodded.

'*You took … the money …*' the man moaned. '*Means … we've got an arrangement …*'

Reggie nodded. That word – arrangement – stayed with him.

'*It won't be … pretty …*' the man rasped.

Reggie paused this time, looking at the man's bloodied middle. He thought of biology class and what was inside people. He remembered the videos they'd watched and the views given by the cameras. The pink and raw things inside everyone.

Slowly, he nodded again.

'*Then let's get this … over with …*' the man said, and the hand holding the wound disappeared in the other side of his jacket, coming back out with a switchblade. A flick of his wrist, and four inches of wicked blade glimmered back sunlight like a jewel.

4.

When it was done there was more blood, all over the place: on the forest floor, on the man, on Reggie's hands. Sticky and wet and slick. The dug-out bullet, dimpled and ruined, lay discarded nearby, gleaming with the wetness.

The man was delirious with the pain and effort, moaning, trembling, falling in and out of consciousness like a restless baby.

Parking the sled next to him, Reggie push-rolled the man onto it, his body shaking and straining with the work.

The man was heavy and solid. It was like manoeuvring a sack of concrete, bulky and unwieldy.

It was evening when he started to pull the sled and its bloodied burden.

His mom would be wondering where he was. Stewing in irritation and maybe a pinch of worry. She might yell at him; shake her finger at him in scolding.

She might even cry.

She'd been like that since his dad had died.

The runners of the sled slid along the forest floor with surprising ease once he got moving. The layer of pine needles provided a rolling surface that eased the progress as Reggie tugged with the ropes looped over either shoulder. Knowing the woods well, he chose the most even, unob-structed path, avoiding creek beds, rocky areas, and fallen trees.

The tree house was about a football field's distance from home, where the woods bordered his family's property. He'd helped his dad build it a few years ago. Reggie still thought of the summer days cutting and measuring the wood boards; nailing the ladder to the trunk of the oak; passing supplies up and down. The sun bright and high and beating down on them. Pepsis and sandwiches in the shade; man and boy shirtless and smiling. Watching the becoming of the thing above them; the floor and the walls and then the roof. The pounding of the hammers and the buzz of the saws like a music of sorts, hypnotic and calming.

Reggie pulled the sled beside the oak. The tree house

above put them in deeper shadow than natural from the early evening. The man seemed almost to disappear dimensionally, only his shoes sticking out from the shadow, so that Reggie had to kneel to see him more clearly.

'*I'll be back later*,' Reggie whispered, though it would take a full shout for his mom to hear him at this distance.

He recalled the man's words before he'd passed out again.

It'll need … stitches, he'd muttered, staring from the bloody, crumpled bullet in his left hand, to the puckered wound in his stomach, dribbling blood like a lazy volcano.

There was nothing to be done about that just now, Reggie thought.

It was dinnertime and his mom was waiting.

5.

His hands in his jeans pockets when he approached the porch, his mom awaited him under the bulb of the porch light, like an archangel haloed by heavenly light ready to pronounce judgment. Reggie shrugged as if it all was no big deal, saying it all at once, their routine – *I'm not a kid, I'm almost fifteen, don't treat me like a baby, I can stay out late* – without a word.

'Wash up,' she said, too tired to fight, saving him the excuse he'd been planning to get to the bathroom to wash his hands before she saw them. She closed the front door behind him as he turned down the hall.

Locking the door, he turned on the faucet and grabbed

the bar of soap on the sink. Scrubbing, he watched the pink swirl away down the drain. The whirlpool effect made him think of the ocean, a sinking freighter, and sailors being sucked down into the depths.

Reggie washed the soap clean as well. Grabbed some toilet paper from the roll and scrubbed down the doorknob where he'd left a scarlet smear. He peed and flushed the bloodied tissue away with his piss.

He looked briefly in the mirror. Saw how normal he looked. Not as if he'd just helped dig a bullet out of a man.

***

His food rolled around his plate aimlessly, like wanderers in a vast wasteland. Then he noticed his mom watching him and he ate to avoid suspicion. Silverware tinkled for a time against china before his mom tried conversation.

'You were gone awhile today,' she said, speaking around a mouthful of roast.

Reggie shrugged.

'I was just walking in the woods.'

Her sharp, short intake of breath was just audible in the space between them.

'You have to be careful out there, Reggie,' she said. 'There's coyotes, bobcats, mountain lions. Not to mention squatters.'

When he didn't respond, she continued.

'You're gone longer and longer,' she said, staring at him across the table. Fellow travellers separated by a looming gulf.

He didn't know what to say and so said nothing.

'I know it's summer,' she said, 'but it'd be nice to see you around more.'

She smiled to show her diplomacy and earnestness.

'Maybe we could go see a movie,' she said. 'Wasn't there a comic book movie you wanted to see? Maybe we could have lunch, make a day of it, like we used to.'

'Like we used to' meant when his dad was still around. It meant lots of things, but mostly it meant when things were still good. When things still made sense. When they still knew how to be a family.

She waited for him, but he had nothing to say. There was nothing worth saying.

He stared at his plate as if the answers were there. But there was only meat and potatoes, so he crammed these in his mouth to avoid answering. Still, she wanted something; he knew this would continue unless he gave her some acknowledgement, so he nodded vaguely, noncommittally.

In his peripheral, he saw her turn her attention back to her dinner. This submission saddened him in some indefinable way.

They ate in silence and went their separate ways.

***

Reggie lay in his dark room waiting for his mom to fall asleep.

With the door ajar an inch or so, he could see the occasional flash of the television from below like the stroboscopic lights of a landing aircraft. He would also be able to hear the buzz saw sounds of her snores, and know when it was safe for him to get up.

In the meantime, he was in the dark with his thoughts.

Sometimes the darkness frightened him. Other times the blackness was calming – or numbing – like a void. A neutral place where he felt nothing.

Occasionally, as now, the dark was a place in-between, where his mind drifted to things unseemly in the light of day.

Arms behind his head, stretched out on the mattress, at first his lazy thoughts threatened to invite sleep. But then, as so often happened, they converged on the wake in the funeral home not so long ago. He didn't want them to, tried futilely to steer his mind in another direction, yet it betrayed him.

The place had a lot of curtains, he remembered thinking. The coffin was open at the front of the room. He had to walk down an aisle of mostly empty chairs to get to it. His mom sat off to one side in a black dress like a phantom, crying.

With each deliberate step the coffin drew teasingly nearer.

Until he could see over the rim of it and what was there

wasn't his dad but a facsimile of the man. Waxen and stiff and immobile. A mannequin or life-sized doll and not his father at all.

He stared at it for a time until his mom stopped crying and one of the employees there came up to him and led him gently away. But he glanced back, keeping the thing in the casket in his line of sight for as long as possible.

Then the coffin was shut and that was it.

***

When the deep, droning hum of his mom's snores started, Reggie rolled out of bed and slipped his shoes back on. He hadn't changed out of his clothes and his mom hadn't checked in on him, so there was a minimum of rustle and noise before he was ready and moving downstairs.

He took the steps to the side nearest the wall to avoid creaks.

All the lights were off.

He felt like an intruder in his own home.

At the bottom he could turn to either the living room or the kitchen or hang a hard right down the hall. In the living room the blue flashes of the television screen lit his mom's sleeping form in an eerie and solemn glow. Intermittent with her snores were higher sounds like whimpers, and he wondered what she was dreaming of. If her dreams were anything like his, it couldn't be anything good.

He watched her for a moment longer, bundled under

an afghan blanket in the glow of the television. She seemed small and fragile there in the dark, in the glow. She was alone in the dark of the room and for a moment he wanted to reach for her. Have her hold him, tell him it was all right.

Then he was heading into the kitchen, pausing briefly at one drawer. Out the back door, moving with a stealth borne of youthful practise, and heading across the lawn to the garage for the second time that day, the building small and squat and solid like a battlefield fortification in the night.

6.

The man was gone when Reggie got back to the tree house. The sled was empty where he'd left it; no trace of the man as if he'd been raptured for judgment.

Then he heard a noise from above, looked up, and saw a pale oval high over him looking down. It moved back and out of sight, and Reggie whispered, '*I'm coming up*' and moved to the rungs of the ladder nailed to the tree.

At the top he crawled-pushed himself onto the floor and rose to a squat.

The old lantern his dad had given him for the tree house bloomed alive when the man lit it and put both them and the space between them in a dim yellowish light. They could have been Neanderthals huddled in a cave in some distant aeon passed.

'*I brought this,*' Reggie said, still whispering, holding out the spool of fishing line he'd taken from the garage and the sewing needle from the kitchen drawer.

He held it out to the man like an offering and the man took it, setting it down with the rest of their surgical equipment – the sterile pads, gauze, aspirin, and peroxide. The man wore only his heavy denim jacket against the night chill, having removed the shirt at some point. It lay in a bloody bundle in one corner. The flesh of his torso above and below the bandaged area was pale and ghostly.

'This won't be ... pretty either ...' the man said, sounding stronger and more lucid than before. 'You may not ... want to stay,' he said, looking across the small room at Reggie with eyes like stone.

'I'll stay,' Reggie said, squatting and watching.

The man unwound a length of fishing line and threaded it through the eye of the needle. He awkwardly and stiffly dug out his wallet from his pants pocket and brought it to his mouth and bit down on it.

Then he started.

Reggie didn't know what to expect, but what he saw was terrifying and captivating at the same time. The man unwrapped the gauze from around his middle and peeled the blood-sticky pads from just below his ribs. He dug into his pockets again and pulled out a lighter. The lighter was shaped like a boot and he flicked the flame to life and ran the sewing needle under it for about a minute.

Then he picked up the hydrogen peroxide, twisted off

the cap, and trickled a good amount over the wound, as he'd done earlier. It fizzled and foamed about the raw flesh like the remnants of ocean waves on a shoreline. The needle poked at the flesh around the wound, reminding Reggie of a tent pole pushing up at the canvas. Resistant until the needle broke and slid through the skin and trailed the fishing line over the wound, then returning the way it'd come, criss-crossing the wound like train tracks.

As he watched, a memory of his mom talking to her sister on the phone shortly after his father's death snapped to life in Reggie's mind. He'd caught a snippet of the conversation from his hiding place just outside his parents' room.

I saw him on the coroner's table! He was patched up! his mom had said, fighting back tears, sniffling back sobs. *Stitched up like a doll!*

The man before him now groaned behind the bit of the wallet.

His eyes teared and he had to stop to swipe at them.

His hands trembled and he had to stop again to still them.

And then the wound was closed, trickling blood like a squinty, weeping eye. He motioned Reggie over. Reggie obliged without hesitation. The man took the wallet out of his mouth.

'*Bandage it again …*' he managed, his voice again tremulous.

Reggie nodded and found the unused gauze and pads and went to work, standing, crouching, moving around the man as necessary, bringing the gauze about his middle and over the sterile pads.

'*Make it ... tight ...*' the man said, and Reggie did so, using the enclosed clasps to bind the gauze. When it was done, he stood and moved back, looking at his work.

The man's eyes fluttered. He settled back onto the floor, slowly, carefully, favouring his aches and pains.

'*No ambulance ...*' he said, losing consciousness. '*No police ... we have an ... arrangement ...*' he muttered, repeating what he had said earlier. And then he was gone, out cold, and Reggie was alone in the tree house that his dad had built and a stranger now inhabited.

Chapter Two

1.

The man awoke in the middle of the night. He sat up, saw Reggie there still watching him. Reggie smiled at the man, feeling dumb, but not knowing how else to greet him. A handshake or wave would have been even dumber.

'*How long ...?*' he rasped. Reggie reminded himself to bring some water back for the man next time he went to the house.

'A few hours,' he said.

The man held up his arm, looking at his watch.

'It's two in the ... morning,' the man said. 'You've been here ... the whole time?'

Reggie nodded.

'Won't your ... parents wonder where you are?' he asked.

'I snuck out,' Reggie said.

The man nodded solemnly, as if considering something of immense importance.

'You maybe ... shouldn't help me ... anymore,' he said, his voice gaining resolve, becoming stronger, more assured.

'Why not?' Reggie asked.

'I'm not a good ... person,' the man said, choking back a cough, leaning to the side and spitting. Reggie looked at the spit, saw it was tinged with blood.

Then he looked back at the man.

'Tell me about it,' he said.

For a time the man said nothing.

Then he turned back to Reggie and did just that.

***

'I kill people,' he began.

'Why?' Reggie asked, mildly shocked by the man's admission, and at the same time immediately interested. A part of him knew he should be scared if the man was telling the truth. Knowing the man *was* telling the truth, however, didn't bother him as it should.

Reggie had seen death, close up, on a parking lot's asphalt. And countless times afterward, replayed in night terrors. Its constant assault over the past year had numbed him.

'For money,' the man said.

'Good people or bad people?'

'Any people,' he said. 'Whomever I'm paid to kill.'

'How many people have you killed?'

'Many,' he said slowly with a small nod of his head, as if confirming the answer. 'Many people.'

'How long have you been doing it?'

'A long time,' he said with another nod. 'A very long time.'

'Does it pay well?'

'What?' the man said, a slight note of surprise in his tone.

'Killing people,' Reggie asked. 'Does it pay well?'

'Yes.'

'So you don't need the money anymore.'

'No,' he said. 'I guess I don't.'

'So why do you keep doing it?'

He didn't answer immediately. It was as if speaking gave the man strength, but in pausing his body rattled with laboured breathing. When he spoke again the tremors passed.

'I guess it's all I know how to do,' he said.

'Do you like it?' Reggie asked.

'Do I like it?' the man repeated, taken aback once more.

'My dad did many jobs until he found what he liked doing,' Reggie said. 'Then when he found the job he liked, he never left it. We don't have to do things we don't like. So you must like doing it.'

The man said nothing.

'You must like killing people,' Reggie said.

'There's a power in it,' the man finally said. His hand roamed and found his gun, stroking it, almost as if he wasn't aware of it. 'Knowing you hold someone's life in your hands. That you can end them and the world will continue as if they'd never existed at all.'

Reggie nodded as if he knew what the man was talking about.

But he didn't speak. Waited instead for the man to continue.

'There's a thrill,' the killer said, 'a rush when I pull the trigger or tighten the wire around the throat or sink the knife in the belly. There's no one to tell me what I can and can't do. I answer to no one.'

'Have you killed women?' Reggie asked.

'Yes.'

'Have you killed children?' he asked.

'Yes.'

'What about God?' Reggie said.

'What about Him?' the man asked.

'What about hell?'

The man shook his head slowly. He smiled but it wasn't a happy smile or even a smile of amusement, like he thought what Reggie said was funny or stupid or both. It was a sad smile, like he missed something he'd once been fond of.

'I've never seen anything that would make me believe in a heaven or a hell,' he said. 'I've seen cruelty, and greed, and men and women pushing and manoeuvring to make it to the top. Only to find that when they're at the top there's somewhere else they want to be. Somewhere higher.'

'Will you kill me?' Reggie asked.

The man stared at him long and hard.

'I haven't yet, have I?' he said.

'That's because you still need me,' Reggie said. 'You're not healthy enough yet to get along on your own.'

The man smiled again and nodded sagely.

'That's very perceptive,' the man said. 'Always mind the details.'

'Will you kill me when you're better?' Reggie asked.

'No,' the man said. 'I don't think so.'

'Why?'

'Because we have a deal,' the man said. 'And in my line of work, a deal's a deal. A man's word means everything.'

'What if I break it?' Reggie asked. 'What if I call the police?'

'You won't,' the man said, looking at him intently, as if he were reading fine print on a contract.

Under such scrutiny, Reggie had to look away.

Not because he was scared, though. And not because of any suggestion of threat beneath the man's words should the deal be broken. But because, Reggie realized, he knew he *wouldn't* call the police.

He'd made that decision the moment he'd run up to help the man and hadn't turned away even after seeing the gun beneath the jacket.

Reggie looked away because the killer, having known him only a few hours, already read Reggie like a book. This was the kind of insight that only a close family member had.

Someone like a mother ... or a father.

They were quiet for a time, looking across the space at each other. The lantern was lit but carried hardly a few feet. Outside the open windows of the tree house the night was heavy and dark. As if the two of them were in the last habitable space in an abyss.

The man looked at his abdomen, then out the window nearest him, then at Reggie again. He looked tired, aware, and restless all at the same time, like how Reggie felt when he had a big test the next day at school. Something important that much else depended on.

'You should probably go to bed,' the man said.

Reggie nodded and moved to the ladder.

'I think I'll need something for infection,' the man said.

Reggie looked back and nodded again.

The man gave him the names of some drugs. Some for pain, stronger than the aspirin, he told Reggie he could find in a store. Others, he'd have to look around at home, maybe search his parents' medicine cabinet. The man told Reggie to be back as soon as possible in the morning with them.

Reggie nodded again and started down the ladder. Then he paused and poked his head back up.

'What's your name?' he asked.

'Ivan,' the killer said.

'I'm Reggie,' he said.

The man nodded in his direction.

'Good to meet you, Reggie,' he said.

'Are we friends?' he asked.

The man smiled that same sad smile for the third time.

'I guess we are at that,' he said. 'Now get along to bed.'

Reggie gave a little wave and descended the ladder. He jumped down the last few steps and turned back towards home.

The distance and darkness from the woods to the house seemed immense; shadows everywhere where things could hide. Yet he wasn't frightened at all. He felt as if there was something watching his back. Something protecting him. Something that killed and wasn't afraid of hell and didn't answer to anyone.

In fact, the walk back was quite peaceful.

2.

Reggie awoke rested and energetic. He ate his breakfast fast and enthusiastically and this seemed to please his mom. He told her the pancakes were great and swallowed them down with a large glass of orange juice. This made her smile.

Dropping his dishes into the sink, he told her he was thinking of riding into town. This seemed to make her even happier.

'It's good for you to get out and do things,' she said. 'You've been holed up in this place too long.'

No doubt she assumed a trip to the comic book or video game store was his destination. Reggie said nothing to make her think otherwise. He just smiled back and walked out of the kitchen.

Upstairs, he showered, dressed, then left the house, wheeling his bike out of the garage for the first time in months. He checked the tyres, hopped on, and was soon down the road and turning onto the highway. The desert road twisted downwards, a serpentine thing, and the town out there ahead of him, miniscule but growing. Like a toy model magically rising to human dimensions.

A mile down the road he saw the sirens, flashing red and blue.

To either side of the highway desert fields stretched to the horizon in great white expanses. Sparse cacti and trees and bushes dotted the bone-white stretches like stragglers of a great migration. Periodically, ditches and arroyos dipped the surface like moon craters. Men and women in police department blue and sheriff's department tan spread out to either side of the highway, moving further from the road and deeper into the fields. Some lingered by the shoulders of the road and leaned against open patrol car doors and spoke into radios.

A young deputy flagged him with a wave when Reggie rode near and he braked in front of the man. Reggie squinted in the morning sunlight and visored his eyes with a hand to look up at the deputy.

'How's it going, kid?' the deputy asked. He chewed gum or tobacco like cud as he spoke, and hooked his thumbs in his belt like a movie marshal swaggering into town.

'Fine, officer,' Reggie said, being respectful as his parents had raised him to be.

'Where you off to?' the deputy asked, not really looking at Reggie as he asked the question. He looked this way and that to either side of the highway, like he wanted to be out there with the others, and not on the sidelines directing bicycle traffic.

'Town,' Reggie said. 'It's summer break.'

'Yeah,' the deputy said, turned and spat a large black wad, 'well, just be careful.'

'What happened?' Reggie asked, following the deputy's lead and turning and looking out into the barren desert fields where others were fanning out, checking ditches, peering behind pathetic gnarled trees and rocks.

The deputy looked at Reggie for the first time. A hint of a smile touched the corners of his mouth.

'There's a dangerous man out there,' he said, not doing a good job at keeping the amusement from his tone. 'A really bad, dangerous man.'

'That so?' Reggie asked, trying to sound interested and worried at the same time.

'That's so,' the deputy said, grinning.

'What'd he do?' Reggie asked.

The deputy looked to either side again and then leaned in confidentially, as if he was sharing a secret. He motioned Reggie forward and Reggie pushed the bike closer with his feet on the ground.

The deputy cupped a hand conspiratorially around his mouth.

'*He raped and killed a woman and killed her kid,*' he whispered.

Reggie didn't say anything.

'You know what rape is, kid?' the deputy said, speaking above a whisper now, but not by much.

Reggie nodded.

'Do you really?' the deputy said, cocking his head a bit like he didn't believe Reggie. 'Because I don't think you really do unless you've seen the results.'

Reggie shifted uncomfortably in his seat.

'We've got pictures,' the deputy said.

Reggie didn't know what to say.

'Of the crime scene,' the deputy elaborated. 'I can show you, if you want.'

Reggie started pedalling again, steering around the deputy.

'I've gotta go,' Reggie said, his heart beating fast.

'*Stay on the road where people can see you!*' the deputy called after him.

The asphalt rolled along under him, the town drawing

26

closer. The laughter behind him grew vague and distant and was gone. Leaving Reggie alone with his thoughts of pictures of raped women and dead children.

***

He chained his bike in front of the drugstore and walked in, the whoosh of the air conditioning meeting him in a cool wave. Brilliant white and sterile walls and floor made the place seem dreamlike. As he passed by the checkout area a clerk waved to him and said hi and Reggie said hi back and moved deeper into the store.

He found the pharmacy and drug aisles towards the back. A line mostly of old people stood in front of the window, behind which clerks in white lab coats browsed shelves for bottles and passed them over to the old people.

Walking past, Reggie peered down an aisle where a teenaged boy a couple years older than him was trying to discretely peruse the rubbers. He saw Reggie looking at him, and Reggie hurried past.

In the aisle with the aspirin and sinus and cold medicine he found some of what he'd come for. He had the names on a slip of paper in his pocket and pulled that out to compare it with what was written on the labels.

The man in the tree house had told him some of the drug names on the list wouldn't be available over the counter, but Reggie thought he recognized them from bottles in the medicine cabinet at home. He grabbed a couple boxes off the shelves in front of him and headed back across the store to the checkout area.

Passing the aisle with the rubbers again, he saw the older kid and the kid looked up again as Reggie passed by. Reggie saw the torn box in the other kid's hands, saw him moving as if to shove something in his pocket, before he stopped and looked up at Reggie.

'What's your problem?' the bigger kid said. 'Mind your own fuckin' business ...'

His words trailed off as Reggie moved past him and back towards the front of the store. He found the ten items or less express lane and put the packages on the counter. The clerk, maybe the same one who'd greeted him when he came in, said hi and smiled and Reggie said hi and smiled back.

He felt more than heard someone step into line behind him.

Reggie didn't want to but looked.

It was the bigger kid who'd been stealing rubbers.

The bigger kid smiled at Reggie, and Reggie turned away, pulled out some money from his pocket, paid for the medicine. He thanked the clerk and headed out of the store and to his bike.

Bending, turning the dials on the lock to unchain his bike, he heard footfalls coming up behind him. Heard them stop very close. He could also hear the breathing of the kid behind him, like the puffs of breath from a prank caller.

'Ain't you the kid that cried last year?' said the older boy.

Reggie ignored him and finished putting in the combination of his lock.

'Hey,' said the condom bandit. 'I'm talking to you.'

Looping the chain out from around the spokes of the tyre, refastening it around the seat bar, Reggie rose and lifted a leg to swing over onto the bike. Caught off balance, the otherwise light shove of the older boy's palms against his back sent Reggie toppling over.

His temple struck the wall the bike rack was bolted into.

Tangled with his legs, the bike clattered along with him and the pedals and spokes scraped him good along the calves and thighs. Pushing away from the bike, disengaging himself, he stood on shaky legs and touched his head where he'd hit it. His fingers came away without blood, but his temple throbbed smartly.

'What the hell's your problem?' he said to the bigger kid, wishing he sounded braver and less pitiful.

'I said ain't you the kid that cried last year?' the older boy said. He had a lazy smile on his face like this was nothing more than another day.

Reggie knew what he was talking about but didn't say anything.

The older boy seemed vaguely familiar, like maybe he'd seen him around school. But being a couple years older, a senior most likely, Reggie probably hadn't seen him much and couldn't put a name to the face.

'I don't want no trouble,' Reggie said. 'I gotta go.'

He pulled his bike up and looked around the parking lot. There were people walking to cars and walking from cars, but none of them were terribly close by.

'Yeah,' the older kid said, 'you're him all right.'

He chuffed a wicked little sound that was something between a laugh and hocking a winner of a snot bomb.

'You were walking to the office and crying,' said the bigger kid. 'Crying like a little faggot.'

Drugstore bag of medicine in one hand, gripping the handlebars, Reggie tried to steer away. The older kid stepped in front of him, placed a hand on the handlebar, a foot on the front tyre.

'Did you poop your diapers that day?' said the older kid. 'Or did your boyfriend dump you?'

Reggie wanted to leave. His heart was thudding, pounding against his chest like a beast shackled. His vision blurred and reddened. He wanted to leave but the bigger kid was in front of him.

For some reason he thought of the man in the tree house. He thought of the crumpled bullet dug out of him. He thought of the shiny black gun.

Something in Reggie loosened. The pounding stopped. The blurry and red vision cleared. His formerly white-knuckle grip on the handlebars relaxed. He looked up at the older kid, looked him square in the eyes.

'My dad died,' he said.

The other kid blinked. His mouth worked like he wanted to say something, but didn't know quite what.

'So why don't you go back to stealing your rubbers,' Reggie said. 'And while you're at it, find someone with a dick who could actually use them.'

And just like that the older boy's flustered moment was gone.

His fist found Reggie's eye and down he went again, bike on top, hard sidewalk beneath. The older kid leaned over him and grabbed a fistful of Reggie's shirt.

'You watch your fucking mouth, dip shit,' he said and shook him, making Reggie's head bounce against the concrete under him.

'*Hey! What're you kids doing there?*'

The older kid looked up, let go of Reggie, turned and ran.

Reggie, slowly standing, touching his throbbing eye gingerly, saw the store clerk who'd greeted him jogging his way. He got back on his bike, turned it, and started pedalling. Across the parking lot, onto the street, the long way home before him.

3.

He handed Ivan the medicine and a bottle of water. The man didn't look good. He was still pale and clammy, but he was conscious and alert, which Reggie took to be a

31

good sign despite the pasty flesh of the man's face, and the shakes that occasionally passed over him.

The man downed a couple of the Amoxicillin tablets Reggie had found in his mom's medicine cabinet, coughed and spit up some of the water, wiped his mouth, and looked at Reggie. He pointed at Reggie, touched his own temple and eye in indication of Reggie's.

'What happened?' he asked, reaching for the antiseptic cream and Ibuprofen Reggie had purchased at the drugstore.

'Some asshole from school,' Reggie said.

'Why'd he do it?' the man asked.

'I told him he had no dick.'

Ivan smiled, and this made Reggie smile. Though a smile on Ivan's face didn't look so much like a smile, as it did a crocodile or shark showing its teeth.

'That's likely to piss someone off,' the big man said. 'Why'd you say it?'

'He made fun of me crying once in school,' he said.

'Why were you crying?' Ivan asked.

'My dad died,' Reggie said.

Ivan looked at him a long moment before he said anything. Reggie wasn't sure he liked those blue eyes staring at him so. They weren't like eyes at all, just as his smile wasn't exactly a smile. His eyes were like gems, bright but lifeless.

'Tell me about it,' the killer said, and to his surprise, Reggie did.

***

'My father died doing that job it was he liked doing so much,' Reggie said.

'The one that took him awhile to find?' the killer asked.

'Yeah,' Reggie answered.

'And what was it?' Ivan asked, trembling briefly with a pained breath. 'What was it that made him happy?'

'He was a minister,' Reggie said, watching the man's face closely for some slight indication of how this made him feel. What killers thought of ministers was something that suddenly piqued his interest.

The killer said nothing; gave only a small nod.

Reggie continued.

'Dad used to say that he was confused much of his life,' Reggie said. 'That he never knew quite where his life was going. As a kid in school he got Cs and Bs, completely average, never excelled at anything. He didn't play any sports. Didn't do any after-school stuff either.'

Ivan nodded.

'I've been there before,' he said. 'Confused.'

'He said his parents were worried,' Reggie said, 'but didn't know what to do. It wasn't like their son was misbehaving or falling in with the wrong crowd or anything like that. So they couldn't yell at him or punish him or nothing.'

'So they left him be?' the killer asked.

'Yeah,' Reggie continued. 'He got through high school, did some college, but eventually dropped out. He went

33

from job to job, worked at just about everything a man could work at. Construction, retail, clerical; he even went back home at one point and did nothing but volunteering, living off Grandma and Grandpa again, saying there wasn't any point in making money.'

'But none of it made him happy?' Ivan asked.

'No,' Reggie said, shaking his head.

'And how'd he come about finding God?' the killer asked.

Reggie searched the man's tone for any sense of mocking or contempt, but found none. The gut shot man seemed genuinely interested, but Reggie kept watching, intent, wary of the man and interested also.

'Dad used to tell me Grandma and Grandpa were what he called social Christians,' Reggie said. 'They went to church because that was what people were supposed to do. But they never really talked about church stuff, never went to any functions. There was a Bible around the house that found itself moving from table to table, shelf to shelf, but no one ever read it.'

The killer was like a child at a campfire ghost story, rapt and attentive.

The words came easier than Reggie would have thought, talking to a stranger about his dad. Almost as if they had always been there, waiting to be said.

'Until one day Dad did,' Reggie said. 'He read it cover to cover on his time off from jobs or volunteering. Then when he was done, he read it again. The third time through he started taking notes, cross-referencing things he read.'

Ivan was nodding again.

'I've known people like that before,' the killer said. 'Get caught up in religion. Only to give it up again.'

Reggie nodded.

'That's what Dad said too,' he said. 'He'd talked to co-workers, heard people at church or in public praising God for everything from cancer remission to baseball games. And that's why he never really took it seriously as a kid.'

The killer nodded his agreement.

'Then he read the book for himself,' Reggie said. 'And things changed. He said much of the scripture made no sense at first. But some of it did. And as he kept reading and rereading, more of it did.'

Reggie paused, looking at the killer. The expression on the man's wan face seemed pensive, attentive, and Reggie waited for the big man to ask a question or say something. When he didn't, Reggie continued.

'Eventually, Dad said, it got to where the more he learned, the more it seemed there was to learn. Frustrated but committed, he figured he'd try to strip it down to the basics. He figured the most important stuff had to be what the faith was named after. So he started to focus on the Gospels, the things Jesus said.'

'I've listened to that sort before,' the killer said, almost speaking over Reggie. 'Jesus this and Jesus that. How we're all sinners and it's the grace of God that saves us. How there's an end to things coming and a new thing starting.'

'What do you think of it?' Reggie asked, cautiously, hearing a note of annoyance in the big man's voice.

'I told you before,' the killer said, and Reggie remembered. 'I've had people pray to God before I killed them, and a few pray for me. Ain't nothing changed the outcome of what happened. Just me and my gun and the silence after.'

Reggie propped his chin in his hands, thinking about this. He was thinking of his dad and there was some of the old hurt. He was thinking of things his dad used to say, and weighing them without really doing so. Just kind of letting the memories float about smoke-like.

'Let me guess,' the killer said, breaking the brief silence. 'Your dad studied, prayed, and eventually started his own ministry?'

'Yeah,' Reggie said.

'How'd he die?' Ivan asked, startling Reggie with the sudden change in the conversation. Though this was where it had been heading the whole time, Reggie realized, and he'd just been taking a detour. Sightseeing before he got to the destination.

Taking a breath, Reggie told him.

'One of his parishioners shot him,' he said, meeting the man's eyes.

The killer's response came quickly but calmly, not missing a beat. Almost as if he'd had such a response planned for a long time.

'I guess that just about says all that needs to be said about God,' the killer said.

36

'I guess it does,' Reggie said, then fell quiet.

He stared at the walls of the tree house and the whirly patterns in the wood. He stared at the floor too. The killer said nothing as well. They stayed that way for awhile, high up in the little house, silent with their thoughts in a place all their own.

Chapter Three

1.

The sheriff's department came around about an hour later. The white and green Ford could be seen over and through the trees from their perch in the tree house, crawling up the road at a leisurely pace.

Reggie moved for the ladder and Ivan grabbed him by the arm.

'Remember our arrangement,' he said, not a question but a statement.

Reggie nodded.

'In my line of work,' he said, 'there's consequences for breaking your word.'

Reggie didn't remember actually giving his word about anything, but nodded again anyway. Then he was moving down the ladder and emerging from the woods and jogging back to the house across the dry field of the front yard. A slight summer breeze stirred things and made a whisper in the air over the expanse. He walked in the back door just as his mom was leaving the kitchen to check on the sound of the car pulling up out front.

He watched from the hall as she opened the screen door and stepped out on the porch to greet the man walking up. The cadence of heavy boots pounding up the steps to meet her sounded like heartbeats.

'Good morning ma'am,' the man said. Through the mesh of the screen door he was a vague form with a wide-brimmed hat and a gun belt. 'I'm Deputy Collins,' said the man and they shook hands.

The voice was familiar and Reggie wanted to reach out and pull his mom back inside and lock the door behind her.

'Good morning, officer,' his mom replied. 'What can I do for you?'

'We're driving around notifying nearby residents about a situation,' the deputy said. How the same voice that had tauntingly asked *You know what rape is, kid?* could now disguise itself with civility, was beyond Reggie.

Such a trick seemed dangerous to him. Something a predator did to lull its prey into a false sense of security. Just before it flashed its claws and dragged the hunted into a dark den.

'What situation would that be?' his mom asked. Interest rather than concern tinged his mom's voice. Serene calm or outbursts of emotion when he was late home for something or wasn't where he was supposed to be were her only two moods since his dad had died. One or the other. Nothing in between.

That was almost as troubling to Reggie as the deputy's dual personalities.

'Not to cause any alarm, ma'am,' the deputy began, 'but it seems there's a dangerous man on the loose.'

'You don't say?' said his mom.

'Unfortunately so,' said the deputy. 'Yesterday morning a man escaped from a police escort taking him to the county jail in Tucson.'

'What'd he do?' she asked. She leaned nonchalantly against the door, her back pushing against the mesh and bending it inward.

'He's a killer,' said Deputy Collins, friendly neighbourhood peace officer and tormentor of bike riding boys.

'Who'd he kill?' his mom asked, her tone still mildly interested, like someone spying a squashed bug on the sidewalk momentarily before passing.

'Many people,' the deputy replied. 'He's a contract killer.'

'My word,' his mom said.

'Yes, I know,' said the officer. 'Who'd think such a man loose in our town?'

They each shook their head at the wonder of it all.

'If you see this man,' the officer said and held up a photo Reggie couldn't see through the screen door, 'stay away from him and get to a phone. Give us a call and we'll be there lickety-split.'

They shook hands again, and the deputy walked away,

climbing in his car and driving off. Plumes of dirt billowed into the air and then settled like battlefield detritus. His mom stood on the porch for a time, looking at the photo without really looking at it, and then came back inside.

Reggie left silently by the back door.

2.

'Tell me about the first person you killed,' Reggie said after climbing back up the ladder and settling down again across from the killer. Together they'd watched the patrol car weaving away in the distance, until, crawling first up and then down a hill, it blinked away in the white horizon.

Despite the deputy's unsettling offer to let him see crime scene photographs, Reggie thought about what the officer had said to him by the side of the highway: *He raped and killed a woman and killed her kid.* And about how Ivan himself had admitted to killing women and children only a short time ago.

Reggie idly wondered if he could get to the ladder before the killer drew his gun. If, peddling fast, he could catch up to the patrol car on his bike before it reached the highway. But these were just fleeting thoughts without substance, like the remnants of vague dreams upon awakening, drifting away.

The two of them had an arrangement, a deal. And in Ivan's line of work, a man's word was everything. Ivan had rightly judged Reggie when he'd asked what if he called the police and the killer had said he knew Reggie wouldn't. Reggie was likewise sure the man would keep to the terms of the deal. He was safe as long as he didn't betray the killer's trust.

At least, he was *pretty* sure.

'My first hit?' Ivan asked. 'Or the first person I killed?'

'There's a difference?' Reggie asked.

'There is,' the killer said. 'A hit is never personal, just business. Killing someone because you want to is an entirely other thing.'

'The first person you killed then,' Reggie said, nodding with the decision. 'The very first.'

Reggie thought it might take him a moment or two to call forth the memories. So many killed over so many years, he figured the killer might have to close his eyes against the tide. Take himself back and carefully reel in the memory out from the rest. But Ivan answered immediately.

'That would be my father,' he said, looking now not at Reggie but at some spot above and past him. He was indeed reeling in the memory, Reggie realized, only it wasn't difficult at all. This was something that was at the core of the man sitting across from him. It was there all the time, merely waiting for him to draw it forth from beneath the surface.

'Why'd you kill your own dad?' Reggie asked. He thought of his mom and his own dad. Such a thing – killing one of them – didn't make sense. He couldn't even fully develop the thought.

43

'I caught him touching my sister,' Ivan said. 'You know, in the way grown-ups aren't supposed to.'

Images came unbidden to Reggie's mind. Dark basements; old corners; unlighted children's rooms at night. A large, hulking figure standing over a frail one with sheet covers pulled to her chin. Again he thought of the deputy on the side of the highway, and later on Reggie's own front porch: *Do you know what rape is, kid?*

'How many times did he do it?' Reggie heard himself asking. He realized what he was saying, and he thought of the gun lying beside the man across from him. But Ivan didn't show any reaction to this question, and Reggie relaxed a bit.

'I only saw him the one time,' Ivan said. 'But there's no telling how long it went on before I saw him.'

'Didn't your sister ever call for help?' Reggie asked.

'She had Down's syndrome,' Ivan said, making a vague gesture at his own head to punctuate the statement. 'She wasn't all there, you know?'

Reggie nodded though he didn't know, not really. He'd seen people with handicaps before, of course. Coupled with their caregivers, guiding them or pushing them in wheelchairs, such people were obvious. But they were just people all the same, and Reggie had never given the mentally or physically challenged much thought.

As a minister, his dad had always told him God created all people as they were for a reason. People with disabilities weren't to be looked down on, or even pitied. But the way

Ivan pointed to his own temple in indication of his sister's condition told Reggie that the killer didn't see things quite the same way.

'We lived up north in a mountain town,' Ivan said. 'I went to school in the city. Took a bus home. It was a short day, they let us out early, and I came in through the back door. The hinges didn't make a sound, and the television was on, so I guess they didn't hear me come in.'

Reggie pulled his legs up to his chest, hugged them about the knees. He rested his chin on his right knee and stared down at the floor at a spot near Ivan's booted feet. He couldn't look at the man just now, and he didn't know why.

'My sister's room was across the hall from mine,' Ivan said. 'I had to pass it to get to my room. The door was ajar and I looked in as I walked by.'

Reggie stared hard at the wooden floor. He felt like he had when the deputy asked if he wanted to see the pictures. The rape pictures. Not wanting to be in a certain place, and yet held there by another.

'She was on the bed,' Ivan said. 'He'd pulled a chair up close beside it. His pants were around his ankles. One hand was on her, one was on himself.'

Reggie wondered what was on television. He tried hard to think if there was a book that maybe he could read. He wondered if his mom still wanted to see a movie, go have lunch.

And at the same time he was rooted to the spot. It was

as if the very floor of the tree house had sprouted invisible vines, shackling him. He couldn't leave and he wasn't sure he would if he could. With an effort he pulled his gaze from the floor and looked at Ivan again. He was staring right at Reggie.

'What'd you do?' he asked.

'Right then?' the killer asked. 'Nothing.'

Reggie waited. He knew the story wasn't over.

'He finally saw me and turned to look at me,' the killer said. 'He took his hands off my sister and himself, but didn't bother trying to pull up his pants or explain anything. He just sat there half-naked in his chair and looked at me.'

Patiently, Reggie remained silent.

'I walked to my room and closed the door behind me,' Ivan said. 'I did my homework at my desk by the window. Watched the day pass into evening. He knocked on my door once and said that dinner was ready. I told him I wasn't hungry and had a project to finish. I heard him go upstairs to his room not too long after.

'I chopped wood for us,' Ivan said. The change of subject jolted Reggie, but he remained quiet. The set of the killer's face – all hard lines and solid planes – told Reggie they were getting somewhere. Somewhere important. This was something told in a way only the teller could determine, in his own time. Like when Reggie had to tell his mom or dad about a lie he'd told, or something bad he'd done at school.

'I loved doing it. It was hard work and repetitive, and

the rhythm of the work set me at ease. And then watching the logs crackling in the fire and the smoke going up the chimney seemed a fitting conclusion to the work. A cycle of a kind.

'The hatchet I'd bought from a hardware store with the money from one of my first summer jobs. I kept it in my room rather than outside in a shed or with the cords of firewood. I kept it under my bed wrapped in an old blanket.'

The snowy expanse of the killer's northern home came alive for Reggie. Hills and forests and mountains. A small town of quaint, warm houses. And in one a young man in a room, kneeling to reach under his bed for a cherished bundle.

'My father was a heavy sleeper and snored loudly,' the killer said. 'The walls in our home were thin and I could hear him clearly when he was asleep. I climbed upstairs without a single squeak of the floorboards beneath me, which was unusual. It was an old house, and the creaks and pops of its structure was a background noise you got used to. That day, however, it was silent, as if the place itself approved of my intentions.'

Reggie wondered about that. Could a place think? Could a house or building have a memory? He thought of the church and its parking lot. He thought of his dad's plot at the cemetery. How he'd avoided both places for the better part of a year. The very air of each of them seemed heavy and difficult to breathe. At the wake in the church and the funeral at the cemetery, Reggie had felt as if he'd been watched the entire time, and not merely by the people who'd gathered to say their goodbyes.

Shifting uncomfortably, he didn't think that was such a strange idea at all.

'He was face down on the mattress,' the killer continued. 'He never awoke, never saw me coming. I did it with one swing. Cleaved his skull in two.'

The killer took a breath, let it out slowly. Then another. Reggie was reminded of a bull chuffing, its nostrils flaring, as it stared at an intended target to gore. Measuring the distance to the tree house ladder, Reggie hoped he wasn't the focus of the man's quiet, bestial fury. When the killer spoke again it was in a noticeably quieter tone, so Reggie had to strain to hear.

'I wonder if maybe he knew I was coming and slept soundly because of it. Maybe in his own way, he wanted to be punished.'

He looked at Reggie with those stony eyes.

'What do you think, Reggie?'

Reggie didn't think much of anything at that moment, and said as much:

'I don't know.'

'How does a man sleep after doing what he did?' Ivan asked. 'I like to think he knew I was coming and slept in comfort knowing that it was over. Maybe he knew the things he did were wrong and wanted them to end.'

'How do *you*?' Reggie said.

'How do I what?' Ivan said.

'How do *you* sleep, knowing the things you've done?'

The cold blue eyes twitched but nothing more. One hand slipped beneath his jacket and roamed, idly searching, and finding what it sought, stroked the item gently. Whether gun or knife or some other secreted instrument, Reggie didn't know, and didn't want to.

'I'd like to be alone now, Reggie,' the killer said after a time.

Reggie nodded and stood up. Moving down the ladder he stopped and looked back at the man leaning against the far wall.

'I'll bring you a sandwich or something for lunch,' he said. 'Lemonade or something to drink too.'

'That sounds fine,' the killer said, his gun now beside him. That Reggie hadn't seen the motion that brought it forth was unsettling.

The man's fingers ticked slightly, as if they yearned to touch the weapon. So close, only inches away.

Reggie moved down and out of sight.

3.

In his room, Reggie moved to the dresser, opened the top drawer, and reached under his socks. His fingers found the bundle of money he'd filched from Ivan's jacket, pulled it out.

He flipped through the bills, made a quick tally. Three hundred dollars. More than he'd ever had at one time.

Once, he'd gotten over a hundred dollars combined for Christmas, from both sets of grandparents. He'd felt rich then, and his mom and dad had to remind him not to blow it all at once.

Now with three times that amount, Reggie felt momentarily overwhelmed with the possibilities. He could get a new bike. Or the new Xbox everyone at school had been talking about.

Then his excitement was quickly squashed as he considered the source of his newfound wealth. Where it had come from. How it was obtained.

We have an arrangement. We have a deal.

There's consequences for breaking your word.

Suddenly, Reggie wasn't sure if he really liked the terms of the deal. If he spent the money, it would be as if he agreed to it. But if he didn't spend it …

Shoving the bundle back under his clothes, Reggie shut the drawer and walked out of his room, then downstairs, putting as much distance between himself and the cash as possible.

***

His mom did indeed want to go to lunch and a movie; Reggie didn't know how to get out of it, and it was all because of the bruise on his face. She overreacted when she saw it, as he'd known she would.

'It's just a bruise,' he said, trying to push her hand away

50

as she cupped his face and turned it in the light of the kitchen for a better look.

'How'd it happen?' she asked.

'I fell off my bike,' he said, not quite lying.

'You need to be more careful,' she said, just short of a shout. 'I can't watch you twenty-four seven, Reggie!'

'I know,' he said, hanging his head low, hoping submission would end the interrogation.

'You've got to be responsible, Reggie!' she said, wetness gleaming at the corner of her eyes. 'No one else is going to look out for you!'

'I know,' he said.

'Your father would be disappointed,' she said, peering so close and intently at his discoloured temple Reggie could feel her breath. 'He'd never approve of such recklessness.'

In Reggie's mind flashed backyard wrestling matches with his dad. Hikes along forest trails. Woodcrafts in the garage, the table saw buzzing, sawdust sprinkling the floor.

He was sure she knew the untruth of what she said. Her husband, his dad, had done many things with certain risks, and invited his son to all of them.

But that wasn't the point, and Reggie knew this as surely as she knew the reason for her harsh words. Without his dad around, certain things just weren't safe anymore. As his death had shown, anything was possible at anytime.

Only vigilance could assuage disaster, and that only with luck.

She went to the freezer and got out a bag of frozen peas, came back and pushed it at his face. He tried pushing it away but she prevailed, pressing the cold bag against his temple.

'Hold it there for a bit,' she said.

'Mom,' he began.

'Don't argue with me,' she said in near hysterics, pushing him onto the sofa.

So he sat there in the living room, reached for the remote and turned on the television. Onscreen, the starship Enterprise blasted at vicious Klingon cruisers. Uninterested in the explorations of the crew that had in years past previously enthralled him, Reggie changed the channel, found a talking head on a cable news station. Sat back and tuned out the world to the droning white noise of the smartly suited anchor. His mom moved about the house in an imitation of work – dusting this, rearranging that – but always found her way back to the living room. After a dozen or so circuits, she stopped in the hall and looked in at him.

'Want to go see that movie?' she asked.

Her arms were crossed and that meant that though she'd calmed down outwardly, internally her gears were still turning, her mind working.

Reggie knew there was no arguing when she was in such a mood.

'And lunch?' he asked.

'And lunch,' she said, smiling.

'Pizza?' he said, figuring he'd go whole hog if this was his sentence for the day.

'Pizza it is,' she said. Her arms fell away from her chest in a motion approaching relaxation, and she strode away to get her purse and keys.

***

The movie was a comedy, not the comic book movie he'd initially wanted to see. For some reason he wasn't in the mood for violence and action, even stylized and cartoonish like in a Marvel Studios film.

The comedy was of the slapstick Leslie Nielsen variety, and made them both laugh in their high seats at the back of the theatre. In the dark of the theatre with the lighted screen in front of them and their laughter echoing it was almost as if that was all there was. The world relegated to four walls and their easy laughter, and for a time things didn't seem so bad.

After the movie they ate their pizza on the patio of the restaurant and the soaring summer sun cast everything in bright hues. In the warmth and a light breeze with the food and cool drinks before them, they recalled some of the best gags in the movie and laughed again.

They walked back to the car side by side and to Reggie it seemed there was a lightness in their step and stride. As they drove he hung an arm out the window and the wind of their passing buffeted his hand like a sail and it felt good. Along the dirt shoulder of the highway, padding heavily in the opposite direction, a pregnant stray mutt made her way down the road, head down and sway-backed with the weight of her burden.

Reggie averted his gaze.

For a time, with the Dodge rolling along in the quiet of the day, the bleached hills sliding past, nothing mattered. Not the man in the tree house. Not the deputy offering up his rape pictures. Not the condom bandit with his hard fists and taunts. Certainly not a pitiful dog treading down the highway.

Then they were approaching a certain familiar turn-off and a large, bold bronze and stonework sign and something in him froze. At first thinking it accidental – that his mom was just taking a different route home – Reggie tried to calm himself. But then they were pulling into the parking lot of the place, and his anxiety kicked up a notch.

He thought of the conversation he'd only just had with Ivan. His ideas about places and memories.

His mom steered the car into a space and put it in park.

He felt sick in his stomach, like he might throw up.

He looked around at the rolling green hills and the stones about them stretching in all directions from the perimeter of the parking lot.

'I know it's hard, Reggie,' his mom said, touching him lightly on the shoulder.

'Mom,' he mumbled.

'But I think this is for the best,' she said.

'Let's go, please,' he said, shaking a little. He had a tight grip on the passenger door handle. His other hand gripped a fistful of his pants legs.

'I think you should visit him,' she said. 'It's been awhile.'

He surprised himself by laughing. It was a short, wicked noise.

'There's no "him" to visit,' he said. 'He's dead.'

'Reggie,' his mom said in a soft voice like a caress. 'You can talk to him. Tell him how you feel. It might help.'

'He can't hear me,' he said, his voice rising. 'He's worm food.'

'Reggie,' his mom said, her own voice changing from softness to warning. 'Don't be like that. That's your dad you're talking about.'

'No,' he said. 'It's not. It's a fucking corpse.'

'Don't use that kind of language, young man,' she said, the softness gone now, leaving only a menacing tone he hadn't quite heard before. There was an unspoken threat in it, but he didn't care.

'Its *fucking* eyeballs have *fucking* popped out and it's *fucking* being eaten by *fucking* worms,' he said, and then added for emphasis, '*Fuck.*'

She slapped him.

He didn't see it coming but he felt it, hard and loud against his face.

She gasped when it was done. He touched his flushed, stinging cheek.

'I'm sorry,' she said, tried to touch him again on the shoulder as she'd done before. He flinched away from the gesture as if from a hornet.

'You're a bitch,' he said, flat and clear.

She slapped him again.

Reggie turned away; stared out the window.

But he could see her vague reflection behind him in the window.

She almost cried, a glimmering wetness at the corners of her eyes before she wiped it away. She gripped the steering wheel as a tremor passed through her. Then she started the car again and they pulled out of the place.

But in the rear-view Reggie could see the gentle hill and the tree atop it and the plot beneath where his father was, and though seen only fleetingly through a mirror, it felt as if he were being watched. A guilt and shame rose in him and he squashed it with indifference and old pain. Then he turned away from the mirror.

It kept showing him things he didn't want to see.

4.

'What happened?' Ivan asked when Reggie climbed back up into the tree house. It was early afternoon and hot and Reggie handed over the sandwich and lemonade to the man across from him.

'What?' Reggie asked, settling down again in what was

becoming his spot against the wall immediately to the right of the ladder.

'Your face,' Ivan said, gesturing with one hand at Reggie's cheek where his mom had hit him, taking a large bite of the sandwich with the other.

Reggie touched his face absently.

'My mom hit me,' he said.

'Why'd she do that?' Ivan asked.

'I called her a bitch,' he said.

'You sure have a way with people,' Ivan said, finishing the sandwich and washing it down with the glass of lemonade. 'Hit twice by two people in one day. Do you see the common denominator?'

'What do you mean?' Reggie asked.

'You know why you were hit, don't you?' Ivan said, brushing crumbs from his hands and off his lap.

'Because I called one guy dickless and called my mom a bitch,' he said.

'It's more than that,' Ivan said.

'How so?' Reggie asked.

'You let people hit you,' Ivan said. 'You let them get away with it.'

'The kid from school was bigger than me,' he said.

'So?' the killer said.

'My mom's an adult,' he said.

'And?' the killer said.

Reggie said nothing. He wanted to argue, wanted to defend himself, but didn't know how. Also, some part of him thought maybe he deserved it – the hard shove to the ground, the stinging slaps. Why and what for, he couldn't say.

'The common denominator is you,' the killer said. 'People know you're weak, so they know they can hit you if they want, and you won't fight back. You have to change the common denominator, and the equation changes.'

Reggie didn't reply, but he considered what the man said.

'Tell me about the man who killed your dad,' the killer said.

At first he didn't want to. Caught off guard, Reggie struggled to find the words. The words to refuse this man before him, but more than that, to refuse the memory. He thought again of the rear-view mirror casting back his father's gravesite, and the shame that simple reflection had stirred in him.

Reggie's thoughts and feelings whirled, collided, then solidified into something clearer. He focused and it came to him, and surprising himself, he told the killer in his tree house about another killer, the one who'd taken his dad from him with a single bullet.

***

'Where'd it happen?' the killer asked.
'In a parking lot,' Reggie said.

'What was his name?' Ivan asked. 'The man who killed your father.'

'I never asked,' he said. 'I never found out.'

'Why'd he do it?'

'Because he was a drug addict,' Reggie said. 'And my dad tried to help him.'

'Explain,' Ivan said.

'He was a parishioner at my dad's church. My dad caught him stealing from the tithing box one day,' he said. 'Dad asked him why he was doing it. The man broke down and cried and told my dad. He said he needed the money for a fix. He couldn't take it not having a fix. It made his body burn. It made him see crazy things. Only the drugs made it go away.'

'What did your dad do?' the killer asked.

'Dad talked to him, and listened,' Reggie said. Suddenly he had to do something with his hands. He rubbed them on his jeans; plucked at his shoelaces; scratched his arms. He needed to move and he stood, took a couple steps, settled down again and brought his legs up to his chest as he'd done before. For a strange and uncomfortable moment, Reggie wondered if this was how the drug addict had felt that day. 'He told the man about programmes that helped people like him. He told him the church sponsored these programmes and could get him in at discounted rates or even free.'

'Did he go?' Ivan asked.

Reggie stared at the man across from him. Lowered his

gaze to the large bandage about his middle, and the great red stain there. Again, he thought it looked like an eye, even through the bandage. A third eye looking at him, seeing him. Seeing *through* him.

'Yes,' he answered. 'He went.'

'But it didn't work, did it?' the killer asked.

Reggie superimposed himself on that large red eye. Looked with it back in time to the past year. He saw the parking lot clearly. His dad lying there in a pool of blood.

'For a time it did,' Reggie said. 'The guy went to a rehab centre for two weeks. My dad went to see him every day. Came back and told me and Mom how the guy was doing over dinner.

'"He's really going to make it," Dad said. "He's going to turn his life around," Dad told us. "That's great," Mom said. "That's good," I said.'

Reggie rubbed his eyes but found no tears. He felt inside like he should be crying, but he wasn't. There was a numbness and a dull sorrow, yet his eyes remained dry. He wondered if it'd be like that until he died, and somehow that was sad too.

'My dad was so happy when he was helping people,' Reggie said. 'And it made me and Mom happy to see him that way. He liked giving people hope. He'd take calls from the congregation at any hour.

'He woke in the middle of the night once to talk to a man whose mom had died from cancer. Another time, he drove twenty miles across town at 2 a.m. to console a couple whose son had died in Iraq. He even helped bury a little girl's dog that'd been hit by a car.'

'And helping this particular man got your father killed,' the killer said.

Reggie nodded.

'How'd it happen?' Ivan asked.

'My dad got a call from the security company that had set up the church's alarm system,' Reggie said. 'It was late when they called and told him one of the window sensors had been triggered. I heard his half of the conversation from my room, where I lay in bed watching TV. He drove off to check it out.

'Mom asked him not to. She told him to call the police. He said it was probably just an animal or kids throwing rocks. And he left us.'

Something started to come through the numbness inside him, and Reggie pushed it down again. The pain was old and tiresome and he was tired of hurting.

'He was gone for hours for what should have been a twenty-minute drive there and back,' Reggie said. 'Mom finally had enough, grabbed her keys, and dragged me along. I'd never seen her drive so fast, and yet the drive there seemed so long.

'I remember how dark it was on the highway,' Reggie said. 'It was like we were driving through a long tunnel. And those little homemade crosses on the side of the road where people mark accidents that have happened? They were so bright in the dark. Like signposts.'

He looked at the man across from him.

'And then we were there.'

Like his mom earlier on the way back from the movie and cemetery, Reggie felt a wetness at his eye and swiped it quickly away.

'We saw him in the parking lot, lying on the ground. The tithing box was broken in pieces around him. The money was scattered all over the place. A couple dollar bills blew around like trash.'

Reggie smiled at the killer across from him.

'The police counted it later and told us,' he said. 'There was sixteen dollars and seventy-two cents on the pavement. After all that trouble, he killed my dad and left the money.'

Whether he'd expected sympathy, some simple display of concern, from the man or not, Reggie wasn't sure. In the two days he'd known Ivan, he'd seen little to suggest the killer knew such simple things as human emotions. But what he definitely didn't expect was what the big man said next.

'Some things live. Some things die. Remember that, Reggie. There's no sense to it, and you waste your time trying to find any.'

At first, a hint of anger rose up in him. Reggie thought of seeing his dad dead there in the parking lot, and the killer's casual dismissal pissed him off. He clenched his fists, on the verge of saying something, like he'd said to the older kid at the drugstore. But as quickly as it had come, the rage slipped away.

Instead, Reggie found himself repeating those words in his head, the killer's voice echoing in his mind. *Some things live. Some things die.*

Reggie found his gaze drifting again to the shoulder holster and the pistol slid snugly into it. Ivan watched him, saw the direction of Reggie's glance. Quickly, Reggie looked away.

With nothing left to say, they sat in silence.

Chapter Four

1.

That afternoon the killer let him hold the pistol.

He wanted to walk around a bit, which Reggie didn't think was a good idea. But Ivan insisted and they went down the ladder; Reggie first, the killer slowly following. He said he needed to know if he could move if he had to. Reggie knew that meant escape if he had to, but he kept that to himself.

The killer limped along, occasionally stopping to lean against a tree, holding his abdomen, catching his breath, but otherwise making steady progress. They had walked for about twenty minutes when Ivan told Reggie to stop.

The killer walked over to a fallen tree and set their empty water bottles on it. Making his way back to Reggie, he sat on a stump and pulled out his gun. He checked the safety and held it out to Reggie.

The gun was heavy and solid and cool.

'Feel the weight of it,' the killer said. 'Become familiar with its contours, how your fingers feel around it.'

Reggie did so, feeling the heft of the thing. It was heavier than he would have thought. It felt large in his small hands.

'Always keep it pointed away from you,' the killer said. 'Never point it at anything you don't intend to shoot.'

Reggie lifted the gun and aimed at the bottles on the fallen tree several yards away. Ivan rose and stood behind him.

'Keep your right arm locked,' he said. 'Now bend your left at the elbow a bit. Keep your legs apart and the left one forward.'

Reggie did as he was told, and looked down the sight at the bottles. Ivan reached over him and towards the safety. Reggie looked up at him.

'Won't someone hear?' he asked.

Ivan smiled and reached in his jacket. From a pocket he pulled out a black metal tube and reached again over Reggie. Screwing the silencer on, he then flicked off the safety.

'Go ahead,' he said. 'Give it a try.'

Reggie sighted down the pistol at one of the bottles. His finger curled around the trigger, but he didn't pull it. He thought of his dad in the church parking lot and the blood on the asphalt.

'Pull, don't squeeze,' said the killer.

Then he was thinking about the older boy at the drug-store. And his mom slapping him at the cemetery.

He pulled the trigger smoothly and deliberately.

There was a low *whoosh* and dirt kicked up about a foot in front of the tree. The recoil shook in his arms and made his muscles twitch.

'Again,' said the killer, soft but firm, and Reggie pulled the trigger again.

A silver-dollar sized crater appeared in the bark just below the bottle on the left. The *thunk* of the bullet sounded like something heavy dropped on carpeted floor. The bottle did a little wiggle and twirl like a tired dancer, but came to rest still upright.

'Again,' the killer said, and Reggie pulled the trigger.

The low *whoosh* again and the bottle disappeared, pulled out of sight like something yanked out of reality. It was there, and then it was gone.

'Good,' said the killer. 'Now the other one.'

He adjusted his stance and aimed. Pulled the trigger and the other bottle likewise was yanked away.

'Very good,' said the killer. 'You're a natural.'

Ivan reached out and over him to take the gun. For a moment both their hands were over the weapon, and Reggie didn't want to let go. When he did and it was out of his hands, Ivan considered him with a curious look.

It felt good holding the gun, and when it was in his hands he wasn't afraid of being hit by anyone.

'Let's head back,' Ivan said, holding his side and starting

to walk, each step placed gingerly and with care. He holstered the gun and Reggie watched it until it was out of sight beneath the flap of the jacket hem.

He could still feel it in his hands, like a phantom sensation.

Like it belonged there.

***

'Was there ever someone you wished you hadn't killed?' Reggie asked when they were back in the tree house.

The walk and climb back up had exhausted Ivan, and the man settled back down in his spot near the far window with a groan. Outside, a summer wind stirred the branches and made the structure moan likewise, as if returning Ivan's grunt like a separated beast calling for its pack. The swinging branches brought the sun in fits and starts of bright light, casting alternating bars of sunlight and shadow across the floor and the walls of the tree house. This pattern fell over Ivan, making the man seem caged, behind bars.

He thought of what the deputy had told his mom earlier.

Yesterday morning a man escaped from a police escort taking him to the county jail in Tucson.

'No,' said the killer, the answer snapping Reggie back to the moment. 'There were two people I wish I hadn't killed.'

'Who were they?' Reggie asked.

'Just a woman and her son,' the killer said. 'No one special.'

'Is it the woman you raped and killed yesterday?' Reggie asked.

Ivan looked at him sternly.

'What are you talking about?' he said.

'When I rode into town for the medicine,' Reggie said, 'there were police all over the highway. One of them stopped me and told me about the woman and kid you killed when you escaped.'

'I didn't kill anyone yesterday,' he said.

'But the cop said ...' Reggie began.

'I don't care what the cop said,' the killer interrupted him. 'A state trooper recognized the car I was driving as reported stolen. Pulled me over. A second highway patrol vehicle happened to be passing and pulled in behind me. They cuffed me, searched the vehicle.'

'What were you doing here in Payne, then?' Reggie asked. 'Were you sent to kill someone?'

'Only if necessary,' the killer said. 'I was sent to find something. Not my usual business, but the money was good.'

'How'd you get away?' Reggie asked, interested in what the killer was supposed to find, but deciding to save that question for another time.

'There are a few ways to work yourself out of handcuffs if you know what you're doing,' Ivan said. 'I waited until the two police cars were separated in traffic before I made my move. The trooper was young, inexperienced, and panicked when he saw me free of the cuffs. He crashed into the concrete divider, the window shattered, and I crawled out.'

Reggie's uncertainty must have shown on his face, because the killer elaborated a little more. That the man wanted Reggie to believe him seemed somehow important, and so he filed that away in his mind.

Always mind the details, he thought, and was slightly disturbed by the killer's voice replaying in his head.

'I escaped yesterday from the police, beat them up pretty bad, got my stuff back, but I didn't kill anyone. And I don't do rape.'

'So the woman and kid you're talking about ...'

'Happened a long time ago,' said the killer.

'The officer said he'd show me the pictures,' Reggie said, thinking of the deputy standing in front of his bike, blocking him, and later on the porch with his mom. 'You know ... of the crime scene.'

'He was fucking with you,' Ivan said.

Reggie thought of the deputy, and the bigger kid knocking him off his bike. He thought of holding the cool, heavy gun and pulling the trigger. He thought of what Ivan had said to him earlier.

The common denominator.

People know you're weak.

He hadn't felt weak with the pistol in his hands.

'What about this woman and her son?' Reggie said,

changing the subject back again. 'The ones you killed a long time ago.'

After a brief pause the killer spoke, and Reggie listened.

***

'There was a woman who left her husband because he hit her. And we're not just talking about how some guys do when they're drunk. He hit her a lot.

'Like many women in the same situation, at first she tried to placate him. She thought it was her fault. Maybe she didn't pay enough attention to him. Maybe she wasn't pretty enough. Lots of maybes with no answers.

'He never gave her answers. He just hit her. And she took it, because a wife was supposed to be obedient to her husband. That's how she was raised, and so she just took it. Until he hit their son.

'That's when things changed. That's when she couldn't take it anymore.

'So one day she left him. She packed a couple suitcases when he was at work, took their son, and left. Didn't leave a note or anything.

'There was only one problem,' the killer said. 'Her husband was someone important. Or, more accurately, his father was. Her husband was a coyote for human traffickers. His father was the man financing that operation, and many others.

'Her husband's family had their hands not only in human trafficking, but drugs, prostitution, weapons procurement, and pornography. This family was used to getting what they wanted, and once they had something it was theirs until they no longer wanted it. And her husband wanted her back, just not alive.

'He didn't even need all of her. Just the head would do, he said.

'Furthermore, since his son was a quiet kid, a reader, and not at all likely suitable for the family business, he saw no reason to let the kid live either.

'So the husband called me. He explained to me what he wanted, and offered me a lot of money. I accepted the job.

'I found the woman less than a week later. She was working as a card dealer in some Indian casino. The kid was going to school nearby.

'I waited for them at their home. The kid came first and I knocked him out and tied him to a chair. The woman called some time later and left a message on the machine. She told her son she was going to cover a shift for one of the other dealers and wouldn't be home until the following morning. She told him not to wait up.

'My initial plan was to do them together. Let the mom watch me kill her son, then kill her. The husband said he wanted her to suffer, but he didn't specify how. I thought that was as good a way as any. Sometimes emotional pain is greater than physical.

'Remember that, Reggie,' the killer said.

Reggie did just that, adding it to the litany of other things the killer had already told him:

Always mind the details.

Some things live. Some things die.

'But I didn't see any sense in making the kid wait that long,' the killer continued. 'He'd woken up at the ringing of the phone, took stock of the situation, and was crying. He'd also peed himself, and I thought that was enough so I shot him in the face.'

The offhand manner in which the killer relayed the story at first bothered Reggie. At the mention of the kid in the story getting shot in the face, Reggie thought of the gun in the holster under Ivan's jacket. He thought of holding that gun only a short while ago, squeezing the trigger, watching the bottles get whisked away. The power he'd felt with its weight in his hands.

But picturing one of those bullets punching into the face of a boy like himself was another thing altogether. And then the faceless boy in this mental movie was replaced by his dad, sprawled in the parking lot of the church.

Shifting uneasily against the tree house wall, Reggie looked out the window, then looked to the ladder again. But he didn't move, and listened as the killer continued.

Ivan likewise shifted against the wall he sat against, a hand to his bandage. A barely audible moan escaped as he shuffled for a more comfortable position. But otherwise there was no hint of pain – either physical, or the greater sort he'd just mentioned as he'd confessed to killing a child.

'It was just after midnight when I shot him.

'She came home at around five in the morning. She saw her son tied to the chair, but she didn't see me. She ran over to him and cupped his head to her, crying, shaking him, telling him to wake up.

'I walked out of the hall and hit her over the head.

'I tied her to another chair. Took a seat on the living room recliner, turned on the television, waited for her to wake up. I watched three episodes of a *Twilight Zone* marathon before she woke.

'She was gagged so her scream at seeing her dead son again was muffled and not that loud at all. I held a finger to my mouth for her to quiet down. That didn't work. So I pulled out my switchblade and that got her attention.

'I turned the recliner so I was facing her.

'I told her who sent me, though I'm sure she knew.

'I told her what was going to happen to her, and she grew quiet and resigned. She got control of her breathing and hung her head like she was tired. I watched her for a time, letting her gather herself.

'When finally she looked up at me, she used her eyes to indicate the gag. I understood she wanted to say something, didn't think she'd be any trouble, and so I took the gag off.

'"When did you kill him?" she asked.

'"Just after midnight," I told her.

'"Did he suffer?" she asked.

'"No," I told her.

'"Would you wait and kill me after midnight?" she said. "Kill me the same time you killed him?"

'I thought about it, thought her request was interesting, had never heard anything quite like it before. People had begged, people had prayed, told me the things they could do for me. The money they could get me. The women they could get me. Cars, houses, drugs. I'd been offered everything. Heard every conceivable plea.

'But no one had ever requested what time I would kill them.

'I was intrigued, so I agreed.

'We watched the marathon together, episode after episode. All the classics were played, and I remembered why I liked the show so much as a kid.

'I got her a glass of water when she asked.

'I followed her to the restroom when she said she had to urinate.

'And when she asked if she could sit on the sofa with her son, I said yes, and watched her untie him, pick him up, and carry him over to the couch. She held him in her lap as the clock slowly ticked away the time. Morning to afternoon to evening, slowly, so slowly, the longest day I've ever lived.

'Until, at five minutes to midnight, she spoke again.

'"You didn't have to do this," she said.

'I was briefly disappointed. I'd heard this many times

before. The appeal to my humanity. That I could choose to be better. That I didn't have to kill the person I was sent to kill. So often, this tactic quickly led back to begging.

'"No," I said. "I didn't. But I did."

'She nodded, and that was it. No pleading. No anger. No cursing.

'I was pleased and gave her a little smile.

'When the clock ticked midnight I walked over and put the gun to her head.

'"Thank you for waiting," she said. And I told her she was welcome.

'Then I pulled the trigger and it was done.'

***

'Why do you regret that one?' Reggie asked. 'Of all the people you've killed, why do you wish you'd never killed her and her son?'

Ivan didn't answer immediately. He cocked his head a bit like a scholar considering a great question.

'I think it was because she was polite,' the killer said.

'Because she was polite?' Reggie asked, surprised. He didn't know what answer he'd expected, but 'she was polite' wasn't it.

'She didn't fight me,' the killer said, nodding. 'She didn't curse me. She didn't demean herself by begging. It was as if she knew it was merely my job, something I had to do.

'Killing for some people is fun,' the killer said. 'They

take pleasure out of hurting others. It's amusing when they kill someone and the target shits or pisses their pants. They get off on it. I knew this one guy who used to collect things from his targets. Little objects they'd owned – a knick-knack, a photo, a piece of jewellery. Sometimes a body part: a swatch of skin or a finger.'

The killer fixed his blue eyes again on Reggie. Those ice-blue spheres were windows, showing Reggie things he'd never imagined. A whole other world was there behind those eyes.

'It's not like that for me,' said the killer. 'It's just some-thing I'm good at. Like some people are fast typists. Or others are good with numbers. I do it because I'm good at it, and I get paid well for it.'

It occurred to Reggie then just how small the tree house was. They were so near each other. The walls seemed too close, squeezing him in. Pushing him nearer the man than he was comfortable being.

'And she knew this?' Reggie asked, the question coming out in a croak.

'Yes,' the killer said. 'She knew it was nothing personal. Knew it was just my job. And so she didn't hold it against me. And I appreciated that.

'I think about her sometimes,' Ivan said. 'Holding her dead son on the couch, watching television. How the light of the television flashed across them. She looked like a ghost there, dead already, on the couch with her son.'

Reggie thought of how he'd come downstairs last night,

saw his mom in a similar fashion, glowing in the television light. Chills went across his flesh in a tremulous wave.

'I'd never seen a person dead until they were dead,' Ivan said. 'Until I'd pulled the trigger or strangled the life out of them or stabbed them to death. But she was dead long before I did the deed. She was dead the moment she saw her son was.'

'I've never seen that kind of love,' Ivan said, 'and I sometimes wish I'd left it alone. I could have lied to the husband and his father. I could have told them there were complications and I'd had to dispose of the bodies. My reputation was spotless. I could have let the woman and her kid go, and no one would have ever known.'

'But you didn't,' Reggie said.

'No, I didn't,' said the killer.

'Because that's your job,' Reggie said. 'It's who you are and what you do.'

The killer didn't speak or nod, but the answer was in his eyes.

2.

Climbing on his bike again, pedalling away from the garage, Reggie thought of what he'd asked Ivan earlier, before leaving the tree house.

How do you find someone? Like you did the woman and her kid?

Everyone leaves a trail. Use what you know.

Ivan's answer had made Reggie think of the school's yearbook, and he'd gone back to the house to dig it out of his closet. It had taken him twenty minutes of flipping through the pages to find the photograph of the older boy from the drugstore, the rubber thief. His name was Johnny Witte. With the name, he was then able to go onto his computer and do the rest. The kid's street address was familiar to Reggie, and he told his mom he was going back into town.

She was on the couch again with the television on. She didn't look at him and waved him away, so he left. He rolled his bike out from the garage and rode off.

The police along the highway were gone and he made good time without being stopped. The route to the older kid's home took him through the downtown business district. People walked along the sidewalks, under the awnings of the antique shops and bookstores and video stores and burger joints. They went about their business as if nothing else existed, as if each of them were the centre of it all. They walked through the world but weren't a part of it.

That each of them went about their lives while a killer was in his tree house made Reggie feel strangely special. Unique. Like he carried an important secret that affected many things.

Turning into the residential streets, the tract houses lined up side by side and nearly identical like clones manufactured on an assembly line, Reggie found the right number and rode on by. He didn't see the older kid but that didn't mean anything. He could have been inside or at a friend's.

So Reggie rode to the corner of the street and waited.

He watched people mowing lawns. He saw the drifting trails of barbecue smoke swirling skyward like incense offerings to the heavens. A little girl gave her dog a bath in a little plastic pool in the yard. A boy and his dad threw a football in the street.

He felt like a detective, watching people. Or a killer scoping out an intended target, minding the details.

Then he saw Johnny Witte turn the corner at the far end of the street. Even from this distance Reggie recognized him. The rubber bandit strolled with a nonchalant gait as if he hadn't made fun of Reggie's dad and knocked him down mere hours ago.

Reggie pedalled hard, an imaginary cross hairs on the older kid.

The condom thief didn't see him until it was too late.

His eyes turned large in surprise and he tried jumping out of the way. Reggie's bike clipped him on the hip and thigh and Johnny Witte fell, rolling, on the sidewalk. A long stretch of shredded skin along his forearm dotted blood and as he pushed up Reggie leaned forward and spat a nice big gob on the kid's face.

'Fuck you, dickless!' he yelled and pedalled away furiously.

He looked once behind him.

The condom bandit was on his feet. Coming after him, arms pumping. The Morse Code thumping of his leather-soled feet spoke of his fury.

The red-flushed rage on the older boy's face said he was going to pound Reggie good. And that was just what Reggie wanted.

He thought of what Ivan had said.

The common denominator. People know you're weak.

He braked in a vacant field. Dust rose behind him.

He got off the bike, looked at the ground around him. He picked up two large dirt clods, one in either hand. He didn't have long to wait. The older kid wasn't that far behind him. The footfalls of his furious approach smacked a mad cadence in the still summer air, thudding like the clamour of a stampeding herd.

Reggie gripped the missiles tight in either hand, hefting them, testing their weight. Channelled his own rage into them.

The bigger kid came running into the dirt field.

Turning to face him, Reggie let fly the first missile. It flew inches to the left of his target's head. The older kid watched it fly by in surprise.

Reggie let loose the second one.

The rubber thief, who'd asked why Reggie was crying that day, did he crap his pants, did his gay lover dump him, watched this second missile also, and it was like slow motion, the rock sailing through the air between them. It found its target. Hit him high on the chest, below the shoulder. Sent him stumbling back. He tripped and tumbled in the dirt.

Reggie ran at him, yelling, fists clenched.

But the bigger kid was getting up, saw Reggie coming, and was ready. His fist met Reggie's jaw and sent him down into the hard dirt. The impact jarred the bones of Reggie's face, sending shockwaves throughout his body.

He tried getting up and a boot to his ribs sent him back down.

It was difficult to breathe but he tried crawling.

Fistfuls of shirt pulled him up and he was looking up into the bigger kid's face.

'You couldn't let it go, could you, little faggot?' the rubber bandit said, cheeks red, spittle flying with each word. 'Fucking faggot! Goddamn motherfucker!'

He punched Reggie square in the stomach. All the air was sucked out of him. He crumpled to his knees.

He was waist high now with the bigger kid.

He thought of Johnny Witte stealing rubbers as he fought for breath. What did he do with them? Try them on?

It suddenly seemed funny and a laugh escaped through the pain.

'What's so funny, faggot?' roared the other kid, cocking his arm back, fist raised.

Reggie remembered something else Ivan had said.

Always mind the details.

Eyes squinted against the pain, Reggie looked dead ahead.

He balled his fist, steadied himself with a trembling breath, threw a punch. Time seemed to slow again. Almost to stop. His piston-fist nailed Witte in the crotch. He felt the mashing of the other guy's balls through the jeans.

The bigger kid let out a long, slow groan before falling to his knees. They were eye to eye now. Johnny Witte's cheeks were teary and red with agony, then, rather than rage. Reggie reached out and grabbed the other guy's shirt, pulled him close as had been done to him moments before.

'You ever bother me again,' he said with effort, 'I'll kill you.'

He rose on shaky legs. The older kid's eyes followed him up.

'Good night, dickless,' he said, cocked his arm and let fly, his knuckles slamming Witte hard on the temple. The condom bandit fell with a thud to the dirt.

Reggie walked back to his bike, got on, rode away.

He took his time riding home. The sun on him felt good, and the busy world quiet and calm.

3.

He stopped in the living room on the way upstairs. His mom was still on the couch. She still wouldn't look at him.

He walked over and sat beside her.

'I'm sorry I called you a bitch,' he said.

83

She turned to him, saw the dirt on his clothes.

'Jesus,' she said. 'What happened?'

She reached to inspect him, and he gently pushed her hands away.

'I fell off my bike,' he said.

'Again?' she said, worried and knowing he was lying at the same time.

'It's fine, Mom,' he said. 'I just wanted to say I'm sorry.'

She studied him, trying to figure it out. Something was wrong. She couldn't read him, needed to know where he was coming from. Had to anticipate him, and she couldn't.

'I just wanted you to see your dad,' she said, tears rising in her eyes.

'I know,' he said kindly, smiling. 'But that's my decision, not yours.'

People know you're weak.

He couldn't allow that anymore. Not with anyone.

'I love you,' he said. 'But I'll figure things out on my own.'

Then he stood up and walked away. The sounds of his mom's soft crying followed him up the stairs, and it was the loneliest sound he'd ever heard.

4.

'Have you ever killed anything?' the killer asked him.

'Just bugs and stuff,' Reggie said.

He'd come straight to the tree house after the fight with

Johnny Witte and his brief exchange with his mom. He'd felt like a streak of light flying through town back home. Charged; powerful. The world seemed to have admitted him to a special place. He felt light inside almost as if he could float away. He needed to talk to someone about it, the feeling inside of him, and there was only one person he could think of.

Yet, having regaled Ivan with the epic tale of the older boy's serious ass kicking, the man merely nodded. Then he'd changed subjects to this.

'You've never killed an animal?' the killer asked. 'Never shot a pigeon with a BB gun? Or stomped a cat to death?'

'No,' Reggie said, a little horrified. But not so much that he wanted to leave. 'Of course not.'

'Of course not,' said Ivan.

He paused, rubbing his stubbly cheek with one large hand.

'How did it feel holding the gun?' the killer asked.

Reggie thought a moment before answering. It had been a mix of emotions when he'd held the gun. There was power and fear all mixed together, and excitement also.

'It felt good,' he said, unable to put his thoughts to words.

'When you pulled the trigger?' the killer prodded.

'Exciting,' he said. 'And scary too.'

'You weren't really seeing the bottles, were you?' the killer asked.

Reggie's heart skipped a beat. How could the man know that? Could he read thoughts, this killer in front of him? Was he something more than a man?

'No,' he admitted.

'You saw the people who've caused you pain,' said the killer.

'Yes,' he said.

'You saw the deputy,' said the killer, and Reggie nodded. 'You saw this kid Johnny Witte,' he said, and Reggie nodded again.

'Did you see your mom?' Ivan asked.

Reggie didn't say anything. This question wasn't right. He knew it wasn't right, and he didn't like it.

'Did you see your dad?'

His heart beat even faster. His head was a storm of thoughts. He wanted to charge the man across from him and punch him like he'd punched Witte. He wanted to deny what the man said, yet couldn't.

'Your dad left you, and you're angry,' said Ivan. His voice was soft, yet not exactly gentle. It wasn't hard either. He was simply stating facts for which he knew there was no denial. 'Your mom hit you because she doesn't understand your pain.'

Inside, the emotions shifted. From anger to resignation to sorrow of a kind deep and raw and heavy. They shifted tectonically like continents realigning.

'Your mom has her pain,' Ivan said, 'and expects yours to be the same. She thinks she knows what you feel, though

86

she never could. Your dad left you, when he was supposed to be around for a long time.'

A tear had come to his eye unbidden, surprising Reggie, and he wiped it away to no effect. Others followed, and soon he was shaking with the release of them.

'When you held the gun,' the killer said, 'all that changed. The world no longer happened around you. You were happening to the world. You made the calls. It was up to you what happened next.

'In your mind's eye were those who'd wronged you. The bullet could end any of them. Or you could spare them. It was your choice and yours alone. The gun was an extension of your mind, and in so being it was really you that was the weapon, and not the gun.

'When you kill someone,' the killer continued, 'you're making a statement to the universe. To all of creation you're declaring yourself the one in charge. You say how things will turn out. It's all up to you.'

Reggie took all this in as the sobs ran their course. By the time Ivan had finished, Reggie had better control of himself. The odd sob still wracked him – he sniffed and rubbed his eyes – but it was dwindling, that sudden pain. Lowering itself back down from where it'd arisen.

'Come here,' Ivan said, waving him over.

Reggie didn't know what to do. This was his side, and over there was Ivan's. They'd been talking on and off since last night and almost all day today. But it was just that

Seth C. Adams

– talking. They'd kept their distance, and Reggie was fine with that.

But now the killer motioned him closer, and Reggie found he was fine with that also. He stood and crossed the space between them.

He sat beside the killer.

The man put an arm around him and held him close. The man was large and present and warm. Like a mountain sheltering refugees.

'It'll be okay, son,' the killer said, and Reggie believed him.

Chapter Five

1.

That night they watched the stars together. The vast blackness of the expanse above was impressed upon both of them. The feeling was palpable in the air between them. They lay with their heads near the edge where the ladder was, looking up between the branches swaying above.

'What did you want to be when you were a kid?' Reggie asked.

'I almost don't remember that life,' Ivan said. 'It was so long ago.'

At first the killer said nothing else, and Reggie almost dropped the subject. Then he thought about what Ivan had asked about firing the gun, and his mom and dad, and he continued. There wouldn't be barriers between them, Reggie realized. Nothing would be off limits.

Somehow, he knew that it was important for things to be that way.

'But you do remember,' Reggie said. 'What was it? What did you want to be?'

Still, Ivan didn't answer immediately. Reggie wanted to turn his head to look at the man lying beside him, but fought the urge. It felt wrong at that moment to look at him, like an invasion of privacy. Beneath the long, black sky, that seemed something important also. That each of them speak in turn, answer all questions, but on their own terms, in their own time.

'I wanted to be a writer,' Ivan said.

'Like Stephen King or Ray Bradbury?' Reggie asked, genuinely interested. That was the kind of stuff he read, and to think he was next to someone who could have been like them was almost as exciting as being next to a killer.

'Like Mark Twain or Hemingway,' Ivan said. 'I wanted to write things to challenge the country. I wanted people to see the beauty and the ugliness of it.'

'What happened?' Reggie asked. 'Why didn't you write?'

'Oh, I wrote,' said Ivan. 'I wrote for hours on end in my room. With the door closed and the world shut out I wrote like crazy.

'But then one day my father walked in without knocking. I usually pretended to be doing homework when I was writing, but he came in too quickly for me to hide my stories and pick up a textbook.

'"What is this?" he said and picked up a notebook with some of my stories in it. He flipped through it, reading some, flipping ahead, reading more. He looked from me to the notebook and back again. "What is this shit?" he said and threw my notebook across the room.

'He searched my room for more of my stories,' Ivan said. 'He tore through the drawers of my desk. He dug through the piles of stuff in my closet. He reached under my bed and pulled out what he found.

'All in all there must have been a dozen notebooks,' Ivan said. 'He bundled them in his arms and took them to the living room. He threw them in the fireplace and squirted lighter fluid on them, struck a match, and as I watched, horrified, he set them on fire.'

'That sucks,' Reggie said.

'All my dreams,' Ivan continued, hardly missing a beat, as if Reggie hadn't spoken at all, 'up in smoke. Years of ideas gone in a flash, just like that,' he said and punctuated it with a snap of his fingers.

'I never tried writing again after that,' he said. 'I never bought another notebook for any purpose but school notes. It was hard at first, but I eventually learned not to even think my stories in my head. I realized that I wasn't meant for writing. Not in this life, not in this world.'

Neither of them said anything for a time after that. Crickets and cicadas made their ticking and clicking music, and somewhere far away a night bird warbled. High above in the great black sky a shooting star streaked by in an arc, and Reggie thought maybe it carried with it the long-gone dreams of a boy turned killer.

'But it's quite all right,' said the killer. 'I eventually found something that suited me better.'

2.

Reggie crept thief-like into the house and up the stairs to his room. Again the house seemed to accommodate his movements so that he reached his destination without sound or disturbance. With the door shut and locked he started to peel his clothes off.

He didn't stop with his jeans and shirt, though. As he'd done only a time or two before, he stripped completely naked and slid the window open an inch before climbing into bed.

The feel of the sheets and the night breeze against his bare body did something strange. The tingling caress of sensations calmed him. It made him hyper aware when so often in months prior he'd felt numb.

When his mind haunted him, turning even his dreams against him, the calming of his body often helped still the rest of him. His troubled thoughts slowly quieted like the serene waters of the ocean after a great storm.

And in this sudden tranquillity it was as if things made sense. As if things had a purpose. What it was, this meaning, he couldn't exactly interpret or understand. It was as of something just out of reach, no matter how he stretched for it.

At these times he thought if he could just get things quiet enough, and just listen hard enough, he might hear something. Someone talking maybe, or words without a voice, but a message, nonetheless. In these fathomless words would be something he needed to hear. Something he desperately needed to know.

But he never heard it.

Eventually sleep would come. Sometimes there would be dreams and sometimes there wouldn't. And, for a time, that was all there was.

3.

The distant baying of hounds woke Reggie up early. The digital clock on the stand near his bed read 6:14 a.m. Then he thought of Ivan telling him he had to find out if he could get around. Reggie had known the implication of those words – the killer had to know if he was physically capable of making a quick escape.

He got up, dressed quickly, and opening his bedroom door slowly, started downstairs. His mom was at the kitchen table, nursing a steaming cup of coffee. She was still in her bathrobe. She greeted him with a weak smile. She seemed subdued, and though this made Reggie a little sad, it made him a little happy too.

That he had beaten *her* down for a change. And, unlike his mom, he hadn't had to slap anyone. Reggie recalled Ivan's words about emotional suffering being as bad as physical or worse, and just like that his mom's demeanour didn't seem like such a triumph after all.

'I'm sorry about yesterday,' she said.

He had no choice but to stop and acknowledge her. The hounds sounded again, far away but for some reason more urgent in their distance.

'Me too,' he said, stepping up to her, leaning over and giving her a hug.

'Want breakfast?' she asked, patting his arm.

'I'm not hungry right now,' he said, noting the tone of hope in her voice. She really was sorry, and wanted to fix things. 'I'm going outside for a bit. I'll eat later.'

'Okay,' was all she said – no arguing, no questioning – and then Reggie was moving away from her and to the door.

Opening the door, stepping outside, he had the brief urge to turn around and ask for breakfast after all. He thought of sitting at the table with her, the two of them eating and talking. Maybe they'd even find a reason to smile.

Then he was out in the yard, and the door shut behind him.

4.

Ivan was coming down the ladder even as Reggie came jogging up.

'You hear that?' he asked, and Reggie nodded.

The dogs were still a ways off, their barks and yelps distant. But still too close.

The killer still wore only his jacket and pants, bare chest and bandage showing. But he carried his bloodied shirt under one arm. He handed it over to Reggie. Reggie saw that it was wet with fresh blood and suppurated discharge.

'It was only a matter of time,' the killer said. 'But I have a plan.'

Reggie looked down at the bloodied shirt. He tried holding it by the clean areas, but two fingers of his right hand were touching the fabric in sticky places. The wetness was warm and thick.

'You go on west with that,' the killer said. 'Smear it on trees and the ground every so often. Take it about a mile or so away from your house,' he said, buttoning up his jacket as he spoke. 'I'll go east, also about a mile. I saw a campground out that way and a stream. I'll try to lose my scent there. I'll clean myself up, get fresh clothes.'

Reggie was nodding, even as a heavy feeling settled in his stomach.

He didn't want Ivan to go.

'Will I see you again?' he asked, not liking the whiny note in his voice.

People know you're weak.

He didn't want to be weak around Ivan.

Ivan looked down at him. His blue eyes seemed afire.

'I'm not well enough to be on my own,' the killer said. 'I shouldn't even be doing this, but we've got to try. Now bloodhounds aren't as easy to fool as they make it seem in movies. All we're doing is giving them three trails to follow, instead of one.'

Ivan pointed out into the woods in the general direction of where Reggie had found him just two days ago.

'Where I came from, leading here,' he said. 'Where you're going,' he said, pointing west into the woods. 'And where I'm going,' he said, now pointing east. 'I'm hoping that a small town like Payne doesn't have a lot of manpower. I'm hoping that the dogs take the freshest track, either mine or yours, and not the original leading them here.'

He turned back to Reggie. He smiled, but his face was solemn.

Though flushed red in the cheeks by adrenaline and action, beneath the eyes his flesh was pale. He seemed a ghost; not fully there.

'It might work,' he said. 'It might not.'

He kneeled down so that he was eye level with Reggie. He groaned with the effort.

'If it does,' he said, 'I'll be back.'

He held out his hand. Reggie took it. They shook on it as if sealing another deal between them; one, two, three pumps up and down.

'We're friends,' Ivan said.

'Friends,' Reggie echoed.

And then he was nudging Reggie west, standing, groaning again, holding his side, and walking steady and fast eastward. Reggie watched him move into the distance, weaving among the trees. In moments, the man was lost from sight through the foliage wall.

Reggie turned westward, holding the bloody shirt.

The hounds bayed in the distance, far, but not far enough.

Reggie started running.

***

The world flew past him, like a rolling stage backdrop giving the illusion of speed. His feet only tapped the earth in brief and tentative touches, as if at any moment he'd leave it altogether and lift off in flight.

Here and there he skidded to a stop to rub the bloody shirt on a fir or on a boulder or a fallen branch or the ground itself. Pine needles and leaves and bits of grit stuck to the red stained shirt like bugs to fly strips.

He charged uphill and downhill, leaping over stones and stumps. He ducked low-hanging limbs and weaved between thick trunks like a receiver on the field, in zone in sight.

The hounds were faint and then gradually louder, coming closer. He tried moving opposite the direction he thought they were coming from. He spotted a rocky cliff face maybe fifty feet high and steered towards it.

There was a natural indentation in the face about halfway up, not quite a cave but deep enough to hide a man. The climb was steep but manageable. Reggie boosted himself up the first stone and started up. Little avalanches fell beneath his heels.

It took him five minutes to reach the alcove. He smeared the shirt on the rocks on his way up. He crawled into the niche as far as he could go. Pushing the shirt into a corner, he used his hands as shovels and scooped dirt on top of it.

Then he started back down, once sliding and banging his right knee smartly. He jumped the last five feet, landing hard. He backed up and looked up again at the recess where he'd put the shirt.

It was just high enough that you couldn't see all the way into it. The police would have to climb up there to see inside.

Proud of his work, Reggie turned and ran home. The hounds grew louder behind him, then quieted. He'd done all he could, and hoped it was enough.

He wanted to see his friend again.

5.

Time passed slowly that day. As if the laws of nature had changed and there were temporal ramifications. Astral realignments shifted the very nature of space and time and stretched the minutes into little eternities.

Reggie sat on the porch pretending to read, but really sitting as a spectator in an audience waiting to see what would happen. He waited to see police cars turning and screeching into their driveway. Ivan would be handcuffed in the back seat of one, and the officers would rush up to arrest Reggie too. They'd drag him to the station and interrogate him. Slap him around and tell him to confess.

In the bright lights of the interrogation room he'd break, cry, and beg for mercy. Instead, he'd get a ten to twenty stretch with a big black cellmate that would make Reggie his little white bitch.

Or Ivan would come limping out of the woods and the two of them would think that they'd done it. They'd fooled the police and their dogs. But then they'd come out of the woods behind Ivan – or come screeching up the drive in SWAT vans – and there'd be a big shoot-out, bullets flying everywhere. Whizzing through the air and shattering glass and walls and flesh and bone, leaving Ivan bullet-riddled on the ground, dying. Maybe Reggie or his mom or both of them would be hit too, caught in the crossfire, their blood pouring into the dirt of the earth also.

All three of them dying and bleeding out into the dirt.

Or Ivan would come running out and he really *had* fooled the trackers. And he'd stop at the porch and ask Reggie to come with him. They'd go and find another place. Reggie would be sad to leave home but Ivan would tell him they'd find another. Off into the world they'd run to disappear and start again.

He'd learn the ways of Ivan's trade.

He'd learn to fire other guns. He'd learn how to fight. He'd go to far-off places and learn new things. He'd start a new life and the old one would fade away. So that, like Ivan, he would one day look back and wonder at the boy he had been and doubt if the memories were real.

But an hour passed and that was long enough of the pretending to read and the daydreaming. He had to get up and move. Reggie went back in the house, sat on the sofa, and turned the television on. His mom wasn't in sight but he could hear her roaming about upstairs in her room.

He switched to the local Tucson news station. He sat through stories of flu outbreaks and sports scores and a mayor's sex scandal, waiting to see Ivan's face on the screen, or his own. Because somehow the police had found out he'd been harbouring the fugitive and now they were coming after him, alerting the country, slapping his fourteen-year-old face on every screen across the nation.

Nothing.

It was as if it wasn't happening. Or as if it was happening in a subworld, an offshoot of reality that didn't quite matter, passing under the radar of everyday concern.

Then his mom came downstairs and walked into the room, setting down a cardboard box on the table in front of him. The flaps were shut and he couldn't see what was in it. She was dressed, finally, in jeans and a blouse.

'I think I've been holding on for too long,' his mom said, sniffing and wiping at her eyes.

He didn't know what she was talking about but knew he soon would and so listened patiently.

'I've kept his things up there like he was just going to

come walking in any day now,' she said, giving a nervous laugh and a sob at the same time. 'Like he was just on vacation and he'd be home before long.'

Reggie knew now what was going on and just let it happen. He didn't have an opinion on the matter. Couldn't afford to – it was either the pain or numbness. He'd stick with the opiate-like numbness.

'I'm going into town,' she said. 'I'm going to give his clothes to the Salvation Army. I kept the photo albums out on the bed for you to look at. You can take whatever you want. Put them up in your room.'

Reggie didn't say anything. He looked down and away, waiting for her to finish.

'You can come with me if you want,' she said. Her voice was shaky as if it might stop working at any moment, like an old answering machine whose tape was wearing out. 'I could use the company. Or you can stay and look through the photos. Or whatever you want. I'm not telling you what to do.'

For a moment Reggie almost said yes, he'd go with her. She looked like she really needed the company. But then he remembered what he was waiting for and he shook his head.

'That's okay,' he said, kindly he hoped. 'I'll stay and look at the pictures.'

She nodded as if this was okay, though she'd hoped for a different answer. Again he noticed how subdued she was. It was as if she'd walked a long way to an uncertain destination, and she was exhausted. It looked as if she could use help walking, now that her destination was in sight. She seemed like an old woman.

'I'll be back in a bit,' his mom said and picked the box up again. 'Could you get the door for me?'

He did, watching her from the porch as she moved down the walkway to the driveway and the car. He watched her open the trunk and put the box inside, shutting the lid with a slam. He remembered his dad's wardrobe of flannels and jeans, and he couldn't remember one from the other, just a universal image of his dad fixed on a point in his mind. He thought of the closet upstairs empty now of those things, and how the whole house seemed emptier without them.

His mom got in the car, started it, and drove away.

Reggie faced the stairs, looking up. Up there was the new emptiness. Up there were the photo albums. Still images and vibrant pain.

He remembered what he was waiting for, but went upstairs anyway.

***

His dad's smile was as bright as he remembered. Brighter still were the eyes set in the kind yet strong face that beamed compassion and a joy for life nearly overflowing. It seemed to Reggie that he could almost reach through the photograph and touch the man standing there on the other side. Even the image of the man possessed more life than most living, breathing, three-dimensional people.

Sitting on the edge of the mattress, he grabbed first one album and then another, flipping through each at a leisurely pace. The images of the past leapt up at him, filling the room around Reggie with their lost sounds and colours. He remembered nearly everything, save those where he was youngest, an infant or toddler. And even some of those brought strange sensations that tickled the back of his mind like the phantoms of memories.

There they were at the ocean, the waves rolling in, white and foamy, washing about their legs, rolling in and rolling out in a syncopated rhythm. Here they were having a picnic, grass emerald green and spread out far like a great throw rug. In this one they stood before the Grand Canyon, the gaping vastness of the split earth behind them.

Reggie touched some photos reverently through the plastic sheets of the album pages. He wanted to be in the places they showed, not the here and now that was confusion and hurt and an aching dullness. These were mocking things, teasing him with times that could never be reclaimed. Lost moments in the grand machinery of the passage of years. These things were gone, washed away in the current, going one direction and he another.

Looking at them threatened the numbness with which he'd armoured himself in the course of the past year. He closed the albums violently; put them aside.

6.

The doorbell ringing made him jump.

He got up, looked out the window, saw the sheriff's department cruiser parked there in the driveway. He'd been so caught up in the pictures he hadn't even heard its approach.

He went downstairs swiftly, taking the steps two at a time. At the door, he paused with his hand hovering over the brass knob.

Reggie thought about not answering. What if they asked him questions that he couldn't answer? Or the answers he gave were all too obvious for the lies they actually were?

But some things had been ingrained in him by his parents. Like respect for elders and compassion for those less fortunate. Deference to law enforcement was another of those, and so his fingers curled around the knob and turned it. He didn't think of who it might be at the door until he opened it. He only knew there was an officer, and he needed to answer the door.

Deputy Collins looked as surprised as Reggie felt, but recovered more quickly. His amused smile was formed of thin, wet lips like earthworms.

'Well, hi there, kiddo,' the officer said, hands hooked at his belt by the thumbs. 'Is your mom home?'

'There was no rapist,' Reggie said, even as he shook his head no to the officer's question. Silently, he cursed himself for giving this man such satisfaction as the discovery of his lie. The growing look of amusement on the man's face was enough to tell Reggie he was right in this regard. This man was a predator, snatching at any piece of information and feeding on it like a spider on a fly.

'Yeah, well, I was just having fun with you,' Deputy Collins said, smiling that wet, delighted smile. 'You home alone?' he asked, knowing the answer.

Reggie shook his head, knowing he should close the door, knowing that wouldn't help. He might be in his own home, but this was Deputy Collins's game, played by his rules.

'Mind if I come in?' the man asked, walking in before Reggie could answer. He took his hat off like most people would do to show respect. For him, however, it was just a motion. Maybe a mockery. He looked around the living room with interest. 'Nice place you have here.'

He stopped at a shelf, touched some of the knick-knacks there. There were little plaster pigs and cows and elephants, and the deputy's fingers moved slowly over each perversely, like he was stroking something else. He picked up a framed family photo, showing Reggie with both his parents.

'Put that down,' Reggie said with a shaky voice.

He thought again about what Ivan had said.

They know you're weak.

He had to try and not be weak.

'Calm down, kid,' Deputy Collins said, setting the photo down. 'I'm here to help,' he added, still smiling. 'I'm an officer of the law. I'm your friend.'

Reggie still held the door open. He wanted the deputy to leave and knew there was nothing he could do to make him. The man moved about their house, an intruder with a badge. Unless his mom came home, Reggie had to play this out by himself.

'I may have fibbed about the rape part,' said the intruder, 'but I was telling the truth about there being a dangerous man on the loose.' Reggie knew there was one right in front of him, but kept this little observation to himself. 'They had us doing sweeps, helicopters flying, K-9 trackers, the whole nine yards. They caught a trail nearby,' he said with a thumb over his shoulder in some vague direction outside, 'about a mile or so from your place.'

Now he was walking past the sofa, one hand trailing the top of it, again with a strangely sensual touch, like he was caressing a living thing. He crossed the room to the kitchen entrance, peered in, looked in either direction. Then he turned back to face Reggie.

'They're having us check on everybody,' said Deputy Collins. 'To make sure they haven't seen anything strange. Have you seen anything strange?'

Reggie wanted to run from his own house, and this angered him. But his anger at himself couldn't translate into anger at the man across from him. He was afraid of the deputy, and that squashed any other emotions that might be below the surface.

He *was* weak.

Before this man, tall and lean-muscled, he was weak, and there was nothing he could do about it.

'No,' he answered meekly, hoping for the man's amusement to run its course. Hoping that in what passed for a mind in his head, the deputy would realize that even he, if caught in someone's house without permission, would face consequences.

'No strangers you haven't seen before?' the deputy asked, stepping closer, closing the gap between them. 'No noises from the woods?' he said, taking another step, and another, bridging the distance.

Reggie shook his head.

Then the man was standing over him. Reggie barely came up to the man's chest.

He looked up, and it was like looking up at the ramparts of a high tower.

'You and your mom live alone?' the deputy asked.

Reggie looked down, didn't answer. He found himself looking at the man's gun belt, and the pistol there.

'Where's your dad?' the officer asked.

Could he reach it in time? Could he pull the trigger?

'Are they divorced?' the man asked. 'Separated? Does he live somewhere else?'

Reggie thought about pulling the trigger in the woods

and watching the bottles disappear, *tugged* out of existence.

'Your mom's pretty,' the deputy said. 'Nice tits.'

Reggie wasn't sure he'd heard what he'd heard. He forgot about the gun, stepped away from the man. His back met the door, the doorknob pushing harshly into his ribs.

'I could suck on those things for a week,' the man said. He made little sucking noises with his glistening worm lips. 'Milk them dry,' he said and laughed.

'Get out,' Reggie said, shaking.

The man laughed harder.

'Get out of my house,' Reggie said, hating his weakness, hating the man in front of him, hating it all.

The man kept laughing.

'The only thing you know how to suck is dick,' Reggie said.

He didn't know where it came from. He just said it. There was no thinking about it. He didn't consider it in his head before he said it. He just said the words.

And the world stopped.

The deputy stopped laughing.

Reggie's heart stopped beating.

Then, slowly, the man reached out, grabbed him by a fistful of shirt, and leaned in close. The deputy's breath was minty and puffed in Reggie's face in little bursts.

'*What the fuck did you just say?*' he asked, just above a whisper.

There was nothing to do but keep on going.

'You like 'em big and hard,' Reggie said, his voice surprisingly steadier.

He was twirled, spun, G-forces stronger than on a rollercoaster pressing against him, and flung away. He bounced off the sofa and sprawled to the floor. His chin met the carpet with a clack of his teeth.

They'd reversed positions. Now Reggie was deeper in the living room, and Deputy Collins was in front of the door. The light outside framed him in a halo, as if giving a physical brilliance to his rage.

'That was stupid, you little shit,' the officer said. 'Really stupid,' he added, loosening his baton from his belt.

He took a step towards Reggie, moving out of the sunlight.

Something else entered it; an even larger silhouette.

Deputy Collins stood over Reggie, raising the nightstick.

The figure behind him raised its own arms, brought them down over the deputy's face and pulled back fast.

Deputy Collins gagged, the garrotte wire pulling deep into the flesh of his throat. He dropped the nightstick and it thumped to the floor. He reached up to pull and pry at the arms cinching the wire tight. He drove his elbows into his assailant. He tried bucking with his legs.

He gagged and spittle dripped and flew from his lips. He shoved backwards, driving both himself and his attacker against the wall. Picture frames rattled and swung askew.

The wire was pulled tighter, the fists gripping it white. The deputy's eyes bulged. He tried inserting fingers between the wire and his throat. There was no room. His eyes pushed out further.

He pissed his pants.

The stench of it was astringent and sharp.

He slid to the ground, his assailant following. The deputy's legs jerked and jived for a few moments more and then were still. His arms dropped heavily.

The killer unwound the wire from the dead man's throat.

He was breathing hard and stood on shaky legs.

'We have to get him out of here,' Ivan said.

For a moment, Reggie couldn't move. He saw the dead man on the floor, and the killer standing over him. As he watched, the killer spooled the wire into a loop and pocketed it.

'Hurry, Reggie,' he said. 'We don't have much time.'

Still, Reggie hesitated. The secreted wire disappearing in the folds of the jacket and the empty stare of the dead deputy seemed to have something in common. A negative space, Reggie thought, recalling the words from art class. That's what it was – a space where something belonged, or once had been.

'Now! Get up, Reggie!'

This hushed shout was a command, brooking no argument. It made Reggie flinch, and his mind cleared.

Reggie got up on uncertain legs. He nodded and Ivan

gestured to the dead man's legs, bending and grabbing the deputy under the arms. Reggie moved into position and grabbed either ankle. On the killer's count of three, they lifted together, shuffled towards the open door.

Reggie tried to tell himself he was lifting a mannequin. This wasn't a man he was carrying. It was a life-sized doll, maybe, like a crash-test dummy. But it didn't work.

He remembered his dad's wake. Seeing the man over the rim of the casket. Waxen, still and lifeless, but a man nonetheless. Reggie paused, bringing their small procession to a halt in the middle of the yard.

He wanted to drop the deputy's legs and run. But across the stretch of the corpse, looming over the dead man's face, was another face, alive, grim, and determined. The killer strained with the burden of the deputy's dead weight, grimaced, yet he met Reggie's furtive gaze. Read Reggie's thoughts in the span of seconds, and shook his head.

'*We have a deal, Reggie*,' the killer muttered. And thinking maybe this wasn't enough, added: '*We're friends. I need your help.*'

Not knowing exactly why, Reggie didn't let go, and nodded.

Their burden between them, they started moving again.

The distance from the house to the woods seemed to stretch forever, and the light of the sun shone down on them, revealing it all.

7.

They loaded the body onto the sled beneath the tree house. That seemed its purpose now, ferrying the dead and dying. No more snow rides in biting winters. Reggie didn't think his dad would have approved.

'We'll have to go far,' Ivan said.

'Can you make it?' Reggie asked.

'I don't have a choice,' the killer said.

'What about the deputy's car?' Reggie asked.

'I'll come back for it. It's better if they're separate,' said the killer. 'It'll confuse the situation, should he or the car be found.'

'Wait,' Reggie said and raced back to the house. There, he grabbed a couple bottled waters, stopped to straighten the pictures and shelves where the deputy and Ivan had collided with the wall, then went outside again and shut the door. He met up again with Ivan at the tree house. The killer was staring down at the dead eyes of the deputy, searching them for something and apparently unable to find it.

Then they were off.

Their small procession moved through the quiet woods in solemn urgency. No one spoke as they passed under the shadows of the trees and the intermittent light of the yellow sun. Birds twittered and then quieted with their approach. The wind seemed to sigh a wordless hymn for the bearers of the dead. As if the heavens noted the passing of the departed, even one so wicked as the man on the sled.

They moved in a general southerly direction, though Reggie could discern no exact bearing. They took turns pulling the sled with the ropes about their shoulders, pausing every once in awhile to break for water and to catch their breath. Ivan's face had a sallow, sickly cast to it again, and Reggie worried. He wanted to know how the man had eluded the trackers and their dogs, but knew this wasn't the time to ask. He also wanted to know how he'd come across his new clothes – blue jeans, a T-shirt, and brown suede jacket – wondered if there was someone dead somewhere, missing those garments, but he didn't ask that either.

Down into a dry creek bed they descended, following the bends and turns. Until they came to a precipice and a far drop into trees and shrubs in a chaotic growth below. Reggie stared down the face of the drop, judging the height, dizzy by the height, and giving up, stepped back.

'Here,' Ivan said, breathing hard.

He dropped the ropes and leaned against a rock like a tombstone. He pulled his water out from a jacket pocket, twisted the cap, and took a long swig. He coughed a little but kept it down.

Reggie braved the cliff again and looked down.

It seemed a maw, a throat, a tunnel to a deep place.

'There's no telling how long it'll take them to find him

here,' said the killer. 'Could be weeks or months. They might never find him.'

Reggie thought of the body bloating, decaying, falling apart, becoming bones.

'They might say he met with foul play,' the killer said. 'Or that he ran off with a woman. Or any of a thousand other stories.'

Reggie thought of that: someone disappearing, no one knowing why. The story of a life unknown, unfinished, left on a shelf to gather the dust of ages. Forgotten and gone.

'Any of which is fine for us,' the killer said, 'because the more they wonder, the less they know. And the safer we are.'

They stared at the body for awhile. Reggie memorized its contours, the details of it. It would be with him forever, every bit of it: how one bootlace was coming loose; how the left pants leg wasn't as sharply creased as the other; how the top two buttons of the shirt were undone; how one sleeve was hiked up the forearm a bit. The glaze of the eyes; the pained crook of the mouth; the hair ruffled and unkempt.

This was their body.

It was for them to remember.

Then the killer moved forward, bent, and pushed it, rolled the body towards the edge. There it hung for a moment, going over, suspended for an instant, and over the edge it went. The tumbling of it was audible, thumps and thuds and falling debris, and a crash far below, distant and carried up like a faint transmission in the ether. They looked over the edge, down the steep face.

Only a hand was visible, pale and sticking out of the brush, as if waving to them goodbye or hello or both: waving, forever waving.

Chapter Six

1.

'What do you think he was thinking when he died?' Reggie asked.

They sat at the edge of the precipice with their legs dangling off, like children dabbling their feet in a stream. Down far below them the hand was sticking out, waving at them, pale against the green surrounding it. Across the stretch of forestland laid out below them, a tall length of stone poking out of the canopy, crooked like a finger, seemed to be returning the dead man's gesture, beckoning him thither.

'I don't know,' said the killer, 'what would you be thinking?'

'I don't know,' Reggie said. 'The things I'd done wrong, maybe. The things I'd done right. I'd be thinking about everything I guess.'

'That's if you knew death was coming,' said the killer.

'Like if you have cancer and you have the time to think of the end as you slowly waste away. When you're fighting just to breathe, you probably don't have time to think much at all.'

Reggie thought about that. That was a good point. But he wasn't entirely convinced.

'Still,' he pushed, 'once you know fighting isn't working, that you're going to die any moment now, you've got to be thinking of something.'

'Maybe,' said the killer.

'What were you thinking?' Reggie asked. 'When you were strangling him?'

Ivan looked at him askance. He had a curious wrinkling of his face as if he wondered about Reggie. Wondered about the questions he was asking and why he was asking them. But still the big man answered.

'I was thinking that many officers are out of shape,' the killer said. 'But he wasn't. He wasn't huge, but he was strong, and me being in the condition I was I had to strike fast. Once I had the wire around his throat, I couldn't let go no matter what. Because if I let go for any reason, I might be the one to die.

'So I pulled tighter,' said the killer. 'I could feel the wire biting into his flesh, sinking deeper. I could feel the strain of my body, working against the pain of my injuries. I pushed away the pain until I couldn't feel it. I couldn't afford to feel it, not then. And so there was only the man and the wire in my hands, around his throat.

'I could feel his heartbeat,' the killer continued, 'we were so close together. It thumped and I could feel it. His body rattled as it died, and each rattle passed through me. When he died, his last breath left his body in a puff. I could hear it and I felt that too.'

'How'd you feel then?' Reggie asked. 'When he was dead?'

'I don't know quite how to say it,' the killer said. 'I was aware of the absence of something inside him. Whatever it was, I had taken it from him. Yet the significance of it was lost on me.

'Society says killing is wrong,' the killer said, 'but I don't understand why. Killing doesn't change anything. He's dead down there,' the killer motioned with a nod toward the pale hand below, 'and we're alive up here. But things could be different. He could be the one alive, and we could be dead. It wouldn't really matter.'

Reggie didn't agree with this. He couldn't verbalize his disagreement, couldn't put his thoughts rightly to words. There seemed a very real difference between Reggie being alive, and the deputy not, though he didn't know exactly what it was. What the dead man deserved for the things he'd said and done (*You know what rape is, kid? We've got pictures.*) seemed a part of this equation. But if that were the case, didn't the things that Reggie and Ivan had done apply as well? Did that change the balance of what was deserved, and who should be alive?

These questions made him uncomfortable. He shifted on the hard ground, as if finding a comfortable position would translate to peace of mind. It didn't, so he remained silent and just listened.

Ivan turned to Reggie. Reached out and held him under the chin. He turned Reggie's face until they were looking at each other.

'There's no purpose to anything,' the killer said. 'It's just life and death. Those are your choices. Remember that. Make decisions that are good for *you*, fend for yourself, and you'll be okay.'

Then he stood and started back, leaving Reggie with the sled and the dead man waving below. Reggie stood, looped the ropes about his shoulders, lifted the sled on his back, and followed.

As they made their way along the path through the woods, there seemed a greater weight upon Reggie's shoulders than merely that of the sled, and it bore down on him the entire way back.

2.

They had to get rid of the deputy's cruiser next.

Fortunately, Reggie's mom still wasn't home.

Ivan got behind the wheel and started the patrol car with the keys he'd taken from the deputy. 'I'll be back,' he said before pulling away and driving the car around the bend in the road and out of sight.

Reggie went back inside and stared about the living room. Everything seemed in place, as if nothing had happened. As if a man hadn't died in that very room. And with the body gone, and now the patrol car, as far as anyone else was concerned that was the case.

Nothing had happened.

At least not here.

They might say he met with foul play. Or that he ran off with a woman. Or any of a thousand other stories.

Reggie could see that was exactly what would happen. No one would ever know what happened, unless he or Ivan told them. And that wasn't an option – they had a deal. There were consequences for breaking a deal. The killer had made that perfectly clear.

Ivan was right: it was almost as if it didn't matter.

Some things lived. Some things died.

As he had after he and Ivan had run off to set their false trails in the woods for the police, Reggie sat down on the sofa, switched on the television, and waited. He clicked fast through the news stations.

In a big budget movie with a big name star, the hero would be watching the news or monitoring the radio, staying one step ahead of those in pursuit. Yet Reggie had also seen Missing Persons alerts on TV, and the last thing he wanted was to see Deputy Collins's face peering back at him from the screen.

No doubt his colleagues in the sheriff's department would all testify to the deputy's character. Hats in hand, held sombrely over their hearts, other officers would regale the viewing audience with stories about their missing comrade. Clips would be shown of the man bringing an old lady's cat down from a tree, or carrying a toddler through floodwaters. Maybe he'd foiled a bank robbery a couple years ago and been given the Key to the City.

Of course, Reggie would know the lies for what they were. But he wasn't sure that mattered.

Didn't everyone have different sides to them? Couldn't the deputy be both the asshole that had taunted Reggie at the side of the highway and barged into his house, *and* a cherished friend and colleague at the same time?

Trying to push these uncomfortable thoughts aside, Reggie found a reality show about married couples swapping spouses. When this ended, another featuring an ex-boxer who now raised pigeons took its place. Realizing why some grown-ups called it the idiot box, Reggie turned the television off.

In the sudden silence, the knock at the door was loud and unexpected. Reggie leapt up from the sofa, smacked his shin on the edge of the coffee table.

Limping, rubbing his leg, he made his way quietly to the door, peered through the peephole. What he saw surprised him almost as much as seeing a SWAT team charging the door with a battering ram would have.

He opened the door.

'Hey Reggie,' Rodrigo Ramos said.

The lanky boy always looked like he was in the middle of shrinking, his jeans and shirts a size or two too big for him. The Hispanic kid was always adjusting the loose, hanging sleeves and pulling at the hems, as if worried he'd trip up on the fabric or lose himself in the folds.

Despite having not seen him in months, despite having only hours ago watched a dead man thrown off a cliff, Reggie smiled at his friend.

'How's it going, Rigo?' He held out his hand palm up, received a slap, gave one back.

'Fine,' the other boy said. 'I just wanted to ... you know ... see how you're doing. Can I come in?'

And just like that, the events of the day came crashing back. Reggie stepped forward into the threshold, pulling the door behind him so that the view into the house was narrower.

He knew he'd straightened the foyer space. He was pretty sure there hadn't been any blood. But he couldn't take any chances.

The deputy's waving hand came to mind. Waving even at this distance. Greeting Reggie or motioning him forward, down, down into the tangled grave.

'I'm not supposed to have anyone in the house when my parents aren't around,' he said, stepping now onto the porch and pulling the door completely shut. 'Sorry.'

This was true enough. No friends inside when his mom and dad weren't home was indeed the rule. With his mom still out and about giving away his dad's things, and his dad ... well, dead, Reggie found the excuse easy to deliver.

More than that, however, Reggie found it easy to block

his friend's entrance because, he realized, he didn't exactly want him there.

They sat together on the top step. Reggie fiddled idly with his thumbs in his lap. Rigo pulled and folded his drooping sleeves.

'Haven't seen you in awhile,' the Mexican kid said. 'We all still do the ballgames on the weekends.'

'We all' meant the loose group of guys from school. Weekly summer baseball scrimmages at the local park were as close to a tradition as they had. As many as a dozen of them would meander on over and meet in the field around noon every Saturday and Sunday until school started up again. Teams and team captains were chosen not by any established process, but by whoever showed up first.

When Reggie didn't immediately respond, Rigo pressed a little more.

'You're one of our best pitchers. Everyone asks about you. When you're coming back, how you're doing. You know, stuff like that.'

'Yeah,' Reggie said, not sure what that single word was directed at or what it even meant.

'You know,' Rigo said, 'if you're not up for that, maybe you and me could do something. Ride out to the comic book store. Maybe go catch a movie. Whatever.'

Reggie only shook his head; even less of an answer than before.

A part of him felt shitty, being this way to his friend.

But another part of him had come to rely on being alone, he realized. Alone, there were no pressures, no expectations. He could say whatever he wanted, or say nothing at all. And not have to worry about what other people thought, or felt.

'When my grandpa died ...' Rigo began, and Reggie felt his twirling thumbs tuck in, curl around his other fingers, as the hands became fists.

This wasn't what he'd opened the door for. This wasn't what he wanted.

Luckily, that was when his mom's car came rolling up the drive, and Reggie rose to meet her. He walked away from his friend when he saw his mom pop the trunk, and reach in to bring out the grocery bags.

Reggie's mom smiled at Rigo, and it seemed a genuine smile. Reggie didn't, however, and with heavy bags in hand told his friend he had chores to do, said goodbye, and closed the front door behind him.

But a closed door couldn't keep out the dead.

3.

A lesson Reggie soon learned was that the dead were as different as the living.

Whereas the lone waving hand at the bottom of the cliff made him uneasy, the urge to visit his dad was a nudging, old sorrow. The scars of time, like scars of the flesh, had memories of their origins affixed to them.

Considering them brought back the events in a wash of recall that pushed aside all other considerations. This was a haunting of the mind, and it demanded an exorcism.

'I'd like to see him now,' he said when his mom returned from the last trip to the car, holding a bag under either arm.

She wasn't even completely through the door, but she saw him there leaning against the kitchen island counter, looking at her, and she nodded.

'Let me run to the restroom,' she said. 'Put the groceries away. Then we'll go.'

***

They didn't speak on the drive there. The morning was bright – almost unbearably so – the sun striking from the west, the world alight in its fire. The hum of the car rolling along the highway had an hypnotic effect. Reggie hung in a middle space between wakefulness and sleep. In this space he remembered his dad, and it was almost real.

When they pulled into the parking lot of the cemetery and his mom turned the car off, this middle space of almost-reality shut off with it. True reality remained, consisting of bright grass and grey tombstones and statuary.

'Want me to go with you?' his mom asked.

There was no anger left in her voice. Neither was she

subdued as she'd been previously. There was only concern, love unfiltered, directionless and needing a focus.

'Sure,' he said, surprising himself. 'If you want.'

Together they got out of the car and started across the asphalt towards the grass. From unyielding cement to cushioned earth, the change of terrain was a startling shift in Reggie's hyper aware state. It was a passage between worlds. Behind him was what he'd known; the pain, old and dull and part of him. Now he was in a different place, of rules he didn't know, and an outcome he couldn't foresee.

'Do you remember where it is?' his mom asked.

Taking a moment to gather his bearings, Reggie nodded and started to walk again. The place was bordered by upright cypresses, giving a wall of privacy to the mournful living, and perhaps the dead as well. Drooping willows hunched scattered about the grounds itself, like old battle-weary sentinels. He found the low hill easy enough, though last he'd seen it the area had been populated by men and women and children in black, so much like phantoms themselves in this land of the dead. Quiet, respectful, uneasy, they'd watched the coffin lowered into the ground, perhaps envisioning the day when the earth would have *them* and others would likewise watch their descent into a similar hole.

The headstone was simple. Only his name and the years of his life. It was the way Reggie's father would have wanted it; unadorned, sobering. He'd want his wife and son to remember him in their hearts and minds, not by some fanciful, elaborate stone.

Reggie understood these things as he never had before.

Thinking on them, it was almost his dad's voice in the silence of Reggie's head, patiently explaining, pointing things out.

Morbidly, he found himself picturing the corpse beneath, rotting, falling apart. Then he was thinking of what had been. The days almost indistinguishable in a span of time that should have continued for decades more. The smiles and the laughter; the meals and trips; the mere presence of the man with them. Corpse mind-pictures and good memories wrestled for dominance, striving for the limelight.

Somewhere, someone was crying.

Reggie heard their sobs and understood. He felt for them and knew the satisfaction of a good cry. How it tired the body and the mind, releasing the things pent-up inside.

But it wasn't for him, not this day. Just being here was enough. There might be time for tears later. This was just an acknowledgement. This opened the door and allowed for possibilities. This allowed the dead into his life, and what they brought he'd find out in the due course of time.

He kneeled on the plot.

He touched the stone.

He closed his eyes for a time, feeling the summer wind on him, the sun bearing down. The sounds about him made a background white noise; cars, people, birds. He was part of it, one thing among many. He allowed himself to be lost in the shuffle, to merge with it all; a stranger in the crowd.

He said hello to his dad.

He told him he loved him.

He said see you later.

And then he was ready to go.

4.

'Whatever happened to your sister?' Reggie asked.

The two of them – boy and killer – were back in the tree house again. They were in their places once more; Reggie near the ladder, Ivan against the far wall. He looked exhausted, Reggie thought. The activity of the morning had cost him. He stunk of old sweat and dank heat. They had changed his bandage because the work of killing and corpse disposal had opened the wound. Shirtless, middle bloodied again but not as bad as before, Ivan caught his breath before speaking.

'She went to a special care home after our father died,' he said.

'After you killed him,' Reggie corrected.

'Yes,' the killer said. 'It was a special hospital for children with ... conditions such as hers.'

'Did you ever visit her?' he asked.

'Not for a long time,' Ivan said. 'Laws on murder and child abuse are strange things. Especially back then.

Though I was protecting my sister from a sick man, I still served a long stint in a detention facility for youths.

'I wasn't kept up to date with my sister's whereabouts,' he continued. 'She moved from place to place as care homes closed or moved. The economy didn't bode well for such amenities. Social programmes are always the first hit when times are tough. Records were unorganized and incomplete at best, non-existent at worst. It took me over a month to find her when I finally got out.'

Reggie thought about that, not being able to see one's only living family member. About being punished for protecting her. What did that do to a person? Doing what was right and being punished for it. Seeing first-hand there was no justice in the world, and only suffering for the just.

'What did you do when you found her?' Reggie asked. 'Did you take her home with you?'

'I couldn't,' Ivan said. 'I had no money, and no home to take her back to. The government condemned our home while we were away. I was living on the streets. Sleeping in parks and in alleyways. She at least had a roof over her head, and three meals a day. I envied her.'

'You had no aunts or uncles? Grandparents?' Reggie asked.

Ivan shook his head.

'We never knew them growing up,' he said. 'Our parents never spoke of them, and we never asked.'

'So you had to leave her,' Reggie said.

'Yes,' Ivan said. 'But I checked on her again when I came

into some money. She was dead then. Died of pneumonia. She snuck out one evening to play outside. There was a winter storm. She wore only a night gown. She got lost in the snow and was gone for hours before one of the caregivers found her.'

'How'd you come by the money?' Reggie asked.

Ivan smiled.

'Now that's a story,' he said, and spoke for a long time.

***

'Like anywhere,' the killer said, 'life on the streets was hard. You fought for the best places to sleep, to beg, and you fought often. And the people were filthy. I'd never seen such filth before. How I hadn't seen it before, I don't know.

'We'd been poor, my father, my sister, and I,' Ivan said, 'but this was beyond poor. Poverty wasn't the right word either. That implied people who worked honest jobs for pitiful wages. People who were trying to be a part of the system, even as that system failed them.

'This was quiet desperation,' Ivan said, 'of the basest sort. These were people lost, with no way to be found again. And they didn't care. They just moved to survive as if by instinct, and not by any true desire to live.

'My first night on the streets I found a sewage culvert that led under an overpass,' Ivan said. 'It was cold but provided some shelter. I tried to sleep but two creatures I took for men arrived soon after. They wore large, bulky clothes caked with dirt and filth. Their faces were hidden under folds of cloth wrapped around them against the cold.'

Reggie pictured these hulking creatures.

They stomped and shambled and lurched as they approached the boy huddled in the sewer culvert.

'They beat me and threw me out,' Ivan said. 'I walked the city in the cold night from place to place. I found an alley and a similar creature chased me out, swinging a stick. I found a park, but the police chased me out too.

'There was no place I belonged, and no place that would have me.

'Until the old man found me,' Ivan said.

'Who was he?' Reggie asked.

'He was a rich man,' said Ivan. 'I'd seen him before, in his big, shiny cars, cruising the streets. I'd passed his home before – a large, gated castle it seemed to me. Larger than any home I'd ever seen. Larger than any home had a right to be.

'He got out of his car sometimes,' Ivan said, 'and other men always got out with him. Large men in expensive suits. He walked the streets with these men. He walked slowly and deliberately with the support of a cane topped by a silver wolf's head. I remember thinking there was a resemblance between that wolf's head and the old man. His silver-grey hair seemed like a wolf's mane, and his eyes were wild. Restrained, but wild. Like he was just waiting to attack something. Biding his time.

'He walked the places where people like me hid,' Ivan said. 'He walked the back alleys and the dark places. He talked to some of the people there. Led them to his clean, shiny car, opening the door for them and herding them in.

'Those that went with him were never seen again.

'He became something of an urban legend on the streets. If you went in the cars, you were never seen again. He took you to places. He showed you things. Where he took you and what he showed you changed you forever.'

'What happened to the people that went with him?' Reggie asked, leaning forward eagerly, his chin on an upright knee.

'I don't know,' Ivan said. 'I can only tell you what happened to me.'

Reggie waited for him to continue.

'I never found a place on the streets that was mine,' Ivan said. 'Every place I went belonged to someone else. I was beaten many times. I got little sleep. I ate from trash cans. I drank from gutter run-off and grimy streams. I wanted to die.

'Then one day the long car pulled up beside me,' Ivan said, 'and the old man got out. The big men got out with him and surrounded me. I looked at them, confused and frightened. I wondered what they'd do to me.

'"I can give you a new life," said the old man, his hands folded on the silver wolf's head. "I can show you new things."

133

'I was scared of them. More frightened of them than of anything else in my life. They were men of the world, men of means. They knew of things I'd never dreamed of. Seen things I never had.

'But I had no other choice. I had nowhere else to go. So I nodded and they led me to the car. I climbed in and sat with my hands in my lap.

'They got in after me, surrounding me again on the spacious car's facing seats,' Ivan said. 'The old man sat directly across from me. His eyes were like the silver wolf's eyes, I noticed. Somehow bright and lifeless at the same time.'

Reggie remembered thinking much the same about Ivan's own eyes not so long ago, but kept this to himself.

'"Sex or death?" the old man asked when the doors were shut and the car was moving again, rolling along in the cold night.

'I was confused. I didn't know what he meant. I said as much and expected them to laugh at me. No one laughed.

'"Those are the businesses I deal in," the old man said. "Sex or death. Choose."

'It took me only a moment to decide. I was thinking of my father in my sister's room, his pants around his ankles. And later, the feel of the axe haft in my hands.

'"Death," I whispered, the word coming with a puff of mist.

'"Yes," the old man said, nodding. He smiled, showing

bright, white teeth. "Death is indeed your business. I can see it in your eyes. You will be very good," he said, and leaned over and patted my knee like a grandfather would.

'And in time, I was,' said the killer. 'I was the best.'

***

'What was it like when your dad died?' Ivan asked. 'How'd you feel?'

Reggie wasn't sure he had the words for what Ivan wanted to know. But he tried.

'You know how some things you just take for granted?' he said, and Ivan nodded. 'Like there will always be another day? The sun will always rise? Things like that? My dad always being there was one of those things. It's just the way things were supposed to be.

'I always thought there'd be time. I always thought we'd get to play catch. Go to the movies. Go out for lunch. He'd always make me tell about my day at school during dinner.

'And then he was gone,' Reggie said, 'and it was like a betrayal, you know?'

Reggie had never spoken these thoughts before. But in the little tree house high off the ground, across from the killer, it seemed a special place with special rules. After what he'd seen, after what he'd done, he could say anything here.

'He betrayed me,' Reggie said. 'But it was more than

that. The world betrayed me. Nothing made sense. There were no rules that could be counted on. So I closed off the world, inside here,' he said, tapping his chest, 'and here,' he said, tapping his head, 'and numbed myself.'

'What's it like?' Ivan asked. 'The numbness?'

Reggie thought the killer already knew the answer to that, and maybe he was just seeking to have his own answer validated. To know that he wasn't the only one who felt that way.

'It's like a wall,' Reggie said. 'It's very high and runs for miles and the foundation's set deep. You can't go around it, over it, or under it. There's a gate that only I control and I only let in what I want.

'Sometimes it feels like it's going to give,' he said. 'Sometimes things really pound on it, you know? And I'm not sure the wall will hold up. Like when my mom tries to get me to talk and I don't want to. Or when thoughts of my dad really come at me hard. Times like that and the wall feels like it could break at any moment.'

'Do things make sense back there?' Ivan asked. 'In the world behind the wall?'

Reggie thought a moment before answering.

'It's not about things making sense anymore,' he said. 'It's about keeping out the things that don't. It's about having a little place for myself that's mine, and only mine. Somewhere that's quiet. Where I can just ... wait.'

'Wait for what?' Ivan asked.

Reggie looked at the man, but didn't answer.

'Wait for what, Reggie?' he asked again.

He couldn't ignore those steel blue eyes. They demanded answers.

'For the end,' he said, and Ivan nodded as if he understood. And God help him, Reggie thought he did.

***

'What were you paid for your first hit?' Reggie asked.

'Five hundred dollars,' the killer said.

Reggie considered that. Five hundred dollars for a human life. There seemed something wrong with that, putting a dollar figure on a person's life. Though his dad had been killed for sixteen bucks, so he guessed Ivan had got a good deal.

'Who was it?' he asked.

'Just some guy,' the killer said. 'It's usually best in my line of work not to know too much about the target.'

'Did he have a wife?' Reggie asked.

'I don't know,' the killer said.

'Did he have kids?' he asked.

'I don't know,' the killer said.

'What did he do for a living?' Reggie asked.

'He was a printer,' the killer said. 'And an editor of a newspaper.'

'Did he have friends at work?' he asked.

'I couldn't say,' the killer said.

137

'He must've had people that cared about him,' Reggie pressed.

'Probably,' the killer said. 'Most of us do.'

'But you killed him for five hundred dollars,' Reggie said.

'Yes,' the killer said.

'How'd you do it?' he asked.

'I shot him,' the killer said. 'Three times in the chest.'

'Was there a funeral?' he asked.

'I assume so, yes,' the killer said.

'But you didn't go to it,' Reggie said.

'No, I did not,' he said.

'So you have no idea who was there?' Reggie asked. 'Family, friends from work. It could have been a big turnout. Lots of people could have paid their respects.'

'It's entirely possible, yes,' the killer said.

'But you don't know,' Reggie said.

'No, I don't.'

'But you killed him for five hundred dollars,' Reggie said. 'Not knowing the people that would be affected by his death.'

'Yes,' the killer said.

'Why?' Reggie asked.

'Because it's what I was paid to do,' the killer said.

'Why?' Reggie asked again, frustrated, knowing there had to be more to it than that. There just had to be.

Maybe, after a time, it had become that way for the killer: just doing a job. Pulling the trigger, tightening the garrotte, slipping the blade between the ribs. Then collecting the payment. But not at first, Reggie thought. It had to have been different in the beginning.

'Because it's what I do,' the killer said, gritting his teeth.

'Why?' Reggie repeated, a tone of insistence creeping into the single word.

'Because it's all I've ever known,' the killer said, his voice rising.

'But *why*?' Reggie said, raising his voice too, stressing that last word.

'*Because I'm not a good man!*' the killer yelled, leaning towards Reggie, face red, spittle flying. '*Don't you get that yet, Reggie?*'

Surprising himself, Reggie didn't turn away from the killer's rage. Not immediately. He caught a glimpse of the pistol in the holster beneath the jacket. He remembered the switchblade as well, tucked away in a pocket, possibly nestled comfortingly against the curled garrotte wire.

Then, slowly, he stood up, making as little noise as possible, like a hiker before a coiled viper. Reggie moved to the ladder. He found the rungs with his feet and scaled down them without looking up.

He had to be away. The wall he'd told Ivan about was shaking, on the verge of crumbling, collapsing. As he lowered himself to the ground, Reggie heard the man's voice above him, trailing off: 'Because I'm not a good man ...'

The words hung for a moment in the air, like an echo captured, and then were gone. Yet they repeated themselves in Reggie's mind well into the night, playing in a loop in his head like a song heard on the radio. An earworm, that was called.

An earworm in his head, in his brain, wriggling around, digging deeper.

Chapter Seven

1.

When next Reggie went out to see the man in the tree house, he was gone. The interior of the wooden enclosure – so like a small game hunter's trap blown up to human proportions – was empty save for little blood-stains on the planked floor. In the silence and vacancy it was as if the killer had never been there at all. The sled was parked at the base of the tree like a taxi cab waiting for a patron. Reggie looked about thinking maybe he'd just wandered off for a piss, but the killer was nowhere to be seen.

It had only been an hour or so since their last words.

He waited fifteen minutes.

Then he went back to the house and tried to forget it all.

***

Reggie couldn't forget it though, and went back periodically to check the tree house. This routine continued through the morning and into the day. His mom, uncommonly permissive of his comings and goings since their confrontation in the car at the cemetery, noticed the frequency with which he left and came back to the house.

She asked him if anything was wrong.

He said he was okay and tried to settle himself.

He watched some television. Got up for a drink and snack during a commercial. Saw the picture the deputy had given his mom the previous day, slid among the pile of junk mail on the kitchen counter, forgotten. Stopping in front of the stack of mail, Reggie shuffled through the rest idly, feigning interest in fast food coupons, an ad for video games, and a public notice from the city warning about rabid wildlife, complete with a larger than necessary picture of a snarling bobcat. Until there was only the photo of the killer on the counter before him.

He picked it up and looked at the profile image of Ivan, the professional killer. The photo was black and white, but the intensity, the silent lethality of the man, came through even in such a grainy picture.

Reggie thought of the man splitting his own father's head with an axe. He thought of him strangling the deputy and pushing the body over the cliff.

Reggie thought of lying side by side with him, looking at the stars. He thought of the man's arm around him when Reggie had cried about his own father.

Reggie didn't know what to think anymore. But he thought of Ivan out there somewhere alone, bleeding, and that didn't seem right. He didn't know what *was* right, but that wasn't it, his friend out there by himself, maybe dying.

So he went up to his bedroom and pulled his backpack out from the closet. Empty now that school was over, the pack was limp in his hands. He draped it across the chair and looked at it for a time. He waited for evening. Watched more television, read a book, went downstairs and talked idly with his mom for awhile. He tried to act natural, not wanting to raise any further concern or suspicion.

She fell asleep watching reruns of old black-and-white shows. Perhaps that window to the past comforted her. Maybe watching a bumbling deputy test the patience of his sheriff best friend or a gangly first mate bungle the rescue of his fellow castaways provided his mom with an alternative to the way things actually were in their sad, quiet house.

Reggie understood this need and left his mom undisturbed. Creeping on cotton-socked feet, he made it across the living room with a stealthy stride fit for a cat.

He went to the kitchen, opened the refrigerator slowly. The suction of it opening made his heart skip a beat. He took out bottles of water and a couple cans of soda. From the cupboards he took out crackers and granola bars. He took a large knife from one of the drawers. He bundled these items up in his shirt just as he'd bundled the First Aid supplies only a couple days ago, and took them back

143

upstairs. Digging the flashlight – purchased by his parents for him in case of power outages – out of the closet, he added it to his gathered supplies. He loaded his backpack and zipped it up.

He took pen and paper from his desk, sat down, and wrote this note:

> *Mom,*
> *I'm going out for awhile. I might be gone for a bit.*
> *Please don't worry. There's something I have to do. I'm*
> *sorry for being so angry. See you soon. I love you.*
> *Reggie*

He left it on his desk where she'd be sure to see it.

Lastly, he stepped lightly to his dresser and opened the top drawer slowly, quietly. Reaching under his socks and underwear, he again retrieved the bundle there. Added it to his pack, pushing it towards the bottom, out of sight.

Then Reggie went to the window and slid it up carefully. The hinges were clean and quiet. Leaning forward, Reggie peered out the window and down. The drop to the yard seemed further from his current perch than it ever had from outside, looking up. Now that he'd made his decision, however, he didn't want to go back downstairs and run the risk of waking his mom.

Reggie hitched the backpack over his shoulders.

Bending, he ducked under the window and onto the roof. He scooted out over the shingles on his butt, inching closer to the edge with his hands and feet. The drop down couldn't have been more than seven feet or so, the way the roof slanted down. But it looked like a fall into the Grand Canyon.

He dangled over and let go.

His feet met the lawn hard and he rolled with the fall. The impact was jarring but he got to his feet without injury.

He turned towards the woods and started walking.

It was night, he could think of only one place to start, and it seemed a long, long ways away in the blackness draped across the world.

2.

The forest was a different world at night.

Heavy shadow clung to everything like a growth. Limbs reached out like scratching claws or hung like shrouds, hiding things. The trunks could have been giants' legs, striding through the dusk and gloom. Night birds warbled sad tunes fit for funereal processions.

Uninvited, his mother's warnings about bobcats and mountain lions pushed themselves forward rudely in Reggie's mind. Squatters, too, she'd said. Doing God knows what in the abandoned shacks and cabins scattered throughout the woods. Shuffling around in lightless rooms, peering out through the slats of boarded windows. Waiting for unwary passers-by.

Reggie dug out the flashlight and turned it on.

The beam lighted the world where he pointed it, but it also made him easier to spot for stalking predators. Slavering beasts or bedraggled travellers with rape on the brain would know right where he was.

He turned it off, and the darkness leapt back around him.

Twigs snapped in indeterminable distances about him.

He turned the flashlight back on.

'*Fuck it,*' he said and started walking.

He knew the general direction, but moved mostly by memory. It had only been that very morning, so he was fairly confident he could find his way to where he wanted to go. It wasn't as if the forest got up and walked about and realigned itself. It was always the same, and all he had to do was take the route they'd taken that morning.

The dark seemed to squeeze in close around him. With every step things crunched underfoot; twigs and dry leaves and small stones. They sounded like bones snapping, and he thought of walking a vast wasteland like in a Mad Max movie, treading upon the remains of people blasted dead and dry by warheads innumerable.

Once, as he walked, a glimmer of something caught his eye, and he turned to face it. Through the dark wall of trees, a glint of moonlight off a reflective surface. Glass or metal. Aware of the dangers of losing his sense of direction in the night, Reggie nonetheless strode towards the dim light.

Soon, he came to the edge of a dip in the ground like a small crater. The soil there was loose and sunk a bit underfoot. Like a dried-out pond, baked empty by the unforgiving desert sun. In the centre of it sat an old car, windows shattered, snaked by weeds and branches.

Skeletal and dead, the car made Reggie feel as if he were in the presence of something malevolent. Or at least best left undisturbed. And so he turned, course corrected, and returned to his previous path through the woods.

At some point he became aware of being followed.

Somewhere about him footfalls padded parallel to his own. Softer and more purposely placed than his, the sound of them carried in the still night air like distant, hushed drumbeats.

He swept the light to one side, saw nothing. Swung it the other way, and saw branches and leaves swaying with the passage of something large. He followed the movement of the thing, the swaying of the shrubbery in its wake. It fell back under the searching light, out of reach of the flashlight beam.

Telling himself animals were wary of people, Reggie pressed on.

He found the dry creek bed by almost falling into it. Like a fissure in the earth it was there before him, shadows hiding the bottom so that it seemed to fall away into forever. A grinning drop into nothingness. But he knew there was a bottom and slid down into it. Small avalanches of grit and dirt rolled with him. Standing, he turned and kept walking, the light showing the way ahead, the twists and turns an earthen maze.

Again, as he followed the bends of the creek he at some point became aware of the padding footfalls, and the whisper-brush of something big displacing the foliage as it passed. Coming from the left, Reggie flashed the light up that way and saw again the lazy swaying of the bushes and low-hanging branches.

Whatever was there was just out of sight behind the growth of the woods. He thought he caught a glimpse of hide – taut, tan, and wide – but he wasn't sure. He thought there was a brief gleam of light reflected off eyes, but then they blinked away as if they'd never been there at all.

Living in Arizona all his short years, Reggie knew the basics of safety when encountering wildlife. Rangers sometimes visited the schools on Career Days. Make noise, they said. Make yourself as big and intimidating as possible. Don't panic and run. Wild animals were cautious of humans, and would usually retreat. The behaviours and things of people – clothes, gadgets, cars – confused them and, unless provoked, they kept their distance.

Yet Reggie also knew animals like raccoons or bears that developed the habit of nosing in human refuse for easy meals – or the stupid people that fed them – were more difficult to deal with. An animal that had discovered a routine of effortless food was hard to chase away, and was even more dangerous because of their familiarity, and lack of fear, of people.

But usually noise, big and intimidating, and don't panic was the way to go.

Reggie bent and with the aid of the flashlight found a couple large, fist-sized rocks. He set his backpack down and took out the knife just in case. At first glance the blade had seemed large and wicked-looking when he'd taken it from the kitchen. Now it looked small and pathetic to his eyes. He yelled a '*Hey!*' that came out a croak, and tried again.

'*Hey!*' he shouted. '*Hey! Get out of here!*' he bellowed and jumped up and down, waving his arms. He stomped his feet and clapped his hands together. He threw the rocks into the forest where he'd seen the moving branches and the flash of eyes. '*Get out of here! Go away!*'

Reggie heard the impact of the stones. He heard something low and rumbling. It was a warning sound, deep and throaty. It sounded like rolling thunder. The vibrations of its decibels almost tangible in the air.

A fear deep and heavy went through his body. His stomach did little flops then curled up in a tight little ball. His legs felt weak. A shiver went through his frame like an electric charge.

The rumble out there and the slow drumbeat padding of the heavy footfalls provided a cadence for the thumping of his heart.

It came near the treeline again, drawing closer rather than retreating. The eyes flashed a bright yellow, like captured fire. Parts of it were clearly seen this time – a dirty tan hide rippling with muscle, canvas-thick.

Nothing could be that large, Reggie thought in immobilized fear.

The rustling of the woods again. Patches of it seen through the trees; the thunder-rumble of it; the pushing aside of the forest growth. But mostly the eyes, afire, glowing golden like spectral orbs.

Trembling, Reggie knelt, found more stones.

He threw them weakly in its direction. The first disappeared, swallowed by the thick woods. The second struck the enshadowed stalker and bounced off ineffectually.

'*Get out of here*,' he muttered. '*Go away*,' he whispered, the words like a prayer.

And it drew away again, but slowly, casually, as if mocking him. The impossible beast slunk away, the woods moving around it. The eyes faded into the darkness and blinked out. The rumble of its low roar likewise diminished, moving away like the thunder of a passing storm. The weighty slaps of its gargantuan footfalls faded.

Gathering himself, fighting back the tears of terror, Reggie started down the creek bed road again, further into the woods, the night, the darkness.

3.

The drop where they'd rolled the body off was infinite at night. It made Reggie think of the beach vacation he and his parents had taken a few years back. The photos of which he'd looked at earlier that very day. His dad had rented a boat and they'd cruised a couple miles off the Pacific coast. Setting anchor in the early evening, they'd eaten dinner in the calm waters. At night all the ocean turned black, and with the dark sky above it was as if the world had been erased.

Staring down the cliff face, that's what it was like: looking down into an ocean of blackness. Reggie wondered what it would be like to fall down into such a void. It seemed you'd fall forever. And would you even know you were falling? If you could see nothing, neither height nor depth, would there be any sensation at all? Or just the endless black all around?

He thought of the dead man down there.

Or was he dead? In that emptiness, that swallowing darkness, who was to say?

Maybe the dead got up and roamed in such blackness. Without the light of the world maybe different rules applied. Maybe the deputy crawled around down there, lost, confused, groping for something solid, something to pull himself back to the land of the living. Maybe he knew Reggie was up here, watching, and he was pulling himself up, up, slowly, and at the top he'd pull himself over, snatch onto Reggie, and pull him back down with him, clinging, back down into the void.

Reggie moved cautiously back from the precipice.

He saw the note on the ground by the light of the flashlight, the paper weighted down by a rock. Had it been

151

there before? He hadn't seen it, but that didn't mean anything. His attention had been on the approach to the cliff.

It was startling; the note there, white in the night, as if deposited by a phantom hand. Cautiously, he approached it. Wary, he bent, picked it up, read it.

If you've come this far, I think you'll come a bit farther. Though I would be remiss not to suggest otherwise. My world doesn't have to be yours. It shouldn't be. But head west if you choose to continue. Come to the high rock, and we'll talk.

There was no signature, but Reggie knew who it was from.

And he knew the high rock as well. It was there, seen from where he stood. The great finger of darkness crooked against the greater night, beckoning. A tower of stone out of the woods like a rampart.

One could see it from almost anywhere in town.

From his perch atop the cliff, the giant stone finger still stretched higher than Reggie. Looming over the treetops below, the vertical spire poked from the earth like the vestige of a buried kingdom. All he had to do was keep walking towards it, and there was no chance he'd miss it. He could see where the cliff face gradually eased downward, and met the forest floor below.

Turning away from the stone tower, so far and yet so near, shoving the note into his pocket, Reggie started to walk again, empty space dangerously close to one side and deep forest to the other, like a vise squeezing tight.

***

There was a clearing about the ash tree from which the body swung. As if the rest of the world had stepped back in regard of the sombre dead. Under the beam of the flashlight the leaves about the tall, broad tree seemed fire-red, brilliant in the night.

At first Reggie couldn't make out what it was that hung from the branches. The rope about it stretching from the bough creaked in the evening breeze. Gashes in the hide revealed the raw muscle and flesh beneath, making identification difficult.

He stepped closer until he was almost under it.

Looking up he could discern the droopy ears, the long snout. The hound's eyes flashed in the light but were otherwise dead. Strung up by the hindquarters, its final gaze was directed at the earth below.

From somewhere about Reggie came the deep rumble again, as if on cue. Whatever had been following him would be attracted by the scent of the pooled, dried blood beneath the swinging canine's corpse. The padding footfalls slapped their approach upon the forest floor in an anticipatory rhythm. The rustle of the creature's passing issued a frictional, serpentine hiss.

Reggie cast the flashlight's beam around him, scanning

153

the edges of the clearing. He waited for it to appear. He trembled at the thought of its approach.

But the footfalls faded again. The thunder-rumble of the monstrous purring drifted away and then was gone as well.

He spotlit the hound again. No beast did that, he knew. The dog had died by human hands and been strung up as a sign, a marker, and maybe as a warning.

The dead dog's eyes no longer seemed to be staring at the ground. Now they were watching him. And one paw seemed bent and crooked, pointing southwest, back into the woods, and the tower above it all, drawing nearer.

4.

A distance ahead of him shone other lights in the woods. So as not to attract their attention, Reggie turned off his and crouched, watched their progress. The lights blinked in and out of existence as they moved behind things – trees, bushes – and reappeared. They bobbed and swerved and jumped in little dances of movement, like fairies. There were three of them, in no specific formation with each other, bobbing, weaving, jerking about.

He thought of the police on the highway two days ago, spread throughout the fields, searching.

He thought of the body at the bottom of the cliff behind him, eternally waving.

He thought of the hung hound he'd just passed, swaying.

Are You Afraid of the Dark?

Were they closing in on Ivan? Did they know he was out here?

Wouldn't the police have sent more than just three men, though? Wouldn't there have been something more organized, say a methodic grid search like you saw in movies? A helicopter buzzing above with a spotlight and night vision scope?

As he watched, the lights before him blinked out, either by design or distance. Reggie counted to himself, waiting a time before doing anything, then he flipped his light back on and continued forward.

A dead man at the bottom of a cliff; a huge beast stalking the woods; a hung dog; phantom lights; all seemed pieces of something in play. It seemed a design or pattern that he should be seeing, if only he looked hard enough.

Something was happening. Something he was a part of and had to see through to the end. Part of Reggie knew that was foolish. He was a kid, and out here in the woods were some sort of animal, police, and a killer. All three dangerous in their own ways.

He shouldn't be here. He should be back in bed, fast asleep. Or staying up late and playing video games or watching movies with naked women, like other guys his age did.

And yet the stone finger beckoned, spurring him onward.

Westward, the wind in the trees seemed to whisper in a

155

ghostly murmur, adding its opinion to that of the beckoning stone. *Westward.*

Reggie listened to this persuasive voice, and moving one foot in front of the other, one step at a time, he started walking again, heading in the general direction of the phantom lights.

***

Somewhere in the forest night someone was singing.

The lilting notes were soft and yet unmistakable. The voice rose and fell, rose and fell, so at first Reggie was certain that it wasn't very far away at all, and then he could only just hear it and thought it must be carried from a vast distance. The song was unknown, the words indistinct, and sometimes it seemed to blend with the nighttime winds so that he couldn't tell what was nature and what was human.

Whether man or woman, that too he couldn't figure. In the snippets he caught as the voice rose, it seemed deep enough for a man, yet gentle enough for a woman. There came to his mind a scene of an old man on a porch front, rocking in an old rickety chair, bellowing notes as the day crawled by. He also saw an old spinster before a strong hearth fire, humming away the endless days.

The direction was indeterminate as well. The voice seemed to come from all directions and nowhere in particular at the same time. He tried standing still, cocking his head this way and that to pinpoint the source, with no luck.

Again there was the sense of something he should be seeing, understanding. The dead, dog and human; the stalking beast; the beckoning stone; the dancing lights; the ghostly singer; all seemed not merely random and separate events on a nondescript Arizona night. Surrounded by shadows and the whisper of the woods, it was easy to think something might be watching him. Unseen, standing just outside his view, this presence was watching, weighing things, and awaiting an outcome.

Waiting on Reggie.

And then the singing stopped. One last note, words heard yet not understood, carried to one last crescendo and then cut off. Ended as quickly as it had begun, leaving Reggie straining to hear nothing. He waited for a time, in case it should start up again.

When it didn't, he kept on walking.

***

By his watch Reggie had been walking hardly an hour since leaving home, when he stopped to sit and rest. He slung the backpack off his shoulders and unzipped it. Pulling out one of the bottles of water, he uncapped it, took a couple swallows, and put it back. He sat with his back against a pine, the flashlight between his feet lighting the ground in front of him.

Not for the first time, he thought about turning around and going home. He wondered what he was doing out here in the first place. He wondered why it bothered him so much that Ivan had left. In the dark and silence, he wondered many things, each thought brief and fleeting before being replaced by another.

What would his mom think when she woke and found him gone? What if, while looking for him, she wandered over to the tree house, went up the ladder, and saw all the blood? Would she think something had happened to him? Would she call the police? Once contacted, would the police have some way of knowing that one of their own had been by the house earlier? What then?

Much of what had happened in the past couple days came whirling back to Reggie in a torrent of confusion. The appearance of the killer out of the woods. The fight with Johnny Witte. His mom slapping him. Holding Ivan's gun, squeezing the trigger, and watching the bottles disappear. Kneeling before his dad's gravestone. So many images, sounds, smells, fighting for centre stage in his mind.

All Reggie knew for certain was that when he'd climbed the tree house earlier in the day and had seen it empty, he'd also felt empty.

Something had been happening between him and the killer. What it was, he wasn't sure. They'd both said they were friends, and Reggie thought they were, to a degree. But that wasn't all there was to it.

Reggie knew that like himself, Ivan hadn't spoken to

anyone about anything important in a long time. What the man did for a living didn't give him the luxury of friends. Then they'd come upon each other, talked of things, and it had felt right. They'd listened to each other and there was no judgement, no condemnation.

The times Reggie and his mom had spoken about things since his father's death there'd been a hesitancy, an under-lying worry about what could be said. What would she think if he said what was really on his mind? And no doubt she'd held back as well, reluctant to give voice to the quiet, insistent murmurings in her own head.

Certain thoughts just weren't supposed to be spoken aloud.

But that's not how it'd been between Reggie and Ivan.

They'd said anything and everything that came to mind. The other had listened and there'd been an exchange of things beyond words and thoughts. That was it, Reggie thought. That sounded right. The two of them had made an exchange, bartering like patrons at a market.

But unlike the mall or a grocery store, there'd been no credit cards or receipts passing from one to the other as a register beeped and tallied their trade. Instead, it was some-thing intangible, unseen, but wholly necessary despite its ethereal nature.

Then Ivan had left.

And all Reggie knew was that it wasn't done yet, this thing between them. He had to go after his friend, the killer. There was something else yet to be done, and if it

159

wasn't done there'd be an incompleteness, an unfinished part of him that he'd carry forever.

Much like the hole in him his dad had left.

He didn't know if he could live with two of those holes. Gnawing on the inside of him, ready to swallow him entirely. So he'd followed Ivan into this other world of deep forest and deeper night. But he was small and it was large, and Reggie felt inadequate and terrified by his smallness.

He'd undertaken something too big for himself.

He was in the unknown. All was mystery. He didn't know what lay ahead.

At home, in his dull pain, he'd known what each day held.

Now it was all new, and it was frightening.

He got up and looked through the canopy of trees above him. The stone finger blocked out some of the stars, defining itself against the further blackness. It beckoned, and Reggie followed.

5.

He saw the campfire from a distance. He heard the singing coming from it. He approached with caution, each step slow and deliberate. As he drew closer, he could discern three shapes around it. The red and orange tongues of the flames lit the faces but nothing else, so that there seemed disembodied heads afloat and singing. Perhaps of previous lives and old regrets.

He crawled to the edge of the light, peering in from the darkness.

The figures were bundled in coats or blankets or both, mummy-wrapped for warmth. Their singing was slow and deep and melodic. Reggie had never heard the tune, wasn't sure he could repeat it, but he liked it. He smelled coffee and cocoa and felt the heat of the fire. It crackled and made little sounds like sharp handclaps.

He inched closer, stopping behind a pine and bush.

One of the figures raised a hand and the singing stopped.

'*Come on out,*' it called in a man's voice. '*We can hear you out there.*'

Reggie froze. His heart skipped a beat. He thought about running. He thought about staying still. Maybe they were bluffing. Maybe they'd heard something else, not him.

'*You, behind the tree,*' the man said. '*Come on out.*'

Which left only two options: run, or go to them.

He thought about vagrants, the squatters his mom had warned him about. He thought about child raping hillbillies. He thought about backwoodsmen, grizzled, gruff, half savage. He thought about hunters, maybe not hunting deer but something else.

These were all shitty options, and he knew it would be best to avoid them all. And the best way to do that was to avoid people until he got to where he was going. Until he got to Ivan.

Yet his goal was beyond them. He had to pass through or around their camp to continue on his way. Or he could turn around.

Which wasn't really an option at all.

Reggie got up, dusted himself off, and strode into the firelight.

The three spectral heads turned to watch him, their attached bodies coalescing out of the night as he drew closer to the light of the camp, but none of them rose. The one that had spoken gestured to an open spot near the fire, across from them, and Reggie took it. He sat down cross-legged and felt like an Indian in a sweat lodge, maybe, starting a vision quest. He saw the tent behind them, like a little black pyramid in the night, the front flap open and waving a bit, a come-hither motion, and Reggie thought about being dragged in there, stripped, violated.

The three men sat side by side across from him, the fire between them, like a shadowy tribunal. What he was being judged for he didn't know, but the judgment – and the sentence to be carried – were nightmarish possibilities in his imagination.

'You're kind of young to be out here alone,' said the one on the left, even in his bundle of blankets slightly smaller than the other two.

'Maybe we ought to call his parents,' said the one on the right, wide and large. 'Or take him home.'

'I think he's just old enough to make his own decisions,'

said the one in the middle, the one who'd called him out from behind the tree. 'Isn't that right?' he asked, directing the question at Reggie.

Reggie didn't answer. He thought about the butcher's knife in his backpack. He both wanted to hold it, and yet thought it entirely inadequate if these three should turn out to be the redneck child rapists his mom had warned him about.

'What're you doing out here?' asked the small one, his face blurry over and through the fire. Through the distortion of the fire, he could have been a demon shaping a human face over its true hellish visage.

'What are *you* doing out here?' Reggie asked, knowing he shouldn't be talking to adults like that. Especially if they were inbred adults anxious for molestation.

'We're camping,' said the large one. His voice was deeper than the other two, and his lips smacked with certain consonants, so that he seemed hungry and slavering. Reggie thought again about the tent and being dragged in there, but instead of rape this time he thought of cannibals.

'I'm camping too,' Reggie said.

'Where's your family?' asked the one in the middle, his voice rich and smooth, so that Reggie knew this had been the singer whose song had drifted ghost-like through the woods.

'They're back a ways,' he said with a nod of his head, indicating where he'd come from. The lie was weak even to his own ears.

'Won't they be worried if they find you gone?' said the singer.

Reggie didn't respond.

'Where are you really going?' the singer prodded, his tone insistent yet not unfriendly. He reminded Reggie of a long-suffering teacher at school, pressing a student for the truth about the spitball that had just smacked the blackboard.

Reggie still didn't say anything. He wasn't a good liar, and thought it better to keep his mouth shut.

'There's animals out there,' said the smaller one. 'Mountain lions. Rattlers. It's dangerous being out here alone. Never know what might find you.'

Reggie thought about the beast that pushed through the forest. The deep rumble of its low roar. The firm slaps of its footfalls.

'People can get hurt out here,' said the large one.

Reggie thought about the man at the bottom of the cliff. The hound strung up and slashed ribbon-like.

'We really shouldn't let you wander about,' said the one in the middle, the singer, who only moments ago had said Reggie seemed old enough to make his own decisions. 'We're out here hunting someone,' he added, this second statement not seeming to logically follow the first, and yet somehow it did at the same time. 'There's someone dangerous out there,' he said, and turned his head a little each way, as if listening for that dangerous somebody.

'Haven't you heard?' said the smaller one. 'It's been in the paper and on the local stations. There's a criminal out here. Escaped from the police. Real dangerous sort. Killed lots of people.'

Reggie's heart beat faster. He thought they must be able to hear it, how fast it slammed against his chest.

'The police are strapped for manpower out here,' said the larger, hungry man. 'We're doing our civic duty, helping out.'

'Plus there's a reward,' said the singer, 'for any information leading to his arrest.'

A posse, Reggie thought. He'd seen enough westerns to know how that turned out, when a group of vigilantes went out in search of the outlaw. Usually lots of bullets and bodies were involved.

He wanted away from these men. But he didn't know how to do so without raising their suspicion. He didn't know if they'd even let him leave.

'You haven't seen anything strange?' the middle one asked, leaning a bit towards the fire, towards Reggie. The man had a bushy mustache that wriggled like a live thing when he spoke.

Reggie shook his head.

'No strangers around town?' he asked, mustache quivering caterpillar-like.

Reggie shook his head.

'No one acting suspicious?' he pressed.

Reggie shook no again.

The man leaned back. He took a deep breath, the sound of it going in and blowing out like a dying wind.

'We really should get you back to your family,' he said. 'Would you like some hot chocolate?' the man asked, gesturing with a pale hand appearing out of his blanket at the pot over the fire.

Reggie nodded, though there was nothing he wanted less than to drink anything from these three. He thought of poison, or some drug that would knock him out, and waking up in the trunk of a car or in a shallow grave, buried alive.

The smaller posse member leaned forward, used tongs to take the pot from the fire, and produced a mug. The splash and swirl of the liquid into the mug could be heard, like the current of a small stream. He stood and leaned around the fire to offer Reggie the mug.

Reggie had the urge to flee from the nearness of the man, but fought it down. He took the mug and held it on his knee. They all looked at him over the fire, and he slowly lifted the mug and took a sip. It was hot and delicious.

He waited to feel weak and dizzy. He waited for his limbs to slacken and grow heavy. He waited for his vision to go blurry. Nothing happened and after several seconds he took another sip, and another.

'Thank you,' he muttered.

'Maybe you should stay the night,' said the one in the middle. 'And bright and early we'll walk you back to your family.'

Reggie had no way to answer that to save his lie. He had only the truth, and he thought that might work for now.

'I'm out here alone,' he told them. 'I live a couple miles back that way,' he said, gesturing again behind him with a nod of his head. 'I'm looking for the killer too.'

Across from him, the spectral heads nodded knowingly.

'The reward?' the middle one asked.

Reggie nodded, suddenly finding that a bending of the truth was the easiest of lies.

'Twenty thousand dollars is a lot of money,' the man said, still nodding his head. 'How'd you plan on taking him back if you find him?'

Reggie slung his backpack off and unzipped it. He reached inside and pulled out the butcher's knife. He knew for such a task it looked pathetic, something a child would think of. An assessment he now counted on.

'Your heart's in the right place,' said the fattest of the camping trio. 'But you'd need something a bit more than that to get a cold-blooded killer to go back with you.'

'That's why we brought these,' his smaller companion said, and as deftly as he'd produced the mug from his bundled form, he brought out a shotgun from behind him. The weapon was large and sparkled darkly in the night.

'If he's out here,' said the singing man, 'we aim to find him.'

Reggie put the knife away, set his backpack aside.

167

'It's a task for adults,' said the singer, 'not for children, however brave they might be. Do you understand me?'

'I'm not a kid,' Reggie said, feeling like a kid for having to say that. 'I'm almost fifteen.'

But he nodded. He was still looking at the smaller man's shotgun, held across his lap. He took another swallow of the hot cocoa and looked back at the fire.

'We have an extra sleeping bag,' said the singer. 'Sleep here tonight and tomorrow morning we'll walk you home. You're not afraid of the dark, are you? It can get pretty dark out here. Especially when the fire goes out.'

Reggie shook his head, but as he finished his hot chocolate and spread out the offered sleeping bag, he looked cautiously at the edge of the woods around the clearing. He thought of the beast out there, roaming around in the shadows, perhaps even circling them. Wondered if he should tell the three-man posse about it.

Instead, crawling into the sleeping bag and stretching out, he pretended to sleep, his mind's eye on the shotgun and what he could do with it.

Chapter Eight

1.

Bumblebee snores not unlike his mom's let Reggie know when it was safe to get up. The sleeping bag hugged him snugly and made his worm-like motions to slide out difficult and awkward. When he was out of it, he rose to a crouch and looked about the campsite at the other three sleeping forms.

The campfire was down to embers, but the men had left their lanterns burning low. In the dim light, with the full moon above, Reggie could make out forms and shapes in some detail.

All three men had their shotguns nestled beside them, like little babies with comfort toys. Reggie eyed the smallest of the three, thinking if there was a struggle he had the best shot at wresting the gun from that man.

But then the trees about them moved. Pushed aside like stalks in a field. A deep rumble-roar accompanied the slap falls of monstrous feet. Twin yellow orbs like headlights blinking to life swept the camp.

Only yards from him, the enormity of the thing melting away from the rest of the night froze Reggie in terror. A shadow from the other shadows, the mountain lion seemed not a mere animal, but something otherworldly, a dark emissary crossing the space between realities. Emerging from the woods nearest the smallest bundled man, it stood over him, eclipsed him.

The beast chuffed and sniffed at the sleeping form. Little plumes of mist puffed from its nostrils like dragon's breath.

Reggie wanted to cry out, wanted to warn the man, and at the same time that was the last thing he wanted to do. Lest those glowing eyes turn upon him.

In his terror, his mother's words of caution from days ago came back to Reggie: *You have to be careful out there, Reggie. There's coyotes, bobcats, mountain lions.*

Now they seemed not merely motherly words of caution, but a warning, a threat. Something that would most definitely happen to stubborn, disobedient boys who disrespected their moms.

The bundled, sleeping figure stirred.

The beast pounced.

There was a scream unlike anything Reggie had ever heard. The man who'd given him hot chocolate earlier in the night was swung side to side like laundry being shook out, up and down, his head caught between massive paws like catcher's mitts. There was a crunch and snap like twigs broken underfoot as the monstrous cat's head darted forward, the jaws grasped, and the teeth clenched.

The other two men snapped awake. They bolted up from the tangles of their bedrolls. They grasped their shotguns. Turned, sought the source of the thrashing, aimed.

They were too slow.

A tearing, ripping sound joined the crunching and snapping under the thing's paws. The smaller man's screams rose an octave, transitioning from scream to shriek, lowered to become a brief whimper, and then ceased altogether.

Somehow Reggie stirred himself to motion, found his pack, opened it, found the flashlight, and turned it on, aiming at the struggle before him. He saw the thick hide, torn and battle marred. He saw claws like daggers, painted red. The jaws worked like a machine, showing teeth as large as spikes from wrought-iron fences.

He saw all of this in a moment. The cat-thing from the woods, its jaws clamped on the small man, turned, was there, and then was gone, dragging the limp form with him. Trees and shrubbery parted and then closed around beast and prey, like earthen lips slurping.

Reggie remembered when he'd taken aim and shot the water bottles in the woods with Ivan. How, when hit, they seemed to have been snatched out of the air, yanked out of reality. There and then not.

The other two men – the large one and the campfire singer – were shouting, swinging their weapons side to side, but there was nothing to fire at.

They were confused. Where Reggie's light pointed there was nothing.

'*What the fuck was that?*' asked the fat one. The shotgun in his hands trembled, and Reggie backed up a couple steps, in case he should reflexively pull the trigger.

'*Mountain lion?*' Reggie offered, speaking softly, reverently, as if at the scene of a miracle. A dark miracle; violent, irrational. The cleared circle of their camp could have been the gathering place of ancient man come to worship the old gods. Gods of blood and death.

'*Fuck that,*' said the singing one. '*I've never heard of a mountain lion that big.*'

'*Had to have been two hundred pounds,*' the fat man said, his tone matching the grim awe Reggie felt.

There was one last scream from far off. It sounded strangely like it bordered on laughter. A sound of pain and the breaking of sanity. A cry from hell.

They all stood silently, listening to it fade.

The two men dug out their own flashlights and switched them on.

The trio of beams cut through the night, trying to eye all directions at once. Reggie saw the third shotgun on the ground where the small man had been. He wanted to go to it and was afraid to move at the same time. As if his very motion might stir the suddenly silent world to chaos once again.

'*We have to go after him,*' said the fat one, though his voice said he wanted to do no such thing.

'*He's dead*,' said the singer, as if they hadn't heard the scream seconds ago.

The flashlight beams searched the woods. Oaks and elms and cedars and ashes and pines; gnarled trunks and twisting branches seeming to mock them; deep impenetrable shadows hiding things. This world wasn't theirs. Man didn't belong here. They were intruders in a territory not their own; trespassers. All of them knew it.

And unless they departed, they'd pay a similar price as their absent companion.

The men started to break down the camp in a frantic scramble, rolling up the sleeping bags and dismantling the tent. Occasionally, one or both of them pulled out cell phones, held them up, cussed loudly when there was no signal. Reggie picked up the dropped shotgun, and no one stopped him. He stood silent vigil and guard with his flashlight and the shotgun. All three of them cast frequent glances at where the third man had been. Trails in the ground marked where he'd been dragged off into the woods. When everything was packed the singing man said, 'Let's go' and took a step east, where Reggie had come from, towards home.

Reggie didn't move.

West was where he was going.

'*We've got to go*,' said the man, looking back at Reggie. '*It could come back at any time*,' he added, still whispering as if they were someplace sacred. Made sacred by the spilling of blood.

'I can't,' Reggie said, shaking his head.

'*Forget about the reward*,' said the man. '*It's not worth it.*'

'It's not that,' Reggie said. But he couldn't tell these two strangers exactly what it was. Ivan's words came back to him: *We have a deal*. That was the short and sweet of it, and yet it was something much more.

Then language he remembered from his dad's sermons came to him, and Reggie knew what it was that tugged him in the direction of the killer. Not merely a deal, it was a *covenant*. He and Ivan were bound by something irrevocable, as powerful as anything between Yahweh and the Israelites in millennia past. Likewise, as between the chosen tribe and their god, it was a covenant of blood and sacrifice.

Reggie's own blood, and that of the deputy cast down the cliff face, flagging the living with his death wave.

West was where he had to go. West was where things would be revealed.

'We don't have time for this,' the man said, angry now. 'We have to go!'

Reggie didn't know what he was going to say next, because he never got the chance to say it. The fat man had drifted some yards from his friend as he and Reggie had been talking. Reggie saw the eyes in the darkness. He saw the large hulking shadow. But still shaken and confused by what had already occurred, he hadn't the wherewithal to shout a warning.

The singer must have seen some change in his expression, though, because he turned in the direction Reggie was looking. The fat man began to scream as a flash of movement in the air before him streaked through the night.

His torn throat spewed blood like a faucet. His flashlight fell, hit the ground, winked out. Reggie and the singer pointed their beams in that direction simultaneously.

But there was nothing there, only the fat man's flashlight on the ground.

Yet they could hear them in the nearby brush. Man and beast. The friction of the man being pulled along the forest floor. The roar of the monster cat. There was a thunderclap and a brief flash as the fat man fired a shot. The singer raised his shotgun and fired in the general direction. The sound of the dragging faded and was gone. There were no screams this time.

Just the absence of the man. The existence of him scrubbed out.

Leaving only the two of them. Singing man and frightened boy.

They waited, trembling. They bore no illusions that there'd be a walk back to civilization. There was no safety. It was them and the beast. Their breath puffed in little clouds. Flashlights in one hand; shotguns in the other.

Together, they stood back to back, man and boy, turning, guarding each other, watching everywhere at once. The woods pressed against them, closing in around them, keeping them snug and tight. There was a little circle of existence at the centre of the clearing they occupied; outside this ring of light, stark blackness.

And they waited.

'You know how to use that?' the man asked.

'Yeah,' the boy answered, gripping the weapon tighter.

'You'll probably only get one shot, if that,' the singing man said. 'Make it count.'

The boy nodded though the man couldn't see him, facing as he was the other direction. The world was silent about them. The night birds and cicadas mute, as if aware of death about them. Showing respect or dread or both.

Movement from his right. A shadow among shadows.

Reggie swivelled and fired into the night. The recoil sent the shotgun's butt stock into his right shoulder in a hard, fast punch. The flash lit a glimpse of torn, mangy hide as tall as he. But the spread pockmarked only tree bark. The creature drew away.

The singing man turned about their shared axis, saw something, fired. The blue flash was seen in Reggie's peripheral, but he didn't take his eyes off the woods.

Branches swayed a few yards ahead of him. Twigs snapped like brittle bones.

Reggie fired again, leaning into the kickback this time, the butt stock set firmly against the small hollow between shoulder and collarbone. Something roared and bounded away. He tried to track it, ready to pull the trigger again, but it moved too fast.

Then it was there again, out of the shadows, charging.

It leapt from a distance, such a monstrous thing seemingly flying, sailing through the air.

Reggie tried to raise the shotgun, but he knew he was too slow. He wouldn't have it in his sights in time. So he could only duck, drop, and roll away ...

... leaving the singing man in the big cat's path.

The man sensed something. He turned, raising his shotgun. Saw the thing coming down on him. He fired wildly. The creature landed on him, crushing him beneath its weight. Claws slashed and teeth ripped. The man's screams were as torturous as the small man's minutes – an eternity – ago. They weren't mere cries of pain but shrieks of agony. Unbearable suffering.

As the mountain lion bore down on the man beneath him, chewing, tearing, ripping, it spared Reggie a brief glance. Then, the singing man's face in its jaws like a wet hanging rag, it turned fully to face him.

Reggie, still on his backside on the ground, pointed both flashlight and shotgun at the feline thing. It walked lazily towards him. Scars adorned it and rippled with the muscled flesh like a living map, a topography of its past kills. It had one ear; where the other should have been just a hole into its head. It came at him slowly, the muzzle stained crimson.

Reggie heard the singing man's words.

One shot. Make it count.

He'd already fired a few times, but it was the second part of that advice that mattered. He'd make this one be the one that counted. Or he'd do nothing ever again.

The monster stepped slow, almost tiredly, as if the smallest of its prey was of no consequence. Reggie thought of a house cat toying with a dying bird or mouse, batting it about. Delaying the inevitable death for fun and amusement. Enjoying the leaching of the life from the weaker being.

He thought of the parishioner who'd shot his father, and he thought of Johnny Witte the condom bandit. He thought of Deputy Collins.

They know you're weak.

He could almost hear Ivan's voice. It pissed him off.

His hands tightened on the shotgun. He drew it up and aimed.

'*Come get me you big pussy*,' he said, and the demon-cat leapt, high and then coming down.

Reggie fired.

A spray of blood and fur blossomed in the cool air.

The beast roared and landed heavily beside him, the thump of the impact shaking the ground. It rolled once and was still.

Reggie stood uncertainly on trembling legs. Prodded the creature with one foot.

It didn't move.

For a time, neither did Reggie.

He surveyed the dead. Considered them and spoke wordless prayers for them. Then he went to the fallen singer, searched the man's pockets, found the cell phone.

Although Reggie wasn't done tonight, he could at least call the police, let them know what had just happened. These men who'd invited him into their camp for the night deserved better than to serve as scraps for forest scavengers.

Holding the cell phone up, pressing the 'Call' button, the LED glow showed only one bar. Pressing it to his ear, Reggie heard only a dead line.

Ivan's voice whispered silently again to him:

Some things lived. Some things died.

For a time he considered both the dead lion and the dead man. He focused more on the big cat. The red meat of the now faceless man was more than Reggie could handle. But he found it in himself to take a sleeping bag, unroll it again, and lay it over the man. Makeshift shroud in place, he lowered his head, closed his eyes for a moment, and murmured something like a prayer again.

Directed at no particular god, but a prayer, nonetheless.

Then Reggie turned and continued west. The tower of stone beckoned.

***

Every so often, Reggie pulled the cell phone out of his pocket, tried 911 or the operator. Each time, he received only the dull tones of a dead line.

He thought of the dead men behind him. He thought of his dad dead in a lifeless heap in a parking lot.

None of it was fair. And at the same time it didn't matter.

Or all of it mattered, but there was nothing to be done about it.

You could turn around, he thought. *Go home, tell Mom what happened. Call the police, tell them everything. Let them deal with it.*

But, again, he knew that really wasn't an option at all. He couldn't say exactly why, but he had to see it through to the end.

So Reggie kept walking. And the crooked stone finger waved him onward.

2.

The dog was a mutt and a stray, ugly really. Skinny and mangy, it was a pathetic sight. It stepped into Reggie's path, froze as if surprised to find another wanderer this far out, and stared at him for a time. Stunned in the beam of his light, like a frightened stage actor considering the audience before him. Reggie knelt, slowly set the shotgun down, unslung his backpack, and pulled out the crackers. He dumped a few into his hand and held them out palm up for the dog.

It sniffed the air between them, cautious yet interested.

But it also seemed preoccupied, fidgety, as if it needed to move on.

There was something familiar about the mutt that Reggie couldn't immediately place. He wondered if it was a neighbour's, and tried to remember the canine residents of his street. Urging the dog nearer, he stretched his arm out further, enticing the mutt with the proffered food.

The dog inched closer to Reggie, stretching its muzzle towards his outstretched hand. It nosed the crackers in his palm, licked one experimentally, then drew it into its mouth and started to chew. It ate a second and a third, until Reggie's hand was empty.

Reggie took out a bottle of water next, uncapped it, and poured a little into the same palm. Holding it out to the mutt, the dog was quicker to accept this time, lapping the water up quickly. Reggie refilled his palm half a dozen times before the dog had enough and turned away.

He had wanted to pet the dog, but it drew away, moving back towards the trees from which it had emerged. It didn't immediately leave, though, but looked back at Reggie, then back towards the trees, then at him again. The way it carried itself, tail tucked between its legs, head lowered, made it seem troubled, uneasy, and though it had taken the food and water, it seemed as if there was somewhere else it had to be.

It looked again from the woods to Reggie.

Reggie looked from the stone tower, nearer yet still a distance to be travelled, then back to the dog. It wasn't as if he'd lose sight of the stony structure, great and soaring as it was.

'Okay,' he said, getting up, putting on the backpack again, picking up the shotgun. 'Lead on.'

The dog gave one weak swish of its tail, not one of joy

or excitement, but something akin to a human nodding, something of acknowledgement and appreciation maybe. The downcast angle of its gaze, the slump of its posture, assured Reggie that he wasn't in for something altogether pleasant, but he followed the mutt regardless, remembering the waving corpse, the swinging hound, the singing, the dancing lights, the beast, and how it all seemed a part of something larger, something looming over him, like a great wave rolling in. This had the same feeling: this sad dog that had stepped from the shadows into his path.

Seeing it had his attention, the dog turned and walked into the trees and darkness beyond them, and lighting the way with his flashlight, Reggie followed.

***

The bodies were small and pale in the grass. There were five of them, still and lifeless. Reggie leaned in close to make sure, looking for the rise and fall of breathing. Nothing. He turned from them back to the mutt, the bitch, the mother.

He remembered the pregnant stray along the highway, on the way back from the theatre with his mom. Before she'd pulled off the road to the cemetery. Before he'd cussed at her, and she'd slapped him.

'I'm sorry,' he said to the dog, a deep shame coming upon him. 'There's nothing I can do.'

But there was, a voice whispered to him in his head,

indicting him. *Then, there was something you could have done.*

The dirty, fur-entangled mutt made a small sound that died quickly, like a whimper starting but she was too tired to finish it. She moved forward and nudged one of the dead puppies with her muzzle, as if to test this prognosis. She did so weakly, though, as if aware of the cold facts before her. She lay down heavily, almost a collapse, beside them. Set her head on her forepaws and let out a long, deep breath.

Reggie looked about himself, thinking.

He knelt and tested the ground with his fingers. It was soft and rich and yielding. He took off his pack again, unzipped it and took out the knife. Kneeling, he stabbed the ground and lifted at an angle. The soil came loose easily. He started to work more earnestly, pushing the blade in deep and lifting. As the hole grew deeper, he used his hands to widen and shape it. When he was done the grave was a couple feet in diameter and a foot or so deep and he was breathing heavily from the effort.

He then piled the small bodies in one by one. He thought the mutt might lunge or snap at him in an instinctive maternal rage, and he tensed, ready to fend her off. But she did nothing, just watched him with tired resignation in her eyes. When the last dead puppy was in the small grave, he pushed the dirt back in with his hands and feet and patted it smooth. He found some rocks nearby and made a small cairn atop the grave.

Then he sat beside the mutt and gently set a hand on her shoulders. She flinched at the first touch, then slowly relaxed under his strokes.

'I know how it feels,' he said, not feeling the least bit foolish talking to a dog. 'I'm sorry.'

He thought of his dad's gravesite upon the hill at the cemetery. The cold plaque bearing his name. The general silence of the place.

Some things lived. Some things died.

The words came to him again, at first with what he took to be a taunting note to them. But as he listened to them repeating in the quietude of his mind, Reggie reassessed this judgement.

No, they weren't so much taunting as they were insistent. As if what they had to impart was of utmost importance. Reggie's understanding was necessary, and the voiceless words must continue until he apprehended them.

And, God help him, Reggie thought he was beginning to.

The two of them remained like that for a time, dog and boy, sitting vigil over the dead, the small cemetery lit by artificial light and moonlight, the darkness about them seemingly extending over all the world.

3.

The climb up to the great finger of stone was steep and slow-going. Regretfully, Reggie left the mangy dog at the bottom, setting the shotgun down as well. *I'll be back*, he'd told the dog, not knowing if he would be or not, but feeling like the option should be put forth. Then he started up, grasping at craggy handholds, pulling himself, pushing up with his legs at carefully plotted places. At times the going was nearly vertical. At others, the hill levelled out into little recesses, and Reggie could stand, stretch, and looking up, plan his further ascent. Then he was at the rim, reaching up, rolling over, and coming up to a crouch, catching his breath.

And there Ivan was, sitting, leaning against a backrest of stone, waiting.

'I found your note,' Reggie said, pulling the paper out of his jeans. His hand was jittery from the strain of the climb or something else, and the wind snatched the note out of his fingers. They watched the piece of paper sailing out into the sky, carried aloft like a lazy bird. It twirled and whirled and danced an airborne ballet, graceful in its descent.

'I knew you would,' Ivan said. 'I knew you were too stubborn to let things go.'

Reggie slung the backpack down and dug a bottle of water out of it. He stepped closer to Ivan and passed it over. The man took it, uncapped it clumsily, and brought it to his lips. When he'd taken a few swallows, he nodded his appreciation and set the bottle down between his legs. Reggie saw what else was there.

The black pistol glimmered like obsidian.

185

'Things weren't done between us,' Reggie said, moving towards the base of the pillar beside Ivan and sliding down to a seated position.

'I guess they weren't,' Ivan said.

Reggie pulled out the crackers too, and passed over a package to Ivan. Ivan took these gratefully also, and opened them with a crinkle of plastic.

'There's other things I want to know,' Reggie said.

Ivan nodded.

'I knew there were,' he said.

And beneath the shadow of the stone tower in the woods, high above the world, Reggie asked the killer the things he wanted to know.

***

'Was there ever someone you killed that deserved it?' Reggie asked.

'What do you mean?' the killer asked.

'You know,' Reggie said. 'Was there ever anyone you liked killing? Not just because you were paid to do it?'

'Like my father?' Ivan asked.

'Yeah,' Reggie said. 'Bad guys, people that deserved to die.'

'I told you I never ask about my targets,' the killer said. 'The less you know about them the better.'

'Come on,' Reggie pressed, smiling a little. 'You never broke that rule? There was never anyone you just had to know more about?'

'No,' Ivan said. 'I never broke that rule.'

Reggie looked away from Ivan. He didn't know what to ask next.

'But there was this one woman who freely told me about her husband,' he said. 'She paid a lot of money to have it done in their house, with her watching. They lived in a large hacienda in New Mexico. He was something of a cattle baron, though he'd invested in so many things that you couldn't pinpoint exactly what it was he did.

'He was also something of a philanthropist and humanitarian,' Ivan continued. 'He worked with Immigration to employ Mexican immigrants legally. Gave them steady work on his ranch as they worked their way through the naturalization process. He also gave the workers' families a place to stay. He had cabins built on his property that served as employee quarters. He was one of the few voices of reason in the immigration controversy.

'And his wife thought him a child pornographer.'

Reggie didn't say anything immediately. He let those words sink into his head; tried to grasp the meaning of what they meant. His parents had told him about staying away from strangers when he was younger. His school had visiting police officers give presentations, telling the students what to do should someone pull over in a strange vehicle or approach them at a park or something. He knew intellectually what could happen to kids who were abducted. But to hear from Ivan about these things – after what they'd seen and done together – made the reality of such crimes hit home.

In Reggie's mind, images played of dirty children in seedy rooms. Shadowy and dark like basements or cellars. He saw big, burly men leering and towering over them. In this mind theatre the children looked like the frail and filthy creatures he saw on those Christian Children's Fund commercials with flies buzzing about their heads. They were hopeless; the plight of their circumstances lost even on them who lived it; their faces devoid of emotions.

'How did she know?' he finally asked, in a voice hardly more than a croak.

'She found pictures and videos,' Ivan said. 'She recognized some of the faces. They were the children of the immigrants working for them. She tried showing them to me, pulling them out of her husband's wall safe.

'I turned my head,' Ivan said, 'slapped them away, but she persisted. Shoved them in my face, telling me how her husband deserved to die. She wanted it slow, and she wanted to watch. She cried as she flung the pictures at me.

'They fluttered down about me like dead birds,' Ivan said, 'settling on the floor all around so that I had nowhere to look that was safe. Some of them brushed against me as they fell and I felt dirty. It was like being touched by something grimy and soiled. I had the instant urge to wash myself.'

The breaking morning seemed to reveal everything. The world was alight and everything shone. There were

no dark corners or deep holes. There seemed no hiding
places for shadowy things. It seemed an impossibility,
such evil, in the presence of such light. And yet Reggie
knew it was out there. He'd seen it in the past couple
days himself. Glimpses of what walked the world under
human guise.

'What did you do?' Reggie asked weakly.

'I gathered the pictures and handed them back to her,'
Ivan said. 'And then we waited with the lights off. In the
dark she told me how she wanted it done. She told me the
tools to use. She told me details that only a wife could
know. Fears and worries shared and discovered over thirty
years of marriage. She instructed me on things to say to
heighten his terror. To trigger emotional responses.
Childhood insecurities. Parental disappointments. Things
to inflict psychological torture as well as the physical.'

Ivan shifted on the stone and groaned. He held his
bloodied middle and winced at the touch. His fingers left
scarlet prints and smears on the stone. The wetness glimmered in the morning sunlight. Reggie looked at the blood
with intense scrutiny. The whorls of the fingerprints and
red of the blood combined in strange impressionistic
pictures.

'She wanted to be a weapon for me,' the killer said, 'is
how she put it. "I want to be a weapon for you. I want to
be part of his suffering", she said. "I want to know that
when he screams, it's because of me." Her hatred startled
me. Yet I understood it.

'Her husband had fooled her,' Ivan said. 'She'd thought they were living one life, and all the while she was unknowingly part of another. Under her own roof, on her watch, something terrible had been happening for years. She'd been oblivious to it, or so she told herself. And in her ignorance she'd been party to it.'

Ivan shifted again. A slight kick of his leg sent a small cascade of pebbles and grit down over the edge of the stony shelf they sat on. Reggie listened and could hear the descent of the tiny avalanche. How far it fell and the dwindling sound of it.

'Her husband came home at three in the morning,' Ivan said. 'We heard the engine before we saw him. His car came up the long, twisting driveway and the headlight beams swept over the windows of the house. We waited for him in the bedroom with the lights off. The shadows in the room grew large in the sweep of the headlights and moved along the walls like skulking monsters.

'I could see the woman's face for a moment as the car drove past,' Ivan said. 'I could see her smile. She rocked in her chair with anticipation. She leaned forward and put a hand on my knee like we were old friends. "I want his cock fed to the hogs," she said.'

Reggie wasn't sure he wanted to hear the rest of the story, and yet, like before, he didn't stop Ivan. There was something about the telling that he felt he had to know. When he listened to the killer speak he felt like a student before a skilled teacher presenting an important lesson.

And this was the sort of information that would definitely be on the final exam.

He thought of his father, dead in a parking lot. He thought of the deputy, dead at the bottom of a cliff. That death could come at anytime to anyone seemed part of this lesson. That some people – like the wife in the story, and the killer before him telling it – thrived in the dealing out of death, seemed another part.

And that Reggie was starting to understand all of this frightened him. In some ways, even more so than the lesson itself.

'It was so quiet as we waited,' the killer continued. 'I could hear him unlocking the front door. The rattle of his keys. I heard the opening and closing of a closet as he set things down. His footsteps as they crossed the foyer tile and reached the stairs. The creak of each step as he started up.

'I got up and walked softly across the room,' the killer said. 'I stood behind the door and took out a vial of chloroform and a handkerchief. I wet the handkerchief and pocketed the bottle just as he reached the room.

'He turned on the lights,' said the killer, 'and saw his wife sitting across the room.

'"Hi honey," he said. "What are you doing up so late?"

'I stepped up behind him and shoved the cloth to his mouth and nose. He struggled, snatched in a breath reflexively, breathed in the chloroform, and passed out.

'I dragged him to the chair and propped him up,' Ivan

said. 'I retrieved a reel of fishing wire that I'd brought from my car, parked behind their house out of sight. I tied him to the chair and turned to his wife when I was done.

'"Are you ready?" I asked.

'"Yes," she said, smiling that same smile I'd seen earlier. She wasn't just a wife horrified at the things her husband had done. She was enjoying this. She was having a good time.'

And what about you? Reggie thought, watching Ivan. Were you having a good time? And what about me? he thought. For wanting to hear this? For asking the killer these questions? Was there something wrong with *me*?

Reggie thought of the satisfaction he'd felt beating up Johnny Witte. Of the similar feeling stirring inside when he'd seen his mom's recent submission, allowing Reggie to do what he wanted, when he wanted.

Now, he felt only shame. He had the sudden urge to tell Ivan to stop, that he'd heard enough. But he didn't, and listened to the rest of it.

'I also had smelling salts in my jacket,' the killer said. 'When he was tied securely to the chair, I used them to bring him back around. I waited for him to gather himself. When he saw me, then saw his wife, you could see the panic building in him. You could see it in his eyes.

'"What the hell's going on?" he said, trying to sound commanding, in charge. But it really sounded like a whine. Like he was about to cry.

192

'His wife gathered the file of photos that she'd shown me and set them in his lap. She knelt beside him and opened the file. Her movements were gentle and graceful, like a waitress of a high-class restaurant setting a table. She flipped the glossy photos one by one, slowly, allowing him to really see each of them.

'"I know what you've done," she said to him. Her tone wasn't angry. She was like a parent scolding a disobedient child. "I've seen it with my own eyes," she said, turning the last of the photos.

'"What the hell is this?" he said. "Get those away from me."

'But his words were weaker than before. He was almost begging.

'"Under our own roof," she said. "In my own house."

'He said nothing. But he was trembling now. There were tears at the corners of his eyes. He looked at me. He tried blinking away his tears.

'"Who are you?" he asked. "Do you know any of them?" he said, nodding towards the photos in his lap.

'I shook my head.

'"Are you with the police?" he asked. "The FBI?"

'I shook my head again.

'"Then we can make a deal," he said. "I can pay you a lot of money. I can leave the country. You'll never see me again. Neither of you will," he said, looking at his wife.

'I shook my head a third time.

'"That's not how it works," I told him.

'"Let's get on with it," the woman said, and I nodded, and he started to scream.

'I hit him in the stomach, cutting off the scream. I tore off a strip of duct tape, which I'd brought from the car along with the fishing wire. I wrapped it around his mouth and the back of his head. By the time he caught his breath and tried screaming again, all that came out from behind the gag was a muffled groaning.

'I had a small valise that I'd stowed out of sight under a dresser. I pulled it out, set it on the bed, and unsnapped it. Lifting it open, I turned it so the husband could see what was inside. There was a hammer, pliers, a nail gun, and a box cutter.

'I lifted the hammer and held it before him.

'"I'm going to break your fingers with this," I told him.

'He screamed behind the tape, lost control of his bodily functions.

'I grabbed his right hand and tried to straighten his forefinger. He tried curling his fingers into a fist so I couldn't get at them. But I got his finger, held it down with one hand, and swung the hammer with the other.'

Reggie stood and turned away.

He didn't want to hear anymore. This wasn't why he'd come all this way. At least he didn't think it was.

'You're the one that asked the question,' Ivan said.

'I know,' Reggie said. 'Just … no more right now, all right?'

'Fine,' Ivan said.

Reggie stared out over the forest for a time. Then he turned his gaze to the south and the long stretch of the desert, red-orange under the morning sun, like a barren Martian landscape. The vast emptiness of it, and the life-lessness.

He turned back to Ivan.

'He really did those things to those children?' he asked.

'I saw the pictures with my own eyes,' Ivan said.

'And you killed him?' Reggie asked.

The killer nodded.

Reggie nodded too.

'That's all I needed to know.'

***

'Do you ever think about writing?' Reggie asked him.

'No,' Ivan said.

'Come on,' Reggie said. 'It was your dream.'

'I told you,' Ivan said. 'I don't think about it.'

'That's impossible,' Reggie said, sitting beside his friend, looking out over the woods. The tops of the trees swayed together like elegant dancers. A murder of crows suddenly launched themselves from the branches, blacking out part of the sky. 'It was your dream. People never forget their dreams.'

Ivan didn't say anything.

'Come on,' Reggie pressed. 'If you were to write something today, what would you write about?'

Ivan turned and looked at him square in the eyes.

'I'd write a story about a kid who asks too many questions,' he said, 'and one day he disappears because he doesn't know when to shut his fucking mouth.'

Reggie looked away. He fumbled with his hands in his lap.

'That's not cool,' he mumbled.

Neither of them said anything for a time. Reggie thought of Ivan bringing the garrotte around his throat, strangling him, and dragging him off somewhere in the woods. He thought of the big man stringing him up in a tree like the hound or rolling him off a cliff like the deputy. He wondered, not for the first time, why he'd come all this way.

He wished he knew why, so he could do whatever he needed to do and get on home. And at the same time he didn't want to be anywhere else. With Ivan, things happened, the world *moved*. At home, all there was for him was the numbing pain of day after dreadful day. The emptiness of the house and the emptiness inside of himself.

'I did try writing one last time,' Ivan unexpectedly said into the quiet that had befallen them. 'Once, a long time ago, during a lull in my work.'

Reggie knew 'work' meant 'killing'. For the first time, the killer's substitution for the word – his sanitization of it – disturbed him. Because killing wasn't *work*. It was something else altogether. Something wrong.

Something ... obscene.

'I was staying in some cheap motel off the beaten path,' Ivan continued. 'Just some run-down joint in Texas. I'd collected a big payout, and didn't need to work for awhile. Always wanted to go to Texas, so I went.'

'Why not stay in some fancy hotel?' Reggie asked, not knowing why he did. It wasn't an important detail, for one. Also, he thought what the killer was saying *was* leading to something important, and so Reggie should just shut up and wait for it.

'In my line of work, it's those that flaunt their money that get caught,' Ivan said. 'Wearing fancy clothes, driving expensive cars, people tend to remember who you are and what you were doing. It's better to go unnoticed, to be unremarkable.'

Another first: Reggie looked the killer over with new eyes, seeing the big man in a new light. Other than his height, the killer was indeed unremarkable. From his choice of clothes to the way he carried himself. If you hadn't seen what Reggie had seen in the past couple days, you'd probably not give the man a second look. Maybe not even a first.

And that only added to the killer's ever-present threat, Reggie realized. To move around in full view, mingling with people like some chameleon blending into the landscape, all the while holding each person's life in your hands.

Reggie again had the feeling he'd had earlier in the tree house. Of the walls closing in around him, pushing him nearer the killer. Even out here, atop the hill under the crook of stone and the broad desert sky, he felt trapped.

'I bought a pad of paper from a market down the street,' Ivan continued. 'Sat in the little motel room with the window open. Stared at the top sheet, pen in hand.'

Sitting against the upright stone, Ivan stared into his lap, his hands splayed out, as if he held the pad of paper even now. Looking at the empty space there, Reggie knew the man was looking through that space into that other time.

'But no matter how hard I tried,' the killer said, 'the words wouldn't come. I moved from the bed to the chair in the corner. I stood at the window, sat on the floor. It didn't matter. Nothing came to me. Not one sentence. Not one word.'

Ivan looked up from his empty hands and met Reggie's eyes.

'It was like I was empty,' he said. 'Up here.' He pointed to his temple. 'And in here,' he added, tapping his chest. 'You see, Reggie, whatever was in me when I was a boy was ... gone.'

The killer leaned forward for emphasis.

'None of us is what we were yesterday or the day before or last year. When things are gone, they're just gone.'

He held his hands up as he said this last, like a magician giving the *poof!* gesture.

Although Reggie didn't want them to, he couldn't deny that the killer's words made a certain sense. Then what the man had said the other day came back to him.

Some things live. Some things die.

Now, sitting atop the hill with Ivan, having heard the man's story of his emptiness in the Texas motel, those words made even more sense. Death was just another type of emptiness. And even for those things that lived, it was only a transitory reprieve.

A sentence temporarily commuted.

Option number two would find them all in the end.

All things die, was what the killer should have said, Reggie thought.

With this understanding came a heaviness. A weariness and resignation that settled upon him like a heavy blanket. Covered by this mantle, Reggie shut his eyes for a time and rested.

Chapter Nine

1.

'I killed something,' Reggie said as noon approached and the sun climbed higher along the blue desert sky.

'What was it?' Ivan asked, interested.

'A mountain lion,' Reggie said. 'Or at least I think so.'

'You think so?' Ivan asked.

'It was mangy,' he said. 'Scarred and dirty. It was the biggest thing I've ever seen.' He held his fingers in front of his mouth. 'Teeth out to here,' he mimed. 'Claws as big as knives.'

Ivan gave an impressed harrumph.

'What did it feel like?' he asked.

'What?' Reggie said.

'Killing it,' the killer said.

Reggie didn't answer immediately, carefully considering his response. The attack on the singing man's camp had been so fast and unexpected that it almost didn't seem real.

It could have been a dream, where time passed in flashes and rapid-fire sequences. Coming upon the men from the camp themselves had seemed unreal and dreamlike also – glimpsing them first far off and the floating orbs of their flashlights, then close up, entering the camp and the circle of light cast by the fire, the darkness all around. None of it seemed like something that had actually happened.

But it had. Seeing each man in turn pulled into the darkness; torn apart by demon claws; the death screams like banshee shrieks.

'I was scared,' Reggie said.

'Of what?' Ivan asked.

'Of being killed myself,' he said.

'But not of the thought of killing?' Ivan asked.

'No,' Reggie said. 'Not at the time.'

'You wanted to live,' Ivan pressed, 'and were willing to do whatever you had to, to make sure that you did.'

'Yes,' Reggie answered. 'I had a shotgun in my hands. I'd never fired a gun before – except that time with you. But I knew what they did. I knew what they were used for.'

'And this didn't bother you?' Ivan asked.

'No,' Reggie replied, shaking his head. 'Like you said, this was survival. I had to kill it or it would kill me.'

'Go on.'

'The mountain lion leapt at me,' Reggie said. 'It seemed to be flying. I watched it coming down on me. I saw its teeth. I could see down its throat. I knew what it would do to me if I let it. So I aimed and pulled the trigger. The blast of the shotgun was louder than anything I'd ever heard.

'It sent shivers through me,' Reggie continued. 'There was a spray of blood in the air. In the beam of the flashlight it floated like red dust. The mountain lion fell and didn't move.'

'Did you leave immediately?' Ivan asked. 'Or did you look at it?'

'I looked at it,' Reggie admitted with a slight nod.

'What did you see?' Ivan asked.

'I watched its chest move up and down with its last breath,' Reggie whispered. The memory seemed something sacred, and his tone as of someone in church or at a funeral. 'One of its legs twitched, and then it was dead.'

'What else?' the killer said.

'I wanted to touch it,' Reggie said.

'Did you?' the killer asked.

'I kicked it,' Reggie said. 'You know, to see if it was still alive. But it wasn't. I wanted to do more. I wanted to kneel down and touch it. I wanted to put my head against it, see if I could hear anything. I wanted to study the gunshot. I wanted to trace the edges of the wound. I wanted to smell it. I wanted to know what the difference was between it being alive, and then dead.'

'Did you do any of those things?' the killer asked. 'Did you touch it with your hands? Did you inspect the wound?'

'No,' Reggie said.

'Why not?' Ivan asked.

'Because ... I think another part of me knew none of that mattered,' Reggie said. 'Because it was dead, and I was alive. It felt like the body was off limits. It shouldn't be disturbed.'

'What do you mean by that?' Ivan asked.

'There's something that separates us from them,' Reggie continued, struggling to voice what he had felt, and was still feeling. 'We're not the same. What's in us isn't in them anymore. It's as simple as that. And it seems wrong somehow, the living bothering the dead.'

'What if I were to tell you you're wrong?' the killer said.

'What do you mean?' Reggie asked.

'That there's nothing special or different about the living and the dead at all,' the killer said. 'It's all just meat. We're walking, talking meat. They're ... well, dead meat. But all of us – living, dead – are on our way back to the dirt.'

Reggie didn't know what to say to that.

He'd taken biology classes in school. Dissected frogs and pig foetuses. He knew his father was dead. And yet there was something to be said about visiting the grave, as his mom had pressed him to do all these past months. He couldn't put it into words, but there was something right about honouring the dead. He'd resisted it for months, but paying respects by giving the dead their proper space lent a finality to the event itself.

'Lean closer,' the killer said. 'There's something I want to show you.'

One hand disappeared beneath the jacket, and Reggie waited for the knife or garrotte or pistol. He moved not an inch, wary that his slightest motion may spur the killer to action. Perhaps now that Reggie had taken a life, Ivan wanted to teach him the next lesson. The final lesson that awaited everyone.

Some things lived. Some things died.

And now the killer would teach him this last thing in exquisite detail.

When none of the three instruments of death emerged from the folds of the big man's jacket, Reggie let a breath out through thinly pursed lips. Rather than blade, strangulation wire, or gun, the killer held a sheaf of glossy prints, like a poker hand fanned out.

The photographs were bent and creased. Some were even yellowed, either by age or moisture, tucked for ages in the leather wallet Ivan dropped onto his lap. He fingered one after the other, flipping them top to bottom like a Vegas dealer. When Reggie saw what they showed, he didn't want to look at them, but had no choice.

'These are the dead,' the killer said, shuffling the photographs with a flip and snap, magician-like. 'I keep them with me, to remind me and to strengthen my resolve. There's power in remembrance. They do not haunt me. They do not bother me. I control them. I have power over them.'

Flip. Snap.

'This was a woman in England,' said the killer. 'She was

the wife of a member of Parliament. Her husband owed a great deal of money and wouldn't pay it.'

The photo showed a pale woman, nude, tied to a tree in a wooded area. It was dusk, the sky purple-dark, but a spotlight shone on her brightly. Her skin shone with the light and reflected it in a sweaty sheen. Her throat was slashed, a gaping second mouth, and below it her body was showered with blood.

Flip. Snap.

'This was a third-generation rancher in Texas,' said the killer. 'His family had owned the land for over a hundred years. He stumbled on a business deal being conducted on a remote corner of his acreage. He refused to be silent about what he saw.'

There was a middle-aged man in a flannel shirt and jeans sprawled in a weed strewn ditch. He'd been shot through each eye, and now stared heavenward with raw, red holes. Ants crawled along his face, in and out of the crimson tunnels.

Flip. Snap.

'This was the daughter of a banker in Paris,' said the killer. 'Her father was approached with an offer to allow certain transactions and exchanges to pass through his establishment. Moral qualms inhibited him from accepting the generous offer that was made, and he threatened to go to the police.'

A stretch of freeway and a car ploughed into the concrete divider. The young woman hung half in and half out of the car's windshield, sprawled on the hood, looking sideways at the camera. Her features were mashed together like a drawing scrubbed out. One arm hung uselessly askew, bent at an unnatural angle.

Flip. Snap.

'Here is the child of a Mexican police chief,' the killer said. 'The officer was informed of certain shipments that would be passing through his jurisdiction near the border. He was informed of the importance of the shipments, and the greater importance of their timely arrival. Despite a handsome offer, he refused to cooperate and allow the shipment through.'

A young boy, no older than ten, hung from a traffic light. His head rested at an odd angle on his broken neck, and he dangled several feet off the pavement. One shoe had fallen off and lay on the street below him, lonely and solitary in the empty lane.

'The dead have no power,' said the killer. 'They hold no mysteries. They have no hold over us save what we allow them to. Human traditions and the myths of cultures, passed down over the centuries, tell us otherwise. But these are merely stories, handed down through the ages by ignorant and stupid men.'

The killer reached out and patted Reggie.

Something within Reggie shrank and withdrew at the touch.

'The perpetuation of fear by those in power,' said the killer, 'is the surest means of securing conformity and cooperation. You tell people how frightening death is, how wrong it is, and back that conviction up with might, and you have a society. Laws and the enforcement of laws by strength of arms makes everyone line up obediently and believe the lies.'

The hand on his shoulder squeezed affectionately, and Reggie's balls shrank and drew upwards. He was knotted inside with a raw fear he'd never known. Yet he listened attentively to every word spoken by the madman beside him.

'This is my gift to you,' the killer said. 'The imparting of knowledge, so that you can discern for yourself what is and isn't so. With this knowledge you can do anything. Nothing will be off limits. You will answer to no authority save your own.'

Flip. Snap.

Flip. Snap.

The images of the dead passed before Reggie's eyes, like a projector slideshow at a macabre family get-together, a series of snapshots of vacations and parties chained together for nostalgia and laughs. He watched the slide-show for a while longer, and with each flip of the photos something inside him was burned away.

***

Surprisingly – or maybe not so – Reggie fell asleep. The exhaustion of the previous night draped across him like a great weight. He'd intended only to close his eyes and enjoy the warmth of the sun on his face for a moment or two, and then he was dreaming.

In the dream he was in the funeral home again. His dad's casket was before him. The lid was open and he could just see a hint of the body within. A tip of the nose. A lock of hair. The knuckles of the folded hands.

Then the lights of the place went out, and Reggie was thrown into darkness. In the deep blackness he heard a shuffling, as of fabric against fabric. It came from the direction of the coffin, somewhere ahead of him. A thump and a thud followed, as of something dropping to the floor.

A dragging, slithering noise came next, as something pulled itself across the linoleum.

Bolting upright, Reggie awoke. Breathing hard, rubbing the sleep away from his eyes, he was aware of Ivan sitting across from him, watching. The killer asked a question, but it took Reggie a moment to register it.

'What were you dreaming about?'

Reggie's curt answer: 'My dad.'

'It bothers you that he's dead,' Ivan said, not really a question.

'Of course it bothers me,' Reggie said, looking about himself, still hearing the sound of the thing from the coffin dragging itself across the floor. 'He's my dad.'

'After everything I've shown you?' the killer said. 'After everything you've seen? You still miss the dead?'

Reggie didn't know exactly what Ivan had shown him

the past few days. It all seemed sort of vague and surreal itself, like a distant memory hard to grasp and hold. He remembered hauling the bloodied killer on a snow sled. He remembered beating a kid bloody. He remembered a deputy being strangled and rolled off a cliff.

Reggie recalled his initial fascination with his talks with Ivan. How nothing seemed inappropriate; how they could talk about anything. Now he was just tired and confused. And the longer he spent with the man, it seemed the confusion got worse.

'When your dad died,' the killer said, 'he didn't go to heaven or hell. No god or devil greeted him. He wasn't reunited with friends or family. His neural impulses merely stopped firing, his brain died, and he was gone.

'This life is all there is,' the killer continued. 'We all find things to fill our time with until the end. For some it's religions. For others careers. But it really makes no difference because none of it matters. There's no one watching out for us, no one condemning our actions or keeping track of rewards we've earned.'

Reggie wanted to tell him to shut up. He wanted to scream and strike out at the man. Instead, he listened, and was scared as he realized the more he listened, the more the confusion fell away.

'When you step on a bug,' the killer said, 'what do you feel?'

Surprised, disconcerted at the sudden change of subject, Reggie initially said nothing. But Ivan repeated his question, and under that intense, steely blue gaze, he had to answer.

'Nothing,' Reggie said.

'Why?' the killer asked.

'Because it's a fucking bug,' Reggie said, irritated.

'But it's alive, isn't it?' Ivan asked.

'But it's only a bug,' Reggie said.

'Who says it's only a bug?' Ivan asked. 'Who says a bug's life isn't as important as a person's? Who made this rule?'

'God,' Reggie said weakly. 'The Bible says so.'

'And who says it's right?' Ivan asked. 'Who was there at the time of its writing, to see God come out of heaven and write it down?'

'Moses,' Reggie said.

'And who was there to see *him* see God?' Ivan asked. 'Who saw these things? How do we know they're right? How do we know they're real?'

Reggie said nothing.

'What we have are stories,' Ivan said. 'Stories told by the few to the many to keep them in line. Societies are formed by laws agreed upon to keep order. But the laws aren't intrinsically right or wrong. They're things made up by men to keep other men doing certain things and not do others.

'So when we say killing a bug is okay,' Ivan said, 'but killing a man isn't, how do we come to that determination?'

'Bugs don't think,' Reggie said. 'They don't feel.'

'How do you know?' Ivan asked. 'When you crunch

them underfoot, who's to say they aren't pleading? Aren't crying out in agony?'

Reggie pictured stepping on an anthill like Godzilla upon Tokyo, crushing a hundred or so ants, destroying their homes, their hopes for ant college, a career, ant marriage and ant children. He felt the urge to laugh and choked it down. Because then he superimposed images of his dad, the strangled deputy, and the dead camping posse, upon the imaginary ants and suddenly it wasn't so funny.

'And when you point a gun at a man,' the killer said, 'and pull the trigger, who's to say what you did was right or wrong? Who among us can claim moral superiority over another? And by what authority?'

Reggie again said nothing.

'When you mourn your father,' Ivan said, 'you burn calories on sorrow and anger. You're not paying tribute to his memory or soul. You aren't beaming prayers of vengeance or justice to God, because there is no god.

'You're wasting time,' the killer said, 'on a dead thing buried in a hole somewhere. Its skin is bloated or shrivelling. Its eyes have fallen out or congealed. It's a dead thing falling apart, and no one gives a shit.'

Reggie remembered his mom driving him to the cemetery. How she said she thought it was important that he visit the grave. He remembered what he'd thrown back in her face before she'd hit him.

Its fucking eyeballs have fucking popped out and it's fucking being eaten by fucking worms.

He'd sounded then like Ivan sounded now, and that didn't make him feel so good.

But he didn't want to argue, either, not with this man. So Reggie remained silent. He let the silence take hold and in the utter stillness his mind was a flurry. Within that mental chaos was a lot of confusion – about what to think, how to feel – but one thing for certain climbed its way out of the storm:

He'd have to decide something very important, very soon.

2.

Before he could come to any determination, though, the cop with the kids showed up, and everything changed. First, Ivan stood, looked south over the desert stretched out there in the distance, and told Reggie it was time to move.

'If I can get to Mexico,' he said, 'things will be all right.'

Having seen the wound after helping Ivan clean and redress it just minutes ago, Reggie doubted that. There were streaks of red around the partially scabbed bullet hole, like spokes or trails on a map. Ivan looked pale again, and though he tried to hide it grimaces of pain played across his face from time to time.

'I got to piss, too,' he added.

So did Reggie, and with that settling the matter, they started down together.

The descent was treacherous, Reggie urging the large man to move slowly and cautiously. Bits of rock and dirt tumbled down before them, and Reggie thought of Deputy Collins tumbling down, breaking, and then he thought of them, himself specifically, tumbling down and breaking. At the bottom the dog and shotgun awaited them. Ivan looked at both curiously.

'What's this?' he said, looking at the filthy dog but bending and picking up the shotgun.

'Just some dog,' Reggie said, shrugging, ignoring the shotgun. Inside, in his gut, something twisted and fluttered.

'Is this what you killed that mountain lion with?' Ivan said, turning to Reggie and hefting the shotgun in one hand.

Reggie nodded.

Ivan looked from the shotgun to Reggie and back again.

'Then it's yours,' he said, and offered it to him. Reggie reached out slowly, worried it might be some sort of trick. Worried that somehow Ivan might read what had been in his mind ever since he'd first touched the shotgun back at the posse's camp.

But then it was in his hands, and it felt right. The weight of the weapon felt good in his palms, his fingers wrapped about it. The weight and power of it; the silent promise of the things it could do.

Ivan knelt in front of him, surprising Reggie.

'I've got to know that I can count on you,' he said, his stony blue eyes burrowing deep into Reggie's. 'It's not that far to the border. But it's far enough, the condition I'm in. No doubt they're out there, looking for me. Maybe looking for you too by now. I have a plan, though. And I need to know that you'll go along with it.'

Reggie nodded.

'These past few days,' Ivan said, 'you've become like a son to me.'

Reggie didn't know what to make of this, and so didn't reply. He was a son, but to a different man than this. That man was dead, yet something in Reggie told him this didn't matter. You had only one father in this life, for good or bad, and to pretend otherwise didn't seem right.

Nonetheless, in spite of everything he'd seen and heard in his time with Ivan – the killer's stories, the strangled deputy, the photograph slideshow – a part of Reggie also liked hearing what the killer said. He blinked away the tears threatening at the corners of his eyes.

'We're in this together,' Ivan continued. 'I can count on you, right?'

Reggie nodded again, and was surprised to find he meant it.

Ivan pulled him close and hugged him. The big man smelled of sour sweat and he felt hot and his skin was clammy. Pulled close to him, Reggie could feel little tremors rolling through the man's body like tiny earthquakes.

He told Reggie his plan.

Reggie nodded.

They stood, peed a few feet from each other, zipped up, and started south through the woods, towards the white stretch of desert they'd seen from above.

The dog, wary, stayed a distance behind them.

***

The man was in hunting garb – boots, jeans, a flannel shirt, yellow hunter's vest, ball cap – so they didn't immediately know he was a cop. But he carried a large rifle, and Ivan wasn't taking any chances.

What happened next was fast and unexpected.

They were moving south through the woods. There was but the sound of their own soft footfalls, the crunch and crackle of woodland beneath them. The trees were thick, so that they could see ahead in only broken and intermittent patches. Up a rise they trudged, and then at the top of it there he was, the hunter.

The hunter and the killer looked at each other across the small space between them. Something seemed to pass between the two men in the silence as they regarded each other. Each read the other, neither liking what they discerned in the reading, and they moved.

Reggie had never in his life seen someone move so fast. He wouldn't have thought it possible outside movies and comic books if he hadn't seen it with his own eyes. The hunter raised his rifle towards Ivan, words on the verge of being spoken, his lips curling and moving with the intent, and then Ivan was there, across the gap between them like a phantom coalesced.

His left arm moved like a piston, swinging up and under the barrel of the rifle. The rifle leapt up and pointed skyward harmlessly, the thunder crack of its discharge as the hunter pulled the trigger ear-splitting and announcing its intent hadn't been harmless at all. With his other arm Ivan made a quick, darting jab at the hunter's throat. The hunter choked and gagged and staggered back, though he held onto the rifle with a vise-like grip.

Ivan kicked out with one leg, a motion as swift as the darting throat jab, and his heel connected with the hunter's right knee. There was a pop as of a child playing with bubble wrap. The hunter fell with a squeal. He released his grip on the rifle, which Ivan cast away behind him.

The hunter's rifle hit the ground with a clatter a couple feet from Reggie. He looked at the firearm, considering it. In his mind he pictured Ivan moving a little slower. The rifle in the hunter's hands, in this imaginary rewind, pointed at Ivan and firing with a cannon-like roar.

Out of the corner of his eye, he saw Ivan reach into his jacket.

Reggie watched the pistol emerge. The one whose barrel he'd stared down only a few days before. He saw the gun pointed at the hunter.

He thought of Johnny Witte, battered and bloodied by Reggie's own hands in the vacant field. He thought of

Deputy Collins again, dead at the bottom of the cliff. He thought of the men at the camp, dragged off into the night by the thing that may have been a mountain lion.

All that blood. It stained things.

It stained the soul.

'*No!*' he bellowed as Ivan levelled the pistol and sighted down the length of his arm at the man on the ground.

The killer favoured Reggie with the slightest turn of the face, so he looked at him askance. Ivan's face could have been an alabaster bust, a lifeless, inanimate thing, and not the face of a man.

'He's a cop,' the killer said.

'No, I'm not!' said the man on the ground.

'He's part of the search party,' the killer said. 'He's looking for me.'

'No!' said the man. 'No!' as if that single syllable explained everything.

'Don't kill him!' Reggie said to the killer.

'Don't kill me!' the hunter echoed.

Nothing moved but the killer's lips. And even those could have been the merest of trembles from a master ventriloquist. His eyes askance on Reggie; his gun arm ramrod straight pinning the hunter to the ground; the rest of his body statuesque, immobile.

'He's after me,' said the killer. 'There could be others nearby.'

'I'm not a cop!' said the hunter, holding his leg gingerly, whimpering.

'I can see it in his eyes,' said the killer. 'His identification is on him.'

'I have kids!' said the hunter, not refuting the existence of such damning credentials.

Both looked at Reggie now. One wanting to kill; one wanting to live. And they both looked to him, as if he would determine the outcome of things.

Reggie looked about frantically. For what, he didn't know. His mind raced for an answer. Flashes of blood and death flitted through his brain.

'Your belt!' he bellowed, pointing at the killer. He started unbuckling his own as he spoke, pulling it free of the waistband and tossing it towards the killer. 'Tie him up!'

'Yes!' the hunter said, nodding frantically and smiling nervously. 'Tie me up!' he said, and started working at his own belt, unbuckling it and pulling it loose. He proffered the length of leather up like a penitent to his confessor. 'I have kids!' he said again, though the tone of his voice made it clear who his concern was for.

The killer looked at the two belts Reggie and the hunter, maybe a police officer, had tossed at his feet. Then he looked back at Reggie, and finally again at the hunter.

'You try anything,' he said, bending slowly to scoop up the coiled belts, 'and I'll stick this in your mouth,' he said with a waggle of the gun, 'and blow out the back of your head.'

There was a radio static-like squawk and the world froze.

'*Jeff!*' sounded an urgent voice from within the hunter's jacket. '*Was that gunfire? Are you okay? Over.*'

Jeff the hunter, Jeff with kids, Jeff who had said he wasn't a cop and yet had a walkie-talkie in his jacket, looked from Reggie to Ivan, back and forth, his eyes rapid and panicked. Ivan gestured with the pistol, didn't fire, but the motion made Jeff the hunter flinch and wince.

'Answer the man,' the killer said. 'Tell him you're okay. Nothing's wrong. A deer spooked you.'

Jeff the hunter nodded, dug into his jacket with shaky hands, pulled out the walkie-talkie, fumbled it, and the three of them watched it clatter to the ground. After a pause in which he thought it was all over, that he was dead for dropping the radio, that that was the last straw that would set the killer off, Jeff the hunter reached out and picked up the radio again. Holding it in his hand, thumb on the talk button, he looked from Reggie to the killer.

'*Jeff?*' squawked the radio again. '*This is Sheriff Connolly. Are you okay? Do you copy?*'

'Gather yourself,' the killer said. 'Calm yourself. Be convincing.'

The consequences for not gathering himself, calming himself, and being convincing were implicit in the pistol in the killer's hands, and Jeff the hunter nodded. He closed his eyes, took a deep breath, and pressed the talk button on the walkie-talkie.

'Copy Sheriff,' he said. 'I'm fine. A deer startled me. I

killed an innocent pine. I might be looking at a five to nine stretch. Over.'

He did well, Reggie thought. He did great. He sounded calm. With the threat of death over him, he'd gathered himself. The man was good under pressure, which was good for him, or he'd be dead and he wouldn't have to worry about his kids or gathering himself or being calm and convincing ever again.

'Copy Jeff,' said the static squawking voice on the other end. *'Try not to be such a dumbass and go killing anymore trees. If the man's still out here, you probably just alerted him and he's halfway to Cancun by now. Over.'*

'Copy Sheriff,' Jeff the hunter said, who most definitely was a cop, a cop with kids. 'Over.'

The hunter, the cop, held the radio out to the killer, nodding as if for approval. The killer stepped forward and took it, pocketed it. Then he motioned for Jeff the hunter to lie down and turn over, and he went to work with the belts.

***

The killer started with the basics.

'How many others are out there?' he asked.

The hunter who wasn't a hunter, at least not of beasts but of men, lay with his head against a tree stump. His arms and legs were bound in front of him, at the wrists and ankles, and a third belt, his own, attached those vertically. The belts didn't make the tightest of bonds, but they hobbled him well enough that the effort he'd have to make to get free would alert them long before he actually was. And they all three knew what would come then.

'Maybe a dozen,' the hunter said. He answered quickly and eagerly, like a prized student wanting to please a favourite teacher. 'But they're not as organized as they were a few days ago. They figure you've already made it to Mexico, and now they're just going through the motions for the public and the reporters.'

Reggie realized something then, listening to the hunter. It was both a brief and flitting thought, there and gone, and also a clear and distinct realization. He felt this thing without it really being fully formed.

He saw the officer bound by the belts on the forest floor, and he also saw himself pinned on the sidewalk in front of the drugstore by Johnny Witte. What he realized was this: most people, when at a disadvantage, when faced with fear of the unknown, became cowards. They were quick to please and fast to beg.

He hadn't done so when faced with the larger kid and the promise of an ass whooping at the drugstore.

Yet here before him was a grown man, reduced to a trembling, quivering mess.

Did this make him better than the man bound at his feet?

Did this make the hunter smaller than him?

Reggie saw the bound man and imagined himself in

Ivan's shoes, having the power and the will to use that power. He could hit the man. He could kick the man. He could go to work with his knife. And the hunter could beg and plead and cry and none of it would matter, because it would be up to him when things ended, if they ended at all.

All of this came in a quick blur through Reggie's mind, like the flipping of pages in a book. Yet it lingered also, somewhere in the back, in a corner, and its repercussions didn't escape him.

'Where about?' asked the killer, waving his gun like a conductor.

'Most to the north and northwest,' the hunter said with a nod in that general direction. 'Probably a half mile or so away at most.'

'But not organized,' the killer said.

'No,' the hunter who was a cop said. 'No grid pattern search or nothing. We're just striking out, searching semi-randomly, keeping in radio contact. Like I said, most of us thought you'd made it over the border already.'

'So the way south is clear,' the killer said, not a question really, just a statement requiring a prompt response. The hunter nodded. 'And you know what I'd do to you if we go south and there's a posse waiting or a blockade or something?'

This was a question and a statement at the same time, intended for the hunter to imagine the possibilities.

By the widening of his eyes, like an owl's round gaze,

Reggie saw the man knew those possibilities or imagined his own that were just as bad.

'Yes!' he said, nodding fast so that his neck waggled like a turkey waddle.

'I might be gone for awhile,' the killer said. 'I'd have to lay low for a bit. But if we go south and I find the way blocked, if I find out you lied to me, I'd come looking for you.'

The hunter's eyes widened even more, if that were possible. They rolled side to side in a panic. He shook his head frantically, begging for the killer to believe him.

'You'd never know when I'd come back,' the killer said. 'It could be a month, or a year, or ten. But you'd be sitting at home someday watching television, or reading the paper, and you'd hear a noise and look up, and there I'd be. And I'd kill you. I'd kill you slow. And your kids, I'd kill them too, and make you watch it.'

'*No no no no no* …' the hunter said, over and over, shaking his head. '*Please please please* …' he said, back and forth, no no no, please please please, like two alternating bridges of a shitty pop song.

'So I ask again,' the killer said. 'Is the way south clear?'

The hunter didn't answer as quickly this time.

His breathing was shallow and rapid. Sweat stains grew about his underarms.

'Is the way south clear?' the killer repeated.

The hunter gave his head the slightest of shakes. So slight that it could have been merely a tick or twitch. The killer stepped closer, knelt beside the hunter, and pressed the muzzle of the pistol against the trembling man's forehead.

'Is the way south clear?' the killer asked again.

The crying man shook his head.

'*No,*' he croaked. His face was red with his sobs. Snot dribbled out of his nose. His eyes crossed staring at the muzzle between them. He closed his eyes after taking it in.

The killer leaned closer, spoke softer, more intimately, so that he was almost a lover whispering in the crying man's ear.

'Why did you lie to me?' the killer asked.

The man didn't answer. He kept his eyes closed and cried.

'Why did you lie to me?' the killer repeated, leaning oh so close, whispering, almost consoling like one at a friend's deathbed.

'*It's … my job …*' said the hunter, the officer, through his tears, his eyes still shut, shut against the world that no longer made sense.

'What about being a father?' the killer asked. 'Is that not your job also?'

The crying man didn't answer. At least not the killer's question. His lips moved slightly. The words were soft and lost in the air. Reggie knew what the man was doing, and he wondered if anyone was listening.

'You know what I have to do now, don't you?' the killer

said, sounding compassionate, sympathetic. 'You know I have to kill you, don't you?'

The praying man didn't answer. But his murmured words streamed faster, so fast they didn't seem words at all, rather almost a white noise or static from a television or radio.

The killer rose back to full height. Then bent at the waist, pressing the muzzle hard against the bound man's forehead.

Reggie darted forward.

'*Don't!*' he yelled.

He reached for the killer's gun. He didn't even think of the shotgun in his arms. He was met with a backhand, a blow like stone meeting his face, and yet the killer's motion was nonchalant, almost lazy.

Reggie fell hard to the ground. His palms and arms were scraped by the grit of the forest floor. The shotgun jumped out of his grip and landed a few feet away. The clatter of it caught his attention, and then he saw it clearly and he wanted it, but he tasted the blood in his mouth from the backhanded blow, the power of it fresh with the pain along his face, and he couldn't bring himself to move.

The mangy dog, formerly a distance behind them, darted forward. There was a deep growl emanating from it that was unearthly. It sounded not like a canine or any other animal Reggie had ever heard, but something demonic, something from the darkest nightmares.

The dog leapt at the killer.

Without removing the muzzle of the gun from the praying man's head, the killer somehow did a half turn, raised one leg in a flash of movement, and the dog met the sole of his boot. There was a yelp, the mutt fell to the ground, rolled once, and was still.

Reggie staggered to his feet, tottered, almost fell again. He felt stuck in some sort of muck, his movements unbearably slow and difficult. The killer looked at him from across the distance between them.

'I'm sorry, Reggie,' he said. 'But I have to do this.'

Reggie turned and ran.

'Reggie!' he heard behind him, and he hunched his shoulders in expectation of the shot that would kill him, and it came, cracking the day with thunder. Yet he didn't fall, he didn't die, and he knew it wasn't he who was shot but the hunter who wasn't a hunter, the cop with kids, now dead, head shattered and pouring blood and gruel into the forest soil, feeding the roots hidden beneath.

Reggie kept running.

Behind him he heard the footfalls of pursuit.

Chapter Ten

1.

In an earthen den of darkness, curled snug within leaves and dirt, Reggie watched for the killer from a peephole formed of twigs and brush. Beneath a thick copse of trees and a canopy of summer blossomed branches, the space he occupied lay in a preternatural dusk. The daylight struggled to reach him, only breaking through in slim beams of light weaker than that produced by the flashlight tucked away in his pack.

Within such unnatural gloom, every nightmare he'd ever had seemed possible. Every creeping, slithering thing; every malevolent embodied shadow; every sinister sound that had ever populated his night terrors came back at once. And with his father dead and his mother miles away, there was no one to come bursting into his room, gather him in strong arms to a comforting chest, and reassure him that these things were just dreams. Products of an overactive mind. The hulking figure just his dresser. The peering eyes just reflected moonlight. The taunting whisper just the breeze through the parted window. That there was nothing to be afraid of in the dark.

It was just Reggie alone in the woods, and a madman on the hunt.

Trembling, as in a winter chill that wasn't there, he waited.

***

The killer walked past very close, so that Reggie saw his legs and the legs only, rising and falling, like the gargantuan limbs of a giant. The killer passed him a distance, stopped, leaves and twigs crackling under his boot heels, came back and leaned against a nearby boulder. He looked about, his gaze roaming near to where Reggie was, but passing high, moving over him. The killer spoke in a loud voice, so that it would carry to Reggie if he was anywhere nearby, which he was.

'You once asked me,' the killer bellowed, 'if I'd ever regretted killing people. At the time, I told you about the woman and her son. And that was true. I sometimes think maybe I shouldn't have killed them.'

He paused for a moment, looked about himself, scanning the woods.

Reggie felt naked in the bushes, under the leaves. He felt the killer saw with otherworldly eyes, and would soon pinpoint his location.

'That wasn't the end of it, though,' the killer called. 'Soon after them, I stopped taking contracts for a time. I couldn't get the woman's face out of my mind. I kept thinking about her holding her child, cradling him, and asking me to kill her too. To kill her after midnight, so that she could die the same time her son had.'

The killer sighed and leaned back, drawing one leg atop the stone, so that he looked like a man resting on a porch step. He lifted his face to the sky. He spoke that way for a time – leg drawn up, face to the sun – and he seemed merely a man for a moment, and not a killer.

'People contacted me for jobs,' Ivan said, 'and I turned them down. I was the best at what I did, and people were concerned. They asked why I was stopping, and I couldn't explain it to them. I had a hard time understanding it myself. I told them I needed a break. I told them I was worn out. I told them I'd made enough money. I'd worked long and hard, and it was time for me to enjoy what I'd made. I said many things, and they were partly true. Yet it wasn't the complete truth.'

Reggie moved the slightest bit, extending his right leg which had started to cramp. There was the barest rustle of leaves, and to his ears it sounded like an avalanche.

Yards away from him, the killer took no heed.

He stared into the sky, then at the ground, then off to the distance, talking loud like a speaker addressing a convention audience.

'I had a house on the coast, and I stayed there for a

time. I tried many things to keep myself occupied,' Ivan
said. 'The first couple days I threw myself into yard work.
I mowed the lawn and trimmed the hedges and watered
and tilled the garden. For awhile the work made me feel
normal. It made me feel like a regular guy.

'But I went to bed that night,' the killer said, 'and still
I saw her face. And still I saw her holding her dead son.

'So the next day I tried exercising,' Ivan said. 'I dusted
off the equipment in the garage. I pulled the weight bench
and the treadmill and the punching bag away from the
wall and set them up in the centre of the floor. I worked
myself to a sweat. I mean I must have looked like I'd just
come back from a swim, I was sweating so much. And it
felt good. It again made me think I was just a regular Joe.
Maybe I'd just come home from a long day at the office,
the wife was making dinner, and I was working out as I
waited.

'But I went to bed that night,' the killer said, 'and still
I saw her. Holding her dead son. Asking me to kill her
too.'

There was a tickle at his nose, a sneeze threatening, and
Reggie wiggled it, sniffed softly, fighting back the urge. The
sniffing sounded small and barely audible, and loud and
alerting at the same time. Again he watched the killer,
waiting for the man to come dashing his way, to grab him
up and strangle him, or shoot him, but the man remained
where he was, sitting comfortably on the rock.

'Next I tried reading,' Ivan said. 'I used to read a lot

as a kid, and I'd tried to keep up with it as I grew older. I always bought books, I still do, but they just pile up on my shelves. I sat down that day on the front porch, cracked open a novel, started reading it. It was a bestseller by a great writer, but I found myself lost after five pages. I tried moving indoors, settled on the sofa, started reading again. I was lost even quicker. My eyes moved over the words, but they wouldn't come together, they didn't make any sense. I saw them on the page, fitted them to sentences, but their meanings were gone as soon as I read them.

'And I went to bed that evening,' the killer said, 'and again I saw her, and I saw her son.'

Reggie saw a spider in front of him; a big, brown, hairy thing, crawling slowly over a leaf. He could see its eyes, black and glassy. He could hear the weight of it, the legs of the arachnid tapping on the sun-dried leaf. It sounded to him like war drums, announcing his location for the killer.

'The following morning I went for a walk along the beach,' Ivan said. 'On winter mornings sometimes a mist rises from the cooling water. So that it seems all the world to the horizon is lost in some barrier of fog. Like maybe out there things just end, and there's nothing left. I went out walking and it was like I was the last man in all of creation. Then the fog started rolling onto the beach, and over the sand. And when other people started to get up and come out, they just appeared out of the mist like ghosts. I watched the faces of those passing me, they smiled or nodded, and I smiled and nodded back.'

The killer turned the slightest of degrees in Reggie's direction. A compass needle honing in on its bearing. But he still looked over and past Reggie's location.

His right leg cramping, left arm under his chest burning with pins and needles numbness, Reggie fought the urge to shift into a more comfortable position. The greater urge to jump up and run again was harder to push down.

'It was like I was summoning them,' the killer continued. 'They came out of the mist to greet me. They came out of the mist *for* me. Then returned to the fog from which they'd come. As if they weren't even real.

'That night I slept soundly,' the killer said. 'The woman and her son were gone from my dreams.'

The killer pushed off of the boulder and strode directly towards Reggie.

Reggie tried not to move, tried not to breathe, telling himself he was out of sight, he couldn't be seen.

Yet the killer came straight to him, knelt, pushed a hand through the bush, through the leaves, found Reggie, pushed away his struggling limbs, found his collar, and hauled him out. Reggie was dragged out and shoved to the ground.

'Do you know why I didn't dream of her that night, Reggie?' the killer asked, looking down on him.

Reggie looked for a direction to run. He got up and tried to dart away. The killer was there, snatched him by the collar again, threw him down again.

'Do you know why my sleep was peaceful that night?' the killer asked again.

Reggie shook his head frantically. He didn't know, and he didn't want to know. He was starting to cry, was ashamed of the feel of the tears trickling down, and didn't care at the same time. He heard the killer's words from days ago – *They know you're weak* – and he remembered the older kid knocking him down in front of the drugstore. His mom slapping him at the cemetery.

Reggie didn't want to be weak, but he was. So he cried.

'It was because I saw those people coming to me through the fog that morning,' the killer said, 'and I knew they belonged to me. It was like a vision, a revelation. They were all lost in a fog, wandering aimlessly through the wasted years of their lives. I called them forth, whether I realized it or not. Everyone else existed for me to do with as I pleased. And when I killed someone, I wasn't changing the world for the better or the worse. What I did had no impact on things at all. All the world was a fog, a mist in which everyone was lost and to which everyone returned.'

He paused for a moment, as if to let that sink in for Reggie. But something in the killer's eyes told Reggie the man was letting those words sink in and settle in his own mind as well.

'I woke the next day,' the killer said, 'walked along the boardwalk this time, among the stores and restaurants, watched the people pass by, and verified this, so that I

235

would know what I saw the previous day was real. People went to jobs, they went to school, they went shopping, they ate at restaurants, they fished and surfed and walked dogs and roller-skated and bought newspapers and nothing they did meant anything.'

Reggie stayed on the ground. Didn't move.

'Do you know what I'm getting at?' the killer asked, staring down on him.

Reggie shook his head, afraid even of that small motion, lest it be the wrong one and he get a bullet in the head like the hunter who wasn't a hunter, Jeff the officer with kids, whose kids no longer had a father.

'Everyone's just filling time,' the killer said, spreading his arms for emphasis, smiling, as if saying isn't that just strange? Isn't that just *absurd*? 'None of them was doing anything with their lives. And even if they were, what did it matter? Nothing they did impacted anything. Other than a small circle of friends and family, no single life really adds anything to the world, has any impact.'

The killer bent, reached for the ground.

Reggie flinched and cried out, ready to be strangled, shot, beaten, or stabbed.

The killer rose again without having touched Reggie. He held something in his palm; reached for it with his other hand and pinched it between thumb and forefinger. He held it out for Reggie to see.

'Our lives are like this grain of dirt,' the killer said. 'They mean absolutely nothing. They have no purpose whatsoever.' He flicked the kernel of dirt away. 'And they're disposed of just as easily, with no pomp and circumstance. Like so much dust in the wind.'

The killer bent, offered his hand to Reggie.

Reggie didn't want to touch it. But he was also afraid that such an offence would mean the aforementioned strangling, shooting, or stabbing. So he took the man's hand. The killer helped him up gently and brushed the dirt off of Reggie like a doting mother.

'So you see, Reggie,' the killer said, 'what I do is the only meaningful thing there can possibly be. I help cull this meaningless world of the meaningless apes that inhabit it. I will always be here, or someone like me. I'm a force of nature. I *have* to be here.'

Standing now, Reggie saw not for the first time just how large the man was. Two Reggies standing one atop the other, totem pole-like, would have only barely equalled the killer's height. Looking up at him was like pondering the heights of a vast mountain, the peak brushing the heavens. From above, the face of a god looked down on him.

'So when you oppose me,' the killer said, his tone gone from nonchalance to winter cold in a single beat, 'you oppose nature itself.'

The backhand came fast. The knuckles met his cheek like a hammer. Reggie tumbled to the ground again, landing hard on his forearms and elbows, the dirt and grit biting flesh. He lay in the shadow of the god, the killer, his face thrumming with the blow, his very bones aching from it.

'Don't ever oppose me again,' the killer said. He bent, grabbed Reggie by the hair, hauled him up, and flung him to the ground again. 'Don't ever run from me again,' the killer said. He grabbed Reggie by a fistful of shirt, wrenched him to his feet once more, and flung him down again. 'You do what I say, when I say it, do you understand?'

Reggie was crying, and through his tears he was nodding, he was begging, *yes, yes, he'd do what he was told, he understood, he was sorry, he'd do what he was told!*

Now the killer walked over to him, kneeled on the ground, and gathered Reggie to him. Reggie flinched and went stiff. And at the same time he knew that might be the wrong response, and so he went limp in the man's arms. His heart raced and thudded, on the verge of exploding. His mind was wild, his thoughts rampant, the fear like a rushing river, carrying all sense and reason and order away in a wild current.

'I care for you,' the killer said in his dead, emotionless tone. 'I do, Reggie, I do. You helped me, hid me. Even when you knew who I was, what I was. I care for you because of that, even though I know I shouldn't.'

The killer stroked Reggie's hair. Reggie remembered his dad doing that sometimes, and hated the feel of this man doing it. Leaning against the killer, he could smell the sick-sweet odour of the man's wound; the blood and the infection; the rot inside the man. He wanted to push away from him, the killer, away from the poison inside the man, and yet he dared not.

'We have to make it to the border,' the killer said. 'And I can't have you slowing me down. You've got to do what I tell you to, when I tell you to do it.'

The killer cupped Reggie's chin in one hand and turned his head so that Reggie was looking him in the eyes. The thoughts that moved behind those cold, blue baubles were of a nature Reggie couldn't even begin to understand. Why he once thought he had was beyond him. The mind behind those lifeless orbs – so like the glass eyes of a taxidermist's kit – didn't house thoughts like those of regular people.

Whether or not the killer was even human suddenly didn't seem too far-fetched a thought.

'Come to Mexico with me, Reggie,' the killer said. 'I can show you new things. We can start over, as a family.'

Reggie couldn't believe what he was hearing. It was like he was in another world. The rules of reason and order didn't apply here in this other place.

'You have nothing here worth staying for,' the killer said. 'Your father is dead; your mother doesn't love you; you have no friends. Come with me and I'll be your father, your family, and you'll be my son.'

The high sun above seemed to shine its light upon a dark, new world. They rose together to their feet, killer and boy, and started to walk again, south, away from what was and towards what would be. As they strode across the landscape, the killer regaled the boy with the new things of the new world, beyond the border, beyond the horizon, far away and yet frighteningly near.

***

'In Mexico,' the killer said, 'there are stretches of desert so vast that they seem to reach to the end of the earth. And yet it's not lifeless, sterile land. There are towns and hamlets that have tamed the wilderness. I have a small villa, purchased under another name that no one knows about. Everyone is corruptible in Mexico. Everyone has a price. I will see to it that no one bothers us. The Mexican police will never come after us. We will have the privacy and seclusion to live out our lives.'

Reggie both heard these things and did not. He walked in front of the killer obediently yet in a state of protracted numbness, knowing that things no longer made sense and that anything could happen, at anytime.

'I'll teach you the things of the world,' the killer said, 'as your former father failed to do in death. He failed you by dying, but I'll be with you always. We'll go sailing on the Pacific in a boat you'll help me restore. The deep brown of Mexico and the great blue of the Pacific, stretched out before us, and a new life without limitations.'

The woods had changed from the wondrous place Reggie had come to know as a child, camping and hiking with his parents. With them there had been a thrill and mystery when in the yawning breadth and depth of the forest.

Walking trails and climbing hills there had seemed the possibility of coming across ancient ruins or a vast and high castle or a subterranean cavern where great and mighty beasts lived, at any moment. Just through the next copse of trees or just over the next rise, and another world would appear looming before him. The quiet of the woods, the stillness of it, lent an ease to such meanderings, nurturing the mind and the imagination.

But now, being herded forward by this other man, this killer, who'd strangled a man, rolled the body down a cliff, and shot another man, all in a matter of days, the woods around them were completely different. The oaks and pines and firs were heavy and gloomy, sorrowful things, rather than the proud and tall species that they had once been. Their limbs were dragged down by the gravity of the world. Their trunks seemed weathered and aged by aeons of strife. Reggie thought of drunken winos, bent, haggard, bedraggled and lost in the world, stumbling down sidewalks, sunk and collapsed against storefront walls. The shit and vomit of the intoxicated mixing with the greater toxins of the world around them.

'I'll teach you responsibility,' said the killer. 'I'll teach you pride. Though Mexico is an old land its people lack both. They lack the discipline and strength to change their own homeland, so they sneak across borders on their bellies and in the back of trucks, in dirt and filth, to find a new one. That's bad for them, but good for us. In their squalor and malfeasance we'll use them as a contrast against ourselves. You'll learn what is great by observing what is pitiful.'

In the midst of the woods they came upon a low wall, no higher than a foot. Made of a mixture of clay and rocks, the wall formed a rough square about twenty feet wide. The inner space of the clay wall was littered with stone and bone chips that seemed cut and fractured in specific ways, rather than just the happenstance crumbling of weathering and age. With a gentle hand on the shoulder, the killer urged Reggie forward, closer, and upon drawing nearer to the low wall, he saw things on the wall. There were black and red scribblings on the rock and clay, figures really, some vaguely human and others animal. About the wall the trees were thinner and the light of day came down from above, seeming to spotlight the wall and its interior space, like a museum exhibit on display.

The killer moved with a deliberate slowness and caution, as if in the presence of something sacred. He stepped cautiously past Reggie and knelt to put a hand against the clay wall. He lowered his head for a moment, as if in prayer. Then he stood again and addressed Reggie without looking at him.

'You know what this is?' the killer asked, still staring at the wall, and then at the spaces inside and around the wall, as if the clay barrier's aspect carried out in a ripple and washed its perceived power about the immediate area.

Reggie didn't know whether to speak or stay quiet, and

so he kept his mouth shut, deciding that saying nothing was better than saying the wrong thing.

'This was a house,' the killer said, reading Reggie's silence as rapt interest, or not caring. 'Probably from the Yavapai tribe,' he continued. 'These were a people with pride, unlike the people where we're headed. They worked every day simply for the necessities. They lived off roots and seeds and small animals. Like most Native Americans, they knew full well the precarious balance of all life. That to live, one must kill. And to die meant merely to be part of the cycle of it all.'

The killer turned and sat gently on the clay wall. He touched it again with both hands to either side. He patted the wall with his left hand, indicating that Reggie should sit as well; and this time, with a direct prompting, Reggie obeyed without hesitation.

'Like all people,' the killer said, 'Native American tribes had their rituals and religions. But they never had the luxury of relying on their gods for supernatural intervention. They had the very real concern of daily survival. Where would the next meal come from? Would the next birth be healthy so that the tribe could continue? Christians are a lazy bunch, having evolved their religion with modernity, so that prayers and God can be for all things. You want your favourite baseball team to win the World Series? Pray for it. Are you in a hurry and need a parking space? Pray for it.'

The killer looked at Reggie and smiled.

The smile and flash of teeth looked hungry to Reggie. Like they meant to tear and rend flesh – like they *wanted* to tear and rend flesh – rather than expressing a moment of contentment.

'This is a great place,' the killer said, his voice low and awed, like an archaeologist having come upon a great and ancient find, which, Reggie realized, wasn't far off the mark. 'This,' he continued, with his arms held wide to indicate the low wall and everything it represented, 'is what existence is all about. The struggle, the unknown, the unpredictable voracity of life. We fight to stay alive, and yet the one sure thing is that we'll all die.'

Reggie didn't want to, but he thought of his dad dead in the parking lot of the church, and the change scattered about him. He thought of his dad dead in the coffin, in a fine suit, and the fine cushions of the casket. And he thought of his dad dead in the ground, by now putrefying and decomposing, the very matter of him breaking down and falling apart.

They sat there for a time on the ancient wall, killer looking up into the bright sky, boy looking down onto the dark soil. Then the killer moaned, a long, protracted sound Reggie hadn't heard from him before. It was a sound of immense pain and suffering, and Reggie, coming out of his own considerations, looked up at the man beside him.

The killer was pale, startlingly so, and he was trembling. Much as Reggie had trembled in his earthen hidey-hole not so long ago. Now rather than patting or caressing the old wall, the big man's hands were clutching it for support, in desperation, or both. He was leaning forward, like a drunk ready to vomit.

Then he fell, spilling to the ground.

Curled there, trembling, moaning, he didn't get back up.

Reggie leapt off the wall, gave the killer one last look, then turned and ran.

2.

He ran maybe a hundred yards before he stopped and turned back. He was thinking of lying with Ivan in the tree house, looking up into the stars. He thought of pounding the bigger kid to a pulp in the vacant field, and whose words it was that had fuelled him. He thought of the deputy pushing his way into the house when Reggie's mom was gone, throwing him to the ground, and who'd been there to save him by choking the life out of another.

There seemed a greater weight upon Reggie's back than merely the pack slung over his shoulders. His father would have called it responsibility. It was a burden, his father would say. That was how good people knew good decisions from bad ones. The weight of responsibility served as a compass or a beacon, letting you know when an important decision was coming, and how to find your way when it did. It was an ever-present thing, this weight, going away or at least subsiding only when you made the right choice.

Guilt and shame hounded you if you made the wrong choice, stealing rest and peace of mind.

Guilt and shame were with him those first hundred yards he ran.

When Reggie stopped, they subsided a bit.

Then he turned, headed back, and with each stride the shame retreated further, until he was standing over Ivan, the man still curled on the ground, eyes clenched shut in pain, shivering, frail, and barely conscious.

The killer's eyes fluttered; saw Reggie through a hardly perceptible squint.

Reggie knelt so they were closer to each other.

'I'll help you to Mexico,' he said. 'But I won't go with you.'

The only response was a wordless groan. The pain in that syllable-less grunt was so immense that Reggie could almost feel it himself. The man's agony made his skin crawl. No one should suffer like that. But he couldn't let sympathy control the situation. He couldn't let his compassion make him weak.

'Say you understand that,' he said to the killer. 'Tell me you agree to that.'

Arms clutching his middle, Ivan unwrapped one like a tentacle unfurling, and reached out towards Reggie. His fingers clutched claw-like at the dirt. Through his squinting eyes, tears gleamed like jewels.

'Say "OK",' Reggie said. 'I take you to Mexico, and no farther.'

Are You Afraid of the Dark?

The word was a croak, a moan, something hoarse and ugly like a word spoken from a severe asthmatic or centennial smoker's blackened throat. But Reggie heard it, and it was enough.

'*OK*,' the killer whispered.

Reggie leaned forward and fished through Ivan's jacket until he found the antibiotics he'd filched from his mom's medicine cabinet a couple days ago. He sat, slung his backpack off, unzipped it, and pulled out a bottle of water. Reading the instructions on the medicine bottle, he shook out a couple pills into his palm, handed them and the water over to Ivan. Watching the shaking, pale man swallow the tablets, coughing, nearly choking before getting them down, Reggie felt the last tendrils of that weight called responsibility fall away from him.

Feverish, trembling, making noises and sounds, some of them sensible, some of them not, the killer rolled this way and that, crying out, falling silent, until Reggie put an arm around him. Holding the man close, smelling his fever, smelling his sickness, Reggie wondered who'd been there for his dad in his final moments, bleeding out in a dark, empty expanse of asphalt.

Chapter Eleven

1.

It started with a whisper.

'*I killed her,*' the fever-stricken killer muttered.

And unable to ignore it, knowing by now that he should – that he wouldn't want to know more, he shouldn't want to know more – Reggie nonetheless prodded the killer to continue. The man was still on the forest floor, his head leaning against Reggie's leg so that Reggie had a strange parental feeling, like a father looking over his son. The change of things, the swapping of roles, disturbed him. It made him feel that he was responsible for the killer, and that was an obligation he didn't want. Reggie had a hand on the man's shoulder, felt the tremors, not as great and frightening as before, but still persistent, passing from the sick man into him.

'*Who?*' he whispered back, for some reason matching the man's tone and timbre. As if that would reinforce the communication, like soldiers across a battlefield finding the same radio frequency for strategic purposes. '*Who did you kill?*'

'It was a ... test,' Ivan said, finding a little more strength in his voice. 'I had to.'

'Who?' Reggie pressed.

'He said ... to fully embrace my new life ... I had to break all ties ... to my old one,' the killer said, this relatively long sentence reducing him to a violent fit of coughing. He tried tilting the water bottle to his lips, took a sip, choked on that, and coughed awhile longer.

It was awhile before they spoke again. From the more even rhythm of his breathing, Reggie thought Ivan fell asleep for a time. It couldn't have been a very peaceful rest, though. The man's arms and legs twitched like a dog's in some frightful running dream.

Chasing or being chased? Reggie wondered.

When next he woke, Ivan seemed slightly more lucid, though his skin was still clammy with sweat, and the occasional tremor passed through him like a wave. He looked up and backward, momentarily panicked, saw Reggie there and calmed a bit. With one hand he squeezed Reggie's booted foot, a strangely warm and grateful gesture.

'Who'd you kill?' Reggie asked after a moment.

At first he didn't answer, and Reggie didn't think he would at all. The fever at its peak had brought forth memories that the killer would have otherwise left buried. Now, though still hazy through the waves of the fever, it was a diminishing tide, rolling back, and though his body was still tormented, his mind was more fully his own. What came out of his mouth was solely up to him. And if there was something he didn't want to talk about, didn't want Reggie to know, he would keep it that way.

'You said it was a test,' Reggie said.

The killer rolled away from him, breaking that strangely familiar contact of his head with Reggie's leg. Contact lost, Reggie thought the subject of the killer's delirium-induced memories would be also. But, facing away from him, looking off somewhere into the woods, the killer started to speak again.

'It was a test,' he said. 'The old man said it was the last test, and then I'd be ready.'

'The old man from the limo?' Reggie asked. 'The one who found you on the streets?'

Reggie watched the back of Ivan's head as he nodded.

'Yes,' the killer said. 'Him.'

Reggie glanced in the direction Ivan was gazing. He wondered what the man was seeing. All he saw were trees. Ivan was seeing something else. Reggie thought he was probably lucky he couldn't see what the killer saw. It was better that way. It was safer. And, yet, even if he couldn't see it, he had to know.

Reggie took a deep breath before asking the next question.

'Who was she?' he asked. 'Who was your final test?'

'My sister,' Ivan said, quickly, his tone flat, as if

committed now to this course he could say what needed
to be said without reservation. Like it was nothing more
than an item on a grocery list checked off. 'I had to kill
my sister.'

'I thought she died of pneumonia,' Reggie said. 'She got
out of the home she was staying in. It was snowing, and
no one found her for hours.'

'That was the official story,' the killer said. 'That's what
was put in the records.'

'But that's not what happened,' Reggie said.

'No,' the killer said.

Reggie felt again what he'd felt before, now stronger than
ever. He felt as if he was in the presence of some vast evil.
There was a taint and filth in the immediate vicinity. It
was as if a sewer pipe had erupted underground and the
filth had percolated up to the surface.

But it was more than that. It wasn't just a physical sensation of the unclean, that skin-crawling, nausea-inducing
threshold of contamination and impurity. This was a sense
of deep-rooted pollution that signified the world around
you just wasn't right, and was unsuitable for habitation.
Like the nuclear meltdown at Chernobyl, the poison seeped
into everything.

And the centre of it all was Ivan.

'He told me that I could never truly begin my new life,'
the killer said, 'without ending my old one. I asked him,
wasn't that what I was doing? I was leaving the old things
behind, going where he led. He said that wasn't enough.

It wasn't enough that I just leave the old things. I had to end them. I had to erase them.'

Reggie wanted to let this revelation sink in. He needed a moment to let it settle in his mind. Killing strangers you were paid to kill was one thing, especially if they were criminals themselves. No great loss there. Even killing one's own father, if that man was a child-molesting son of a bitch, wasn't so difficult to accept either. Now, though, the killer was saying he'd killed a child, and not any old random kid, but his handicapped little sister.

'*I* had to do it,' the killer continued, denying Reggie the time to let it all sink or settle in, instead jamming it all in roughly. '*I* had to kill her.'

He turned and met Reggie's eyes then, and the expression on his face seemed to say *If I had to do that, then you have to listen*. Reggie thought this was indeed true, but not because the killer said so. Someone other than the monster before him had to bear witness to the dead girl's passing, even if it was a testimony decades overdue.

'He offered to have someone drive me to the group home. I said no. I walked across town alone. It was cold, and it was dark, and in the cold and the dark I thought about what I was going to do. I never thought about not doing it. I just thought about the logistics of it. How would I get in and out? How would I kill her? Would I dispose of the body or leave it to be found?

'The group home was a two-storey structure,' Ivan said. 'It rose out of the white wall of the snowstorm like a

253

fortress. My sister's room was on the first floor. I found the window to her room and stared in at her for a time. Watching her I couldn't drudge up the affection I'd had for her in the past. I couldn't remember what it had been like to love her as a brother.

'I watched her watching a wall. Then she shuffled across the room and stared into a corner. Then she sat in her bed and stared at the sheets. I knew then what I was doing was okay. Watching her watching nothing, I was at peace with what I had to do.'

Likewise, in that moment Reggie was at peace with his budding hatred for the killer. As certain as the killer said he was of the acceptability of his looming fratricide, Reggie was equally certain there was nothing good about the man. In his own grief, Reggie had been very confused to ever think otherwise.

He wanted nothing further to do with Ivan, and yet there was this sick compulsion to hear more, to see things through. It was almost as if their relationship had gained its own momentum. Though he was disgusted by the things the killer said and did, there was a gravity or magnetism that kept pulling him back.

Reggie said nothing and continued to listen.

'I tapped on the window and she turned to look at me,' the killer said. 'At first there was this stupid look on her face. She didn't register anything. She wasn't thinking of anything. She was just responding to a stimulus, like an animal. Impulses were firing in her brain, but they were just biochemical reactions, not actual thoughts. Looking at her made me sick.'

'After a time,' the killer continued, trembling occasionally with the fever, 'me staring in at her, she looking out at me, she came to the window. I motioned her to open it, and again it took her a moment to process and understand this request. She fumbled with the window latch like she was trying to work some advanced NASA computer. Finally, she got it open, and, finally, she recognized me.

'"*Petra*," I whispered. "*Come outside. Let's play!*" the killer said, his voice dropping and becoming sly and suggestive, as it must have been that night. 'We used to play together as children, those days when our father wasn't around to stop us. When he was home, we couldn't do anything. The slightest thing could set him off. So we sat like little statues or hid in our rooms.

'But when he was gone, at work or at a bar,' the killer said, 'we'd play. There were many games that didn't require toys, of which we had none. We played hide-and-seek, tag, follow the leader. These were the only times I saw any hint of normal emotion on my sister's face.

'Standing at the window of her room in the hospital, asking her to come out and play, did the trick. She smiled a drooling, crooked smile, said "*Brother! Brother!*" and climbed out the window in her nightgown. Seeing her bare feet and legs in the snow momentarily made me feel like her brother again. But I squashed that emotion down, told myself I didn't care, and then I didn't. Neither did she apparently, and I was going to kill her anyways, so what the hell did it matter?

'"*Petra*," I whispered to her, hunching against the biting wind. "*Let's play tag!*" I said. Her level of joy was foolish and inappropriate for such a setting. She laughed and nodded and giggled and pulled on the sleeve of my jacket. "*I'm it!*" I said. "*Run and hide!*" I said, pointing off into the storm. Obediently, she turned and ran, kicking up plumes of snow behind her. Walking at a leisurely pace, I followed.'

Reggie found himself doing something strange. He found himself praying for a dead girl. Knowing she was dead, it wasn't a prayer for her safety. It was more of an apology that her brother had been such a person, that the world had been such a place which saw her die in such a horrible, undignified way.

I'm sorry, he whispered in his mind. *I'm sorry*, he said, sending the words out into the world, the universe, hoping they drifted to a place where dead little girls rested in peace after such a stretch in this forsaken land.

'I followed her through the snow and wind,' the killer said, his voice the calculated boredom of a telemarketer. 'Her idiot laughter trailed her, drifting back to me. She tripped at times, stumbled, and once she ran headlong into low-hanging branches. But each time she got up, looked back at me, saw me following and, giggling, she faced forward again and kept running.

'After a time I started to gain on her,' the killer said.

'Her running, or trying to, and I walking, the distance between us steadily shrank. I soon saw why. She paused to touch her legs. Even through the storm, even across the distance between us, I could see how deathly white her legs were. They were white and blue, and her breath came out in great plumes of mist. She stumbled again and slid into a seated position against a pine. She looked up at me as I approached. Snot and drool were frozen around her mouth. "I'm cold, brother," she said, still smiling, still looking like she wanted to laugh, like she wanted to play.'

Reggie knew what was coming, or something close to it, and closed his eyes against the words. Crawling, sliding, seeking, they slipped beneath his eyelids like invisible slugs, however, latched onto his mind with their slime-slick bodies, and showed him the images he'd tried to block out.

'"I know," I said to her,' the killer continued. '"But that doesn't matter anymore." I knelt beside her, reached out, covered her mouth with one hand, clasped her nostrils with the other. I felt the frozen drool and snot beneath my fingers. Disgusted, I squeezed tighter.'

His eyes closed, Reggie tried to imagine himself else-where. But the killer's words drilled through the mental constructs Reggie conjured up, shattered them, and left only the sad world they were in.

'She didn't struggle much. She reached up and grasped my wrists, then let go and patted my arms, as if saying

257

"Okay, that's enough" but it wasn't enough, and I kept squeezing. Then she began to kick and flail. She didn't strike out at me, though. She just kicked and swung her arms in the air, like a person treading water. That continued for a few moments until her arms fell, her legs settled, and then she lost control of her bladder and pissed in the snow.

'And then she was dead.'

2.

After his confessional – if confession was what it was; it had sounded more a disinterested recitation – the killer fell again into a troubled sleep. He bucked and thrashed along with his feverish trembles, but he slept.

That was when the dog appeared.

Reggie had been thinking about the mutt in the back of his mind since it had taken the hard kick trying to protect him. He had wondered if she was even still alive, if maybe the kick had shattered ribs, and one of the splinters pierced a lung or something.

But here she was, stepping slowly and softly out of the bushes encircling the clearing around the old Indian wall. She stopped and sat and considered Reggie from the space between them. The dog eyed the killer, ears pricked up and back, hearing his fever sounds and not liking what she heard.

Reggie wanted to call to her, wanted the mutt to come nearer so that he could inspect her, make sure she was okay. But he likewise didn't want her near the killer, and so just returned her gaze from across the clearing.

Considering her, he tried to place her breed, saw some black Labrador and maybe some pit bull in there, a greater part of mangy beast, so that he really couldn't confidently settle on anything. She was in every sense of the word a mutt, and yet he didn't think he'd ever seen a more beautiful dog in his life.

And, in a moment free of the confusion he'd felt so often in the past months, Reggie knew why he felt this way about the dog.

This stray had tried to protect him.

His father had died on him, and would never be protecting him from anything ever again. His mother, lost in her own pain, couldn't see how to continue their family without her husband. She wouldn't be protecting him anytime soon either. Ivan, the hit man, pretended to be many things and was altogether nothing. Merely a shade of a man trying to play the part.

Yet this dog hadn't needed to consider things, hadn't needed to weigh pros and cons, hadn't tried to be one thing when she was something else completely. This dog had seen him in trouble, and had acted. Drawing upon her simple nature, whether it was instincts or something learned, this dog had accomplished what everyone else in Reggie's life had failed to.

She'd cared.

Without reservation, lacking any ulterior motives, absent

any hidden agenda, this ugly dog in front of him had cared. And he would never forget that. It was etched now, indelibly, inside him.

Reggie raised one hand and waved at the dog. She cocked her head, and her muzzle split in a wide doggie grin.

The killer, muttering, stirred in his fitful sleep, coming awake.

The dog stood silently, turned, and retreated stealthily into the woods.

Reggie stared at the place where she'd been, already missing her.

3.

The killer's fever broke an hour later, and though he still shook and trembled, and getting to his feet was a task of monumental proportions – during which he buckled, vomited, fell to his knees, and had to shakily begin again – stand he did, and together he and Reggie once more started south.

They walked for a time in silence before coming to a river. It was wide and deep and the gurgle-rush of its clear waters was a chime-like music. The killer stopped before the river, glanced either way along the course of the flow. Standing on the bank, leaning forward a bit, clutching his middle, the man swayed, looking like he might fall forward at any moment to be carried away in the rush of the water.

Reggie thought about pushing him.

In his mind he saw the man washed away downstream, waving frantically for help, coughing out the water that surged over him.

But he didn't push the man.

The killer turned unsteadily around to face him. The water rushed whitely behind him. It seemed a wall of sorts, or a barrier, separating them from something else.

'Across the river,' the killer said. 'A little more than a mile away is the border checkpoint. Just through there,' he gestured with a wave behind him at the woods continuing on the other side of the river, 'the woods end and the desert starts again. The highway is over there. That's where the police blockade will be. They'll be watching the highway, so we'll have to go around through the desert.'

Reggie nodded and gestured at the river.

'Let's go,' he said.

The killer nodded but didn't move.

'There's a whole other world in Mexico,' he said, looking at Reggie with what he would have said was longing in any other face. In this one, though, Reggie knew it wasn't. It was a deception. It was a mock-up of human emotion. This was a monster playing at being human; nothing more, nothing less. 'It will be strange and frightening at first,' the killer said. 'But you'll learn the language. You'll make friends. In Mexico the past and the present meet in a wondrous fashion. There's pride in the past and a certainty of a better tomorrow. Deserts stretch out bone-white and woods more green and vital than this one explode across the land.'

Ignoring him, Reggie walked towards the river.

'There's nothing here for you,' the killer said. 'The world moves past you like you're nothing. In Mexico, with my resources, you could be anything you want. You could have anything you want. The world would be yours.'

Reggie moved past him towards the water, that crystal barrier.

A strong hand on his shoulder stopped him.

He turned to look up at the large man before him. Not for the first time, Reggie noticed the lines of Ivan's face. Where he'd previously seen the hard face of a ruthless killer, he now also saw the creased and leathered contours of a weathered, old man.

'Why won't you come with me?' the killer said.

'I thought you knew things that I didn't know,' Reggie said. He hadn't known what he was going to say until he said it. The words just came out. This had happened many times in the past few days with this man. Where previously this freewheeling talk had been liberating – like friends sharing secrets, unburdened by authority such as parents or teachers – now his uncensored words came from another source. In another place and time, Reggie might have called it strength. Right then, next to the killer, before the white river, it just felt necessary. 'I thought you were strong and could show me things I needed to know.'

The killer smiled and nodded, as if affirming this.

'But when you were lying on the ground,' Reggie said, 'your head in my lap, cold and shivering, I knew you were as weak as anyone else.'

The hand on his shoulder tightened. Birds of prey grasped their quarry in such a manner before carrying them off to their dens to feed.

'There's nothing you can show me,' Reggie said, ignoring the tightening fingers, or pretending to. 'There's nothing I need from you.'

The hand on his shoulder balled into a fist, gripping his shirt.

'I could force you,' the killer said. 'I could make you go with me.'

The water whispered its tinkling song behind them. The hum of it, the white-noise rush of it, the friction of it against the banks containing it and the stones lining its bottom, was indeed a barrier: a wall dividing *here* from *there*. This static-like rush brought clarity, however, unlike the interference from a poorly tuned radio or television.

Reggie stared up at the man. He didn't break eye contact. He looked deep into that face; the ancient contours, the lines like a map. The eyes were vast and deep and shallow at the same time. He tried to decipher the thoughts behind them, and was met with an alien force. Something that couldn't be understood. It had been a mistake on Reggie's part to ever think he could.

Something of Reggie's thoughts must have been apparent

on his face. The killer first relaxed his grip, and then the hand released him.

Making a short sniffing-snorting sound of disgust, Ivan moved past him into the waters. It took him in, the river, cutting his bottom half from his upper so that he seemed again like a figure dimensionally torn, as he had on the sled under the oak's shadow so many days ago. Something of this world and yet of another, caught between realities. Reggie followed him; the cool water seeping through his jeans, caressing his legs, welcoming him in its embrace.

They crossed the barrier and the current pulled at them, threatening gently to yank them downstream into its flow, but they crossed, and rose out of its baptism on the other side.

***

The killer walked ahead of him, stomping a path through the woods.

'My dad died trying to help another human being,' Reggie said, the killer moving at a steady pace ahead, not giving any indication that he was listening. That was okay. Reggie knew he was, and so he kept talking. 'I was angry for a long time. I thought, how stupid could he be? Going out at night by himself to check on the church. And when he discovered who it was breaking in, he probably tried to console the guy. He probably tried to talk him out of it. He may have even prayed for the man.

'And then he was shot, and my mom and I were left alone.'

The killer slapped low-hanging branches out of his way angrily, like they were there just to annoy him. He moved faster than Reggie would have thought possible in his condition, almost as if he were trying to get away from something.

Reggie trudged after the killer, pausing only briefly to take a swig of water from the bottle in his hand. He eyed the woods about them and the sky above, and was startled to see the brightness of the day and of the things about him.

'I hid my Bible for a time after my dad died,' Reggie said. 'I couldn't stand to look at it. My dad was always carrying his around the house; and in public, when we were out and about in town, he had a little pocket Bible stuffed in his jacket or jeans pocket. People around town knew him, and often told him their problems, and it wasn't unusual for him to stop in the middle of the grocery store, or the mall, or at the gas station, and say a prayer right then and there for someone.'

Some woodland thing – flora or fauna, Reggie didn't know – had the tenacity to get in the killer's way, and he muttered a '*Fuck*' as he manoeuvred past it. Feeling more and more as if he were on a leisurely stroll, Reggie continued to speak as he followed.

'I would cram the Bible under the bed,' Reggie said, 'or far back in a desk drawer. Or I'd bury it in a box on the top shelf of my closet. But wherever I put it, it never seemed to be dark or deep enough and I always knew it was there. So then I'd take it out, throw it on my bed, and yell at it. I'd call it names, horrible names, and I wasn't talking to the book, but to God, and not really God, but through Him to my dad.'

Reggie smiled the embarrassed yet amused smile of someone remembering some small foolishness. Like the day they'd tripped in public, or been caught by a passing motorist picking their nose in slow traffic. Those little awkward things that reminded us we were human.

'I thought he was weak,' Reggie said, 'for caring for others. I thought he was a failure, for dying on his family. I called him a bastard, a son of a bitch, a fucker, for leaving us. All because a phone call one night got him up to go check on the church alarm. Because he found the man breaking in and confronted him, and probably tried to help him.

'Caring for people was stupid, I told myself,' Reggie said. 'Giving a shit in a world full of shitheads was a waste of time. Worse than that, it wasn't just a waste of time. You set yourself up for major hurt. As my dad learned, and as my mom and I learned after him.'

'You were right,' the killer grunted ahead of him, his words only just audible. It was like someone heckling in a crowd – they wanted to be heard, but didn't want to be singled out at the same time. An act of cowardice masquerading as brazenness.

266

'No,' Reggie said, 'I was wrong.'

Reggie took a breath before continuing. He was on to something, and he was excited by the building revelation. He felt a lightness inside him. A tingling through his body.

'By putting others before himself,' Reggie said, 'my father showed himself to be better than this world.'

'He was a fool and an idiot,' said the killer, heckling again from the safety of the distance between them. 'He sold lies and lived a lie.'

'No,' Reggie said, stepping sprightly over a fallen trunk. 'Liars don't die for their lies. He believed in something for a reason.'

The killer said nothing after that, and so Reggie paused for a time also. They strode through the woods like migrants through a new land, destination somewhere ahead. The killer moved decidedly and aggressively still, his footfalls loud and angry. Reggie walked casually, the birdsongs and the wind and the crunching of leaves beneath him settling him, providing a rhythm for his thoughts. When he spoke again, he could see the tightening and hunching of the killer's shoulders, like the flinching of one hearing fingernails dragging across a blackboard.

'My mom doesn't hate me,' Reggie said, the spoken words giving the truth of the statement, so that he weighed them, considered them, and knew them to be right. 'She was lost, just like me. It was her and my dad long before I came around. It was the two of them versus the world. When he died, she didn't know what to do. She broke, and didn't know how to put the pieces back together.'

'She hates you,' said the killer. 'She sees you and knows she'll never see her husband again, and knows she got the raw end of the deal.'

'No,' Reggie said, smiling. 'When you have a family, people you care about, whose lives you share and who share yours in return, you know about death as an idea. But you never really feel in your heart that it'll come your way.'

There were stones and boulders in their path, and they scaled them. The killer climbed down the other side, but Reggie paused for a moment at the top. He closed his eyes, breathed deep the clean air, and hopped down.

'When my dad died,' Reggie said, 'death became a reality for my mom. For both of us, but she was the only adult left, I was just a kid, and so the responsibility of what came next belonged to her. And it scared her, having to figure it out for both of us without him. There's no way to plan for something like that. There's no way to deal with it until it's right there in front of you. She's doing the best she can.'

'She hates you,' the killer said. 'She despises you.'

But his words were weak, the lies obvious. He had no power anymore, and Reggie felt sorry for the man. He was just like the rest of the world. He held no sway over the fundamentals of life, was lost in that realization, and tried

Are You Afraid of the Dark?

to squash it with pain and anger sterilized into a mock coldness, a false pretence of detachment.

And all the while the killer was drifting down the same wild river that everyone was caught in. Cascading down the currents and twists and bends, carried to an unknown destination called life, and death, and all the things in between.

***

From the treeline they could see the highway to the east and the border checkpoint. There were several police cruisers parked alongside the road, along with the border patrol vehicles. The border fence stretched out of sight to either direction like a great metal serpent and shone brightly under the sun. About a half mile away, the gathered authorities were still too close for Ivan's comfort.

'We'll move further west,' he said, falling back into the woods and starting to move that way. 'If they see us, they'll move fast. I'll need a head start to make it to the fence.'

Reggie thought about running across the desert expanse to the police right then and there. Then he thought about the killer's gun, pointed at him only days ago when he'd come upon the man in the woods. He thought of getting a bullet in the back, falling, dying in the dirt.

Finding he wasn't ready to die, Reggie once more followed the killer.

He also thought about how the killer expected to get

269

through the police and border patrol if they saw him as he made for the fence. Reggie didn't have to ask. He'd seen the man's manner of solving things these past few days. The deputy at the house; the officer in the woods; everything Reggie needed to know was right there in the man's title: killer.

He'd do whatever was necessary to make it to the border, past the fence, and into Mexico. And Reggie was powerless to do anything but stand by and watch it all happen.

'We'll wait until nightfall,' said the killer, after they'd gone a ways. He spoke over his shoulder without looking back at Reggie, almost as if he weren't speaking to Reggie at all, but just to himself. Reggie didn't think they were friends anymore, and he wondered why the killer still kept him around. 'The patrols move around more at night, because that's when most of the immigrants try to make their moves. They won't be concentrated in one area, like they were at the highway.'

After they'd walked for twenty minutes or so away from the highway and the border checkpoint, the killer stopped to lean against a tree, and then settled on a stone. He put his elbows on his legs and his head in his hands. He breathed unevenly and trembled some. Reggie took a seat on a fallen limb nearby, and watched.

He saw the spreading red-yellowish stain on the killer's shirt, but said nothing.

The killer saw it too, fingered the area, pulled up the T-shirt and pried away the bandage to take a look.

Reggie grimaced, wanted to look away, but didn't.

This was infection he was seeing, he had no doubt about it. He'd seen it in movies; read about it in books. The smell wafted to him immediately. The sight was terrible.

The wound was red and inflamed. Tendrils of red spread from the centre like spokes from a wheel. Bile-like pus oozed from the bullet hole like magma from a slow stirring volcano. When the man breathed, the whole thing moved up and down and seemed to wink, again reminding Reggie of some monstrous eye.

'We tried,' the killer said with a wicked smile. 'But I'll need a doctor to fix this.' He lowered his T-shirt like a veil over a secret altar, and then slid off the boulder to the ground, so that he was leaning his back against it, his legs out before him. 'I'll make it through the night.'

He took out the medicine bottle, motioned for Reggie's water bottle. Reggie handed it over, then stepped back again. The killer swallowed a few tablets with an agonized expression, then tilted his head back and closed his eyes.

'I can trust you for this last short while?' he asked.

Reggie looked at his watch, saw it was early afternoon. Thought about spending a few more hours in the presence of this man. He could still see the wound clearly, though it was now covered. The red, raw eye winking at him; the terrible eye that saw all things; the scarlet eye that was more a part of this man than any other feature. Such a thing would see to the heart of him; would know what Reggie would do before he did it.

271

He couldn't keep secrets from such a thing.

He nodded.

'Yes,' he muttered. 'You can trust me.'

Nodding, the killer closed his eyes and slept.

And the boy tried to shield his mind from the piercing terrible eye.

4.

Despite his better judgement, Reggie slept too.

He dreamt of a vast wasteland, a grey and white expanse more barren and forsaken than any desert. No plants grew; no cacti, no shrubs, not the slightest struggling weed. The ground was cracked and marred like a dry lunar landscape. There were craters and valleys like cannon had struck and dimpled the earth. The sky was equally grey and sterile, as if aeons of industrial factory pollutants had settled into place, becoming the new atmosphere. There was a soft wind like dragon's breath; hot and arid.

Far ahead of him there was a figure in the distance, standing on the bleak landscape, looking back at him. They watched each other across the wretched land, across the craters and cracked ground, neither moving. They were like gunfighters staring each other down across the longest stretch of dirt road in a town that didn't exist.

The sun rose over the horizon, but it wasn't the sun. It was a great blood-red eye, and it oozed and bled into the sky. It watched him and the other in the distance across from him. It watched all things; saw all things. When it winked it pulled the sky taut and sent ripples through it like a fabric.

He ran across the barren land, frantically looking for a place to hide. Any crevice, any hole, would do. Anything to be away from that bleeding eye.

But there was nowhere to go. Everything lay bare beneath the great bloody orb.

Then the dark figure in the distance held its arms out, beckoning him. With nowhere else to go, and the bloody sky-eye watching him, Reggie ran towards the figure.

It knelt in anticipation of his arrival. At first Reggie thought it was his dad, and ran faster, pumping his legs harder. Until, the space between them dwindling, he saw it wasn't his father.

It was the killer, and in one hand was the knife, and in the other the garrotte wire.

He tried to skid to a halt, but the land like a conveyor belt moved beneath him and propelled him forward. And as the killer wrapped Reggie in his arms, the knife came down, and the wire twined around his throat, cinching tight.

He bolted awake to falling darkness.

Through the treeline he could see the edge of the western sky. The sun receding and the last redness of its passing staining the horizon. Reggie lifted his arm and looked at his watch. It was after seven in the evening. He'd been asleep for over five hours.

His body was achy and sore from the hard, unforgiving forest floor, and he stood with groans and joint creaks. He looked about him, saw the killer huddled nearby, sleeping or feigning it.

The man, lying still in the draping dark of evening, could have been dead, and Reggie, considering the fading details of his nightmare, wondered how long before that was actually so and if the dying man would decide to take Reggie along with him.

Chapter Twelve

1.

When the killer awoke, he had Reggie hand him a flashlight from the backpack. He turned it on, pointed the beam at the ground, and set it down between them so they could see each other without the light casting along the trees, potentially alerting the police or border patrol. The outer reach of the light found the killer's face, casting it a shade of red and partially in shadow, so that he looked like the host of a horror anthology show or creature feature. When Ivan spoke it was in muttered tones, though they were far enough away from the border patrols not to be heard even if he spoke loudly.

'*When I cross the border,*' the killer said, '*and leave you behind, your life will go back to the way it was. You'll wake one day and wish you'd come with me.*'

'*Maybe,*' Reggie said, matching the killer's whisper. '*But I don't think so.*'

'*And if you're wrong?*' the killer said. '*When you're back in school and bigger kids smack you around? When your mother feels her hatred for you rising and smacks you around? When, in the coming years, she dies on you, leaving you just as your father did? When you're twenty, and then thirty, and one day you're sixty, and you feel death coming for you? What then? What will you say of your life?*'

'*I don't know,*' Reggie said. '*But I'll find out when I get there.*'

Thinking of his mom, Reggie thought of a question, surprised he hadn't asked it before then. Suddenly, it seemed very necessary that he know the answer to it.

'What about your mom?' Reggie said, speaking in a normal tone now, the question seemingly so important that it not be misunderstood in soft spoken whispers. 'You've never mentioned her. What was she like?'

Ivan answered immediately. Reggie was surprised, thinking after asking the question that perhaps – now that they approached the end of their time together – the killer was done entertaining his questions. Or maybe Reggie had hit on a sore spot, and the man would edit his answers. But the directness of his reply spoke of its truth.

'She died when I was young,' Ivan said. 'Petra was only a baby. She was in an accident driving to the market. I remember my father yelling about the wrecked car. He never cried over his wife being dead. But the wrecked car drove him into a borderline rage.'

'Did you love her?' Reggie asked.

'I remember my mother loved to cook,' Ivan said, not directly answering the question. 'We never had much money. My father worked in a factory. My mother was a teacher's assistant and tutor. Neither of them worked full time. Not because they didn't want to, but because no one was hiring. No benefits. Shitty wages. My mom had to shop at a cheap dollar store, and yet somehow she made each meal a special occasion. I remember coming home after school, smelling her stews, her bread, and thinking I'd walked into some gourmet restaurant.'

Reggie tried to envision this man, this killer of others for money, as a child, a boy about his age, and couldn't. It seemed a bad fairytale, that such a man had ever been anything than what he was: a killer. And yet he knew it to be true, and it troubled him.

'When she died,' Ivan continued, 'and my father had stopped yelling about the wrecked car and how he'd get back and forth to work, he turned to me and yelled at me that my stupid bitch of a mother was dead, which I'd already pieced together from his ranting. He said he wouldn't pay for a funeral. He couldn't afford it. He'd let the county dispose of her however they chose. He said if I wanted to say goodbye, I'd have to do it at the morgue. He didn't offer to take me. We didn't have a car. There was no way for him to take me. That was implicit, but I don't think that was the reason. He wouldn't have taken me anyway even if he had been able.

277

'But I knew of the morgue by way of young boys' stories,' the killer said. 'I knew a boy from school who claimed to have snuck in there once in the middle of the night on a dare. He said he'd jimmied a window open and crept in. He said inside it smelled of formaldehyde and other chemicals. Like a lab in school, he said, only much stronger. He said there was one room with a wall full of metal drawers. The drawers were large, he said, large enough to fit a man or woman. He knew what was inside, didn't have to open them, even though the terms of the dare said he had to. There was no one in the morgue with him. All the other boys had stayed outside. He could have just said he'd opened a drawer, and no one would have known any differently.'

Reggie was thinking of a cold white room, smelling of chemicals, and a wall lined top to bottom with metal drawers, like the world's largest filing cabinet. He was thinking of his dad, clammy and cold and dead, in such a drawer, slid away into the wall like a specimen, stored like a file.

'But he was a boy,' Ivan said, 'and like most boys he had to prove something to himself more than he had to prove anything to the others. And so he crept through the dark room to the wall of drawers, and pulled one open. He saw a woman, blue and dead, and he saw the stitches of her autopsy, where they'd sewn her back together after examining whatever they had to examine. He ran, climbed out through the window, past the other boys, and couldn't sleep for a week. He saw her whenever he closed his eyes, stitched up like some Frankenstein monster.'

Just hearing about it was bad enough. Reggie wondered if next time he closed his eyes to sleep he would see her too, stitched together and shambling along, blue tinged with the coldness of her storage.

'I thought about what my mother would look like,' Ivan said, 'as I walked the mile into the city where the morgue was. I wondered if I'd recognize her. I wondered if she'd leap up and snatch me as I looked at her. Pull me into the drawer with her and slide it shut, shutting us in the dark together forever, where she'd hold me in cold, dead arms.'

That the two of them had shared such grim thoughts disturbed Reggie. It was almost as if he and the killer shared a wavelength or were tuned in to the same signal. He didn't like this, and tried mightily to change the station.

'The morgue itself was a drab, grey building of concrete and brick,' Ivan said. 'It reminded me of a small bunker. There was a giant pipe coming out of the roof. A crematory chimney that blew out this heavy black smoke every once in awhile. And there were no windows that I could see; I remember that also. Just this block of a structure with a pipe coming out of it, and no windows.'

Night fallen, the two of them could have been sitting together in just such a windowless, dark structure themselves. Save for the light of the flashlight, dim, shining towards the ground so it wouldn't give them away, the world was dark around them and above. Night sounds from the woods seemed alien and intentionally menacing, like they were being watched by stern and disapproving spectators. The blackness about them could have been walls, and the ebony sky above a shroud. Not unlike a vast mausoleum chamber – or a morgue drawer like Ivan's childhood friend had described. Even now the dead could be around them, closing in, encircling them.

'When I went inside,' Ivan continued, 'there was no one there. There was a counter, but no one manning it. I had the sudden and terrible fear that I would have to navigate the place alone, wandering down hallways, roaming from room to room, peering under sheeted mounds on gurneys until I found my mother.

'I started to panic,' Ivan said. 'My heart was beating fast. My breathing was shallow. My legs shook and the corners of my vision went grey and hazy and I thought I would faint. Then, unconscious, they'd rise, those sheeted mounds on the metal gurneys, and they'd shamble out of their rooms and down the halls, surround me, and tear me to shreds.'

Reggie took a breath, steeled himself, and intentionally stared at the dark of the woods around them. He waited for his eyes to adapt better to the darkness, so that he was able to see the vague outlines and shapes of the trees. He remembered his recent nightmare about the funeral home, the lights going out, and his dad's cadaver slithering out of the casket. The dark wall of the forest around them was just such a place the shambling, dragging dead could be moving in right now.

Inching closer. Hungry for the life they no longer had.

Refusing to give in to his fear, Reggie gazed long and hard at the woods. Reaching arms resolved themselves into hooked, gnarled branches. Eager, hungry faces into the whorls of tree bark upon thick trunks.

As far as he could tell, no zombies lurked, and this helped calm him a little.

He remembered what the singing posse leader had said just last night:

You're not afraid of the dark, are you?

Reggie had said no then, would have said the same now if asked, but it wouldn't have been completely true. Because it was easy to be afraid of the dark when sitting in it with a killer as he shared his tales of death.

'But then a man appeared,' Ivan said, continuing his narrative. 'He stood behind the counter in a black suit and he looked very official. His presence calmed me and he asked how he could help. Somehow I found my voice and told him who I was, gave him my mother's name too. He gave me a sympathetic look and motioned me through the door to the right of the counter.

'Like I imagined, he led me down halls and through doors, though not as numerous as in my head. And we came to the room of drawers that my friend had told me about, or one like it. He walked over to the wall of drawers and motioned for me to follow him. He put one hand on my shoulder as he opened a mid-level drawer with the other.'

Reggie didn't need to hear the rest of the story. He could picture it well enough.

But Ivan pressed on, and Reggie listened.

'She was naked,' Ivan said, 'which should have shocked me, but didn't. I'd never seen my parents naked. But her nudity didn't bother me. It was just very sad. There were stitched areas on her torso, and a small one on her face – injuries from the crash that the mortician had closed to make her more presentable. But she wasn't monstrous. She was just ... dead.

'I stared at her for a time,' Ivan said, 'and the man in the suit was patient. I think he thought I was mourning, but that wasn't it. I was just interested. I was wondering how this came to be: one moment my mother was alive, and the next she was dead and a thing in a drawer.

'I was seeing something for the first time,' Ivan said, his voice changing from a monotone lecture-hall tone to one of curiosity and inquisitiveness. 'I was seeing something of the world that had always been hidden from me. I knew about death, of course, but I had never *known* death. Yet now here it was, right in front of me.'

These words were familiar to Reggie. He'd heard them before. He'd *thought* them before. His train of thought had been very similar when he'd first seen his dad in the parking lot of the church, and later at the open casket viewing.

He'd remembered his dad, living and *there* and all the memories of their time together rolled up into a collage of images in his mind. And then there'd been his dad, dead in the parking lot, dead in the casket. The two things didn't fit together, seemed irreparably opposed to one another – his dad alive, and his dad dead.

Like the killer as a boy, Reggie had felt a similar sense of the mystery of it all. That with the death of his dad he was peering in through a veil that had previously always been drawn across the world. Things had been hidden from him; secrets had been kept.

Then, before his dad's lifeless form, he'd seen the truth of things. The temporary nature of everything. The fragility of life. Things lived, and things died. Those were absolutes that should have never been kept from him.

And it had been the killer – not his mom, and not his dad, gone forever – who had been the first to give voice to this dark lesson. Nearly a year after the funeral. Until this man had come along, stumbling through the forest, Reggie had been on his own, stumbling likewise himself. Trying to make sense of the senselessness he'd felt inside.

Some things lived. Some things died.

For that lesson alone, however painfully delivered, he owed the man a debt of gratitude. Or, if not gratitude ... fidelity. At least until the end.

'And it was absolutely senseless,' the killer said, breaking Reggie's train of thought. 'My mother had lived, and then she was dead, and neither state changed anything. Living or dead, she didn't matter, because I was still here. I still had to find a way through life, until I died, and focusing on her was doing nothing but wasting time.'

The killer looked at him across the pool of light between them.

Illuminated red, the man looked ghastly. This was his true face, Reggie thought. He was seeing the real thing now, not the man-mask that the killer wore to move about the world undetected.

'So I pushed the drawer shut and walked away,' the killer said. 'That was that, and now here I am.'

2.

They heard the border patrol officer coming before they saw him. Which wasn't the surprising part; the officer was calling out to them, announcing his arrival. The surprising part was that they hadn't heard him approaching until the unseen man started calling.

'*Don't kill him,*' Reggie whispered to the killer.

The killer had pulled out his pistol, was screwing on the silencer.

'*If you kill him,*' Reggie said, '*I'll run.*'

It wasn't lost on him that this exchange was almost a repeat of the incident with Jeff the hunter, who hadn't been a hunter at all. He was sure it wasn't lost on Ivan either.

And they both knew how that situation had turned out.

The killer looked at him. He had switched off the flash-light when they'd first heard the officer shouting out, but Reggie's eyes had grown used to the dark. He could see the shape of the killer, and his posture, and the man was facing him, considering.

'*If you kill him,*' Reggie repeated, '*I'll run and warn the others.*'

Reggie had come to know the killer's thoughts, to a degree. As repulsive as it was, he realized that tuning in to that shared frequency could have its advantages. Though he couldn't see the man clearly, he could sense the ideas going through the killer's head. Hell, they were the same thoughts that would be going through his head if he was in the killer's shoes.

'*If you shoot me first,*' he whispered, '*there'll be no one to help with your plan. You'll never make it across the border by yourself.*'

'*Reggie—*' the killer started, but Reggie cut him off.

'*Don't kill him,*' Reggie repeated.

'*I won't kill him,*' the killer said, and though Reggie couldn't read the honesty of his tone, there was nothing else to be done about it.

'Come on out!' the border patrol officer called again, coming nearer, but his shape still lost in the greater shadow of the trees. 'I saw you! Come on out with your hands up!'

He repeated the instructions in Spanish.

Ducking behind the nearest tree, Reggie tried to imitate

a statue, willing his body still, slowing his breathing to a near comatose rhythm.

'We saw the light!' the officer said. Reggie didn't like the use of the word 'we'. It meant others might be out there, on their way or already here, circling about. 'We know you're out there!'

Again, the officer repeated the words in Spanish.

Reggie heard a snap of twigs, a crunch of leaves. It hadn't come from him, and he knew the killer would never betray his own location so carelessly. A dim flash of light came from an easterly direction, maybe twenty yards away.

'Soon a helicopter will fly over!' the officer called out. 'It'll be equipped with heat sensitive equipment! And the pilot will radio down to me your exact position! So you may as well come out now!'

Reggie listened carefully. The night was silent save for the officer's bumbling footfalls. Maybe the border patrol officer thought he was dealing with a couple immigrants. Maybe a family. At worst, a small-time trafficker or drug dealer.

Which seemed impossible. Some sort of alert had to have gone out over the various law enforcement radio channels. Warning the search parties about the killer on the loose. But if he'd known the danger he was approaching, the officer surely wouldn't have come alone.

Crouched in his hiding place, Reggie turned his head the slightest of degrees. Far off, a faint *whup whup* sound carried through the night. A helicopter's blades cutting the air?

If that was what it was, the chopper would be over them soon.

'No one's going to hurt you!' the officer said after repeating his last words in Spanish. 'But you're here illegally, and you'll have to go back! Come out, surrender yourself, and it'll be easier on all of us!'

Again, he repeated this in Spanish for the imagined immigrants.

Reggie hadn't noticed, but the killer was gone. It was as if the man had melded into shadow. Reggie hadn't even heard him move.

He saw another flash of the officer's flashlight. Dim, he must have been covering it with a hand, thinking it hid his position.

Reggie prayed his threat to Ivan would save the man.

But he knew the killer didn't respond well to threats. He responded to nothing but his own thoughts, his own impulses, which, Reggie was coming to realize, made Ivan more dangerous than he'd ever considered.

The border patrol officer was closer. Snapping twigs and rustling leaves preceded his clumsy approach. Now Reggie could make out the shape of him. He could see the crisp outlines of the pressed uniform. The brimmed hat and the outstretched arms at sharp angles. And at the end of the arms, the pistol and the muted light of the flashlight, pointing out ahead of him.

Then the figure fell back. The motion was a fast blur. Reggie thought of a cartoon character slipping on a banana peel.

The officer cried out briefly, and then the cries were cut off. There was another short-lived rustle of branches and leaves as arms and legs flailed, before everything went still again.

The night and woods were impenetrable in their silence.

Then, separating from the night, one shadow sliding out of others, the killer emerged and was there again beside Reggie. He snatched Reggie's arm and pulled him along. Reggie resisted, or tried to, but it was like resisting a gale force wind blowing him ahead of its path.

'He's alive,' the killer said, knowing Reggie's thoughts.

'I want to see him,' Reggie said, trying to pull away.

The killer stopped pulling and instead, with one great yank, brought Reggie face to face with him. Reggie's feet dangled off the ground. The killer's eyes darted side to side, the irises bloodshot, the hollows beneath purple and sagging.

The large man looked both extremely tired and intensely aware. Perhaps running on sheer force of will. Reggie had no doubt even in this exhausted state the killer could end him in seconds.

'Listen you little fuck,' the killer growled. 'If we don't move now, that helicopter will spot us. And then they'll come in swarms. And if that happens, I can't promise that a stray bullet won't find your stupid little face.'

Reggie needed to pee. He didn't think he could hold it. He also wanted to cry, and didn't think he could hold that back either. He hung in the air and felt like a field mouse clenched in a hawk's talons. He knew then, grasped in those strong arms, more fully than ever before just how powerless he was.

'But if I get to the border,' the killer said, 'then there will be little or no killing. I'll be gone, they won't be able to stop me, and you'll go back to your pathetic life, crying over your faggot daddy. But for that to happen, you need to help me this one last time. Got it?'

Somehow, Reggie retained control of his bladder and tears. But he nodded at the killer's words. That was one bodily function he wouldn't deny the man. All he wanted was to survive. He thought that was one thing he still had in common with the killer.

Satisfied, Ivan set him down, knelt at Reggie's level.

'You understand the plan?' the killer asked him, fishing in his pocket, coming out with a lighter.

Reggie nodded, remembering what the killer had told him earlier in the day, about what they'd do when they reached the border.

'Good,' the killer said, and pointed east. 'You'll go that way, and I'll go this way,' he said, pointing west. 'It needs to be big. Like the flames of hell itself.'

Reggie nodded again.

He went east, the killer went west, and together they lit the world afire.

3.

The world shone brilliantly with the light of the blaze. It cast the ground in a red, burning coal-like glare, and lit the sky a deep and flashing scarlet. The landscape looked like a fireplace or the interior of a wood burning stove. Everything burned, flaming tongues crawling along in every direction, licking the sky and skittering along the earth.

It was frightening to see how quickly things burned. The flames seemed hungry and anxious to burn the world, licking and grasping, as if they were living things desperate for sustenance. Reggie knew it was wrong, holding the lighter underneath a leaf or branch, thumbing it and sparking it alight, and running the flame back and forth until the foliage was burning. People could be hurt or worse if the fire got out of control.

Not if, he thought to himself, *when*. That was the whole point of it; a wildfire to distract everyone, to create chaos, so that Ivan could make a break for the border. The border patrol officers and police would become firefighters, rather than immigrant or fugitive hunters. The approaching helicopter would become a wildfire watcher, radioing down instructions about burn paths, rather than watching for migrants or federal escapees.

For it to work, for the fire to build and spread rapidly, the killer had explained, they needed to light many areas, really fast. And so wanting to be rid of him, believing what he said about maybe Reggie getting shot too should they be found out and a gunfight break out, Reggie had done what he was told, running east and stopping from tree to tree, bush to bush, lighting the vegetation up like candles. The killer had done the same, running west.

Soon, the inferno spread across the earth.

The officers, border patrol and police alike, had come quickly as the flames grew. At the sounds of engines roaring to life and coming closer, and the sounds of boots hitting the ground in a rhythmic stomp, Reggie had moved inward, away from the edges of the woods where it gave way to the desert stretch leading to the border. The vehicles and boots stopped outside the woods, also, and so Reggie knew that between the climbing, dancing flames, the intermittent shadows of night, and the woods between them, it wasn't very likely they could see him.

But it was unsettling, being so close. Part of him screamed he should race to the officers and explain everything. He thought about it, looking around as he considered it. The fire made the shadows writhe eerily like dark worms, and this undulating living darkness made it somehow more plausible that the killer was somewhere out there right now, watching him. And he'd know if Reggie went to the officers, and he knew where Reggie lived, and he'd come calling someday, in the middle of the night, maybe stepping out of one of these living, roiling shadows like a phantom.

So instead of running to them, Reggie kept sparking

the lighter under the branches and bushes. When the flames were so hot he could hardly bear it, the fiery walls rising and spreading on all sides, he stopped, turned, and ran back the way he'd come. West, following the fires and the other who'd lit them, the one who he should be running from, and yet who drew him back like a dog to its master.

There were shouts from behind him, heard over the crackles and snaps of the fire. Calling after him or calling out directions to each other, he didn't know, and didn't stay to find out. The helicopter was overhead now, its bright spotlight like the eye of God. It didn't play on him, though, but away from him, dancing among the firestorm. That could change at any moment, Reggie knew, and so he ran faster.

Reggie thought he'd run in a more or less straight path when he and the killer had turned in opposite directions to start their fires. And so running back he tried to keep a straight route again. Heedless of his intent, however, the incorrigible blaze made him turn and jump and duck frantically with its every twist and turn and pop and snap, eager to light him up also, to charbroil flesh as well as burning vegetation to ash. He tried to edge nearer to where the woods met the desert, but now there were vehicles everywhere, engines revving and tyres grinding dirt as they paraded up and down the length of the woods. Shouts of *goddamn* and *holy shit* were thrown about in tones of awe.

So that when the arm found him and pulled him down,

Reggie wasn't expecting it, hadn't thought he was back where they'd parted, and he screamed when he hit the ground, screamed like a girl before he rolled over on the dirt and saw it was Ivan. The killer squatting above him, pressing him down with one massive hand on Reggie's chest, one hand clamped atop Reggie's mouth, cutting the scream short.

But he *had* screamed, loudly, and now they both froze, Reggie on the forest floor, killer poised in a half crouch, like a panther ready to pounce, and they listened. The fire was loud, its snaps like the crisp slaps of a flag in a high wind. The vehicles rolling along the earth and their engines roaring; their thuds and bumps and grinding of desert grit. The helicopter overhead; its blades stirring small tornadoes, the winds parting trees with a hurricane-like force.

Reggie's scream could have been lost among those sounds. Probably had been.

Or maybe it hadn't. Maybe now the shouts and cries they couldn't quite understand were calling the police and border patrol together for one vast raid into the woods, where killer and boy alike would be killed in a hail of bullets.

Ivan atop him, Reggie tense and breathing hard, they were silent and waited. The crackling heat of the flames was close, and crawled closer.

When the storm troopers still hadn't come some moments later, the killer hauled Reggie to his feet and took his hand from across Reggie's mouth. But he leaned close and spoke clear.

'You fucking scream like that again,' he said, 'I'll cut your fucking head off.'

Reggie nodded, feeling numb and slow as if coming out of a heavy sleep. None of this seemed real anymore. How could it be? Not a week ago, life had been mundane. Even the death of his dad had been so. The man's very absence had been real, but the pain had become a routine, just a part of the day. It was a prescribed path of life he'd come to accept, like getting up and going to school, or eating breakfast in the morning.

This, though – guns, murders, monster cats, wildfires, and police chases – was unreal. It was the stuff of movies and books, fantasy, and however many times he'd dreamed of stuff like this, now Reggie wanted nothing more than for it to be over.

The old, boring pain was preferable to this madness.

'We go a little further west,' the killer said, 'away from the checkpoint. Then we go for the border. Someone will be there, waiting for me.'

Reggie heard the 'we' and wanted to say something in defiance. He didn't want to go any further with this man. Fuck the responsibility he'd felt earlier when the killer had passed out and Reggie had run, only to stop a short ways and turn back.

With the killer's very presence, Reggie could feel the ticks and tocks of his life clicking away, like the second hand on a clock. Even being near this man was to tempt and invite suffering. Every moment he was with the killer was another that could be his last.

And Reggie knew now with a certainty that he wanted to live a little longer.

The killer started walking again, and Reggie resignedly followed. His legs weren't his own. His mind not his entirely, either. The fear controlled him. Or maybe Ivan had tuned in to that shared frequency, and now controlled the dial. At the controls, working the dials and knobs, the killer had found he controlled not only the signal, the thoughts in Reggie's head, but the body as well. Punching in commands and operating him like a machine.

The killer beside him had one hand in his jacket, working idly there under the fabric. As if caressing something; the switchblade that had dug out the bullet, maybe, or the garrotte wire, or the gun, the pistol. Reggie remembered it well, and its muzzle, the black eye.

No, the killer controlled the situation, but not through some psychic manipulation. It was through violence and threat of violence that he commanded things. But Reggie was minding the details, watching things, and waiting.

The blaze was behind them and about them. The world red and afire.

At the edge of the woods they looked out; a stretch of desert and the fence there at the end of it. So close and yet so far away. The police cars and border patrol Humvees there to the east, their headlights washing over the desert

295

soil and along the treeline. Far but not far enough, Reggie thought. Then the killer was moving again, and a handful of Reggie's shirt in his fist, Reggie was moving with him.

Here we go, he thought, waiting for the bullet that would stop him, that would end him, and the only thing Reggie could think about was if it would hurt, and whether he'd get to see his dad again.

Chapter Thirteen

A long with the gunfire and the heat of the bullets passing dangerously close – kicking up dirt around them like mortar fire on a battlefield – there was the large shape Reggie saw moving almost parallel with them a bit to the west.

It was low and fast and glowed at the eyes with reflected firelight. He wondered if this was the feline demon returned from hell, sent to retrieve him for the part he'd played in the events of the past days. Because he knew that now, if he hadn't known it earlier, which he thought he did but had just ignored.

He'd indeed played a part.

The death the killer had brought with him was partly on Reggie's shoulders. He had been complicit in it. Allowed it by his very inaction. But more than that, Reggie now acknowledged that his responsibility had started that very first day in the woods when Ivan had stumbled out, holding his bloodied gut. Even then, he'd known something was wrong about the man.

Reggie, wallowing in his own selfish grief, just hadn't given a shit.

Now, however, he definitely gave a shit. When the killer – sick, paranoid, and frantic – racing across the desert towards the border fence, shiny-slick with infection, feverish again and pulling Reggie in tow, inexplicably turned, pointed towards the police and border patrol, and started shooting … Reggie gave many shits.

At the same time the yellow eyes to the west drew closer, the thudding of its enormous girth across the earth like a colossus striding upon the land. Reggie turned to it, saw not the giant demon-cat risen again, but a Humvee jouncing across the pitted, uneven landscape. Men in the passenger seats leaned out of windows, holding rifles.

One long barrel lowered in Reggie and the killer's general direction.

Moving before thinking, Reggie did a crazy little pivot-dance, barrelled sideways into the killer, and sent them both tumble-tripping through a tangle of thorny bramble. An instant later a small thunderclap cracked in the night, and a sharp, hot breeze buzzed past Reggie's head.

Yanking him back on course, the killer turned towards the jeep, emptied the pistol at it, reached in his jacket, found another magazine and jammed it home into the stock. The Humvee careened off to one side, dipped fast and hard into a divot in the earth and rolled over in a plume of dirt. Men shouted out in surprise and pain.

None of this had been necessary, Reggie thought, running. Not Ivan's shots at the border patrol, and not the officers' return fire. They'd been halfway to the fence, unseen, and Reggie thought they'd have made the other half likewise undetected.

Looking at it all from this perspective, out of the woods, seeing the entire range of it, the depth and breadth of it, the fire the two of them had started was immense. It was impressive and frightening to realize he'd helped start such flaming chaos. The tips of the conflagration reached the firmament and reddened the star-speckled heavens, so that the very sky itself was like a great tapestry catching fire.

No one had initially seen them because everyone was watching this inferno dance and leap across the land.

Yes, Reggie thought, they would have reached the border just fine.

The killer would have made it through the fence with the help of his friend on the other side, Reggie would have been free of him, started the trip back home, and it would all be over. He would have climbed in his bed, pulled the covers around himself, and slept as long as sleep would have him. Then he'd wake up, go downstairs, and give his mom a hug, maybe not let go of her for awhile.

But then the killer had turned, pistol in hand, and pulled the trigger. Whether out of fevered paranoia and confusion or pure malevolence, Reggie would probably never know.

299

Yet even feverish the killer was a deadly marksman. Telling himself only to run, Reggie nevertheless turned to watch.

He saw the headlights and flashlights and the helicopter's searchlight criss-crossing the desert and forest. He saw the muzzle flash of the killer's gun. He heard the shouts of pain even above the *whup whup whup* of the copter's blades.

There were curses and more shouts. And then the night erupted in gunfire.

As the first Humvee skittered and rolled, two others broke through the night, headlights glaring, to take its place. More heads, arms, and rifles leaning out windows. More coughs and barks of fire as the men pulled the triggers.

The earth pockmarked about Reggie, torn and bitten by the snatching bullets. He heard a smack nearby, saw the killer stumble, regain his footing, turn and fire again, even as he lurched towards the border fence. It was a strange dance the killer performed – pirouettes, leaps, flourishes – as they raced towards the fence line.

Something struck close to Reggie's foot. He felt something like a pebble knock against his shoe. He wanted to shout at them. He wanted to wave his arms. He wanted to give some indication that it wasn't he who'd shot at them. He wasn't the killer. He was just a boy that wanted to get home.

And yet he was deathly afraid that any move he made other than running would single him out as a primary target. Following that blunder, instead of shooting some-what wildly in their general direction, all the bullets would be coming right at him.

But he couldn't just stand in the way of such a flurry, either. He couldn't just hope he'd not be hit. So Reggie dove, hitting the ground with a forearm-and-knee-shredding slide to put any bottom of the ninth World Series game winning runner to shame.

He heard another smack as he crawled. Ahead of him he saw the killer stumble and stagger again, only to regain his footing, turn, and return fire. Reggie kept his face to the ground. Dirt was in his face, in his nose, in his mouth, and he didn't give a shit.

In fact, if there was shit on the ground he'd gladly keep his face in it as well. He didn't want the bullets to hit him. He didn't want to die. He wanted to get back home again. He wanted to see his mom again. And if he did it with a mouthful of shit, that was just fine by him.

Ground level, feeling like a bug looking up at the land of giants, he saw Ivan reach the fence. There was indeed someone on the other side. The myriad lights of the police and border patrol were now flashing in their direction, scanning the desert for them. By the outer reaches of these lights Reggie caught flashes and vague details of the figure on the opposite side of the fence. It was large and it was working on the fence with a V-shaped device like tree limb clippers.

Then a portion of the fence was pulled and drawn back.

The killer stepped through. Killer ahead, would-be killers behind, Reggie struggled to his hands and knees and followed, scuttling through the opening like a roach into a trap.

2.

Passing through the opening in the fence it was as if they'd passed from one world to another. The bullets stopped flying immediately. Even in his young mind Reggie knew about national borders, but the change was so fast, so immediate, it was startling. As if someone had thrown a switch that turned the insanity on and off.

But the officers were still racing up behind them; the angry, persistent stomping of booted feet, and the clatter-thud of the vehicles over the uneven, unforgiving desert ground a discordant rhythm. The lights followed Reggie and Ivan through the fence and into Mexico, tracing their path.

Having the strange notion that being identified would somehow further 'entrap him in the situation – like an aborigine frightened of the camera that would steal his soul – Reggie covered his face with his forearms, staggering forward after the killer and his guide, and away from the searching, prodding lights. Radio crackle and shouts faded behind him.

After a time they dropped into an arroyo. The decline was steep and though Reggie tried to manoeuvre slowly and cautiously, he ended up on a slide down it on his ass. At the bottom Ivan was sitting, breathing hard. The guide had a flashlight out and was aiming it at the killer. Reggie followed the pointing light and gasped.

Ivan's left leg was in shreds at the thigh. Strings of flesh and meat hung like bits of cheese hanging from a grater. His left arm was dipped in red like he'd immersed it in a deep can of paint. The guide, though Mexican, spoke in English.

'*You did not say you'd have half the state of Arizona after you*,' the Mexican man said in thickly accented yet finely enunciated English. He spoke in a whisper, staring at Ivan's wounds in an awestruck terror. '*You don't look well my friend*,' he said, sounding like Reggie felt. Dark terror and tired resignation jostled for position on the Mexican's face.

'Just get me to the safehouse,' the killer muttered. His face was pale and gleamed with a sheen of sweat so that he seemed a melting wax figure of a human, and not a man at all.

'I can do nothing for you, my friend,' the Mexican said. 'This is beyond me.'

With a sad, slow shake of his head, the Mexican turned, started to walk away.

'Don't,' the killer said, raising his gun. 'You've been paid. You have a job to do. You're going to do it.'

The Mexican turned, having heard the threat in the killer's voice. He eyed the gun, his flashlight spotlighting it as if to validate that it was pointed at him.

'You would really kill me?' the Mexican said, his expression and tone again mirroring Reggie's own silent thoughts. What the man was really asking was *What did I get myself into?* And maybe *Why am I here?*

Ivan pointed the pistol towards the Mexican's feet, pulled the trigger. There was a flat click and nothing else. The Mexican gave a wan smile, turned, and continued walking. Beside Reggie, the killer fumbled in his jacket for another clip. He found one, ejected the spent magazine from the pistol with shaky hands, and slid the new one in. He pointed and aimed with a wobbly, uncertain arm.

A distance away, the Mexican scaled the wall of the arroyo and was gone, taking his light with him, leaving Reggie and the killer alone in the night, in their hole, all the dark, silent world about them.

***

'This wasn't how things were supposed to be,' the killer told him in the darkness.

After the hail of bullets and the roar of engines and the stomping of pursuing boots, the quiet in the ditch was a stark contrast. From such clamour and chaos to such silence was a startling thing, like stepping from a bustling lobby into an empty elevator cab, the doors shutting off one world from another. In the dark silence Reggie could hear a wet patter, a steady drip, and he realized it was the sound of Ivan's blood smacking the dry desert ground.

Are You Afraid of the Dark?

The killer's hand found Reggie's, and he didn't pull away.

The man's fingers were wet and slippery. There was a soft squelch when the killer's hand squeezed Reggie's, and a warm moisture seeped between his own fingers, crept along the lifeline of his palm.

'I want you to know that,' the killer said, his voice hoarse and gruff. His breathing was slow and laboured and Reggie thought of a huffing bear settling in for the winter's hibernation. 'I just couldn't go to prison,' he said and coughed. The coughing was short-lived but moist and harsh. 'So I got away from them, and found you.'

'That's a lie,' Reggie said, surprised at his own boldness. 'You knew that people might get hurt when you escaped. You knew you might hurt me when I found you in the woods. You hid in the tree house because you thought it was safe. But if the time came when it wasn't safe anymore, and you had to do something about me, or my mom, you'd have done anything you had to, to save yourself.'

The killer didn't answer, and Reggie didn't give him a chance to anyhow.

'You chose to be what you are,' Reggie said. 'Maybe the way your dad treated you had something to do with it. Maybe your mom dying had something to do with it too. Maybe being on the streets, and then getting picked up by the old man, played a part. But I don't think any of those things did it by themselves.'

Without their own flashlight, lost at some point in the gunfire, the night was at first thick between them. Then the black veil between them lifted a bit as Reggie's eyes adapted to the dark.

He could see the walls of the arroyo, rising crater-like in the night. He could see the scattered weeds and growth about the ground. And the killer beside him; a silhouette, a shape, humanlike but vague in form. Like an afterimage of where a man used to be, steadily fading.

The killer was watching him – that Reggie could also see. The whites of the man's eyes hung in the night like ghostly orbs. The eyes were desperate, though still holding a hint of their old ferocity. Reggie waited for the bullet or the strangling hand. When neither came, he kept talking.

'Because you freely gave yourself away,' Reggie said. 'It was your choice. You got in the car because you wanted to. You do what you do because you like it. Anything else is just excuses.'

In his mind it wasn't Reggie speaking. In his head, for some reason, the voice he was hearing sounded like his dad's. He could even imagine he was sitting on his bed, and his dad was sitting there too on the edge of the mattress. His dad was telling him these things. Reggie's mouth was moving, doing the speaking, but he was really just taking dictation and then reciting what he heard.

'When you hurt people because you like it,' Reggie said, 'you become something less than human. You're an animal.'

The wet, bloodied hand holding his tightened and Reggie thought, *Here it comes, here it comes*. There'd be a firecracker pop, maybe, when the gun fired, just before the bullet shattered his skull. Or the squeezing bloody hand would leave his, and rise like a cobra before finding his throat, striking and choking.

But neither of those things happened. He wasn't shot or strangled.

After a few moments, the wet hand let go, withdrawing. Though they could see each other vaguely now, there was another veil settling between them. A wall rising, or a gulf opening, separating one from the other. Reggie felt it, and knew the killer did also.

It was Reggie at the dials and knobs, now, controlling the frequency between them. Finding the station he wanted, and turning up the volume. Drowning out the former that the killer had dialled them into.

They were no longer in this together. Whatever had happened between them only a few short days ago when Reggie had stumbled upon the gut shot man in the woods, whatever had developed over their talks together, was fading.

'You're evil,' Reggie said. 'I hate you.'

And with those five words spoken there was a new understanding between them, a new deal negating the old. Signed, sealed, delivered, each awaited their just due.

3.

There was a stillness to things when the killer lost consciousness. Reggie thought perhaps the man was dying when he started to cough and the man's body wracked with chills and shivers. Hearing such distress and pain, Reggie's first thought was still *Get him to a doctor! He needs a doctor!*

Then he thought of the people the killer had murdered. The ones he'd told Reggie about: the woman running with her son from her husband; his own sister; the dozens of photographs showing the multitudinous dead, like a demented child's flipbook. Those he'd witnessed: Deputy Collins; the second deputy in the woods, hogtied and helpless. And the undoubted many others – dozens, hundreds? – that the killer had never told anyone, much less Reggie, about. Those unnamed that would never be missed by the world at large, though maybe, perhaps, missed by a husband or wife, a son or daughter.

In this suspension of all things Reggie thought of his dad, shot and killed in a parking lot. The criminal's vast potential heist of sixteen dollars in change scattered about the asphalt, forgotten in a drug-induced panic. Somehow that was as insulting as the sum itself: the money forgotten, left there like change tossed to a hobo in passing.

With these thoughts what last remaining compassion rattled about inside him for the killer faded away. The man trembled, the man moaned, and Reggie sat by not giving a damn. The killer pissed himself in his shakes and shudders, the astringent smell bitter and sharp, and Reggie smiled to himself at the man's indignity. Soon after, the killer's tremors slowed and stopped, his moans quieted, and for one frightful yet intoxicating moment, Reggie thought him dead.

He leaned over, listened for breathing. He thought he felt or heard the slightest exhalation, like the briefest of breezes through a slightly parted window. He set a hand on the man's chest, felt or thought he felt the slightest of risings and fallings.

Then the killer was still, dying but not yet dead; unconscious, sleeping, but not the last Big Sleep.

Reggie's eyes settled on the gun in the man's right hand. The hand flopped like a landed fish on the ground having breathed its last. Or a dead spider upturned, legs bent and lifeless. He reached out slowly.

His fingers touched the pistol, and he sucked in a breath. They curled around it, and he let the breath out. He lifted the gun and brought it to himself, and his heart hammered.

The killer didn't bolt awake. Didn't even stir.

Reggie settled back down with the pistol, examining its shiny black surface. Held it close to his face to see it in the deep night. He tested its weight in one hand, then the other. It was both lighter than he remembered from the first time he'd fired it in the woods and heavy at the same time. It's very *purpose* it seemed to Reggie was what made it heavy.

He remembered firing at the water bottles. He remembered them being *yanked* out of existence by the slugs. He remembered the absence of the space where the bottles had been.

309

Reggie held the pistol, considering these things, and waited.

***

When the killer finally stirred, then awoke, he felt among his jacket pockets, like a man trying to locate his wallet. But it wasn't anything as benevolent as a wallet he was looking for. Looking up, he saw Reggie standing above him, and found the object of his searching.

'Always mind the details,' Reggie said.

The killer stared at the pistol in Reggie's hands with intent interest.

'It's after midnight,' Reggie said. He didn't whisper the words, but his voice was soft and lowered, as if he were speaking in a library, centuries of the knowledge of man bound in shelves around him. 'Like when you killed that woman and her son.'

The killer, despite his wounds, despite his already waning life, was alert. He didn't try to stand, but he manoeuvred himself to a more upright position.

'That was a long time ago,' the killer said.

'You know who else was killed after midnight?' Reggie asked. 'My dad,' he said after a pause.

'I'm not the one that killed your dad,' the killer said.

'No,' Reggie said. 'But it was someone like you.'

The killer didn't say anything in response to that.

'And if he had been a target,' Reggie said. 'If someone

had paid you to kill him, you would have, wouldn't you?'

The killer nodded.

'Yes,' the killer said. 'I would have.'

'For murdering people,' Reggie said, 'you deserve to die.'

The killer nodded again.

'But you don't want to be the person to do it,' the killer said. 'Take it from me. When you kill someone it never leaves you. You never forget a person when you take their life. They stay with you forever.'

Reggie could detect no lies in the killer's tone. He wasn't trying to talk his way out of the situation. He was just telling the truth as he saw it.

'You try to sleep,' the killer said, 'and you see their faces. You walk in a crowd, and a passing face looks like theirs. You always see them. You can never get away. I've tried to many times, in many ways, and I can't.'

Reggie held the pistol in two shaking hands. He tried to steady them, but they wouldn't settle. He stared down the sight of the gun at the killer, and the killer looked back up at him. Across that bridge there was an exchange, unspoken, unseen, and as real as anything passed between hands.

'I think I'm dying anyway,' the killer said. 'Even if you don't shoot me, I have to make it across this desert and find someone who can help me. A doctor – a surgeon – who can help a man shot multiple times and with widespread infection. What do you think my chances are out here?'

Reggie didn't say anything.

'Leave me alone,' the killer said. 'Go back across the border, leave me here, and I'll probably die anyway. There's no need for you to shoot me. There's no need for you to take the burden on yourself.'

Reggie still said nothing. But his hands were steadying. The killer's face was centred by the pistol's sightline.

He heard the killer take a deep and expansive breath.

'We had a deal,' the killer said, without conviction, as if he knew the answer to this proclamation anyway.

Leaning to one side, holding the gun in his right hand, Reggie found his backpack, zipped it open, and removed one of the last things he'd put inside before leaving the house what seemed an eternity ago. He tossed the wad of money back at the killer, watched it bounce and settle in the man's lap, where it sat curled like a dead creature.

'Deal's off,' Reggie said.

The killer breathed deeply again, and they both heard the loud, moist gurgle from somewhere inside him. The broken hidden pieces sputtering their last.

The killer looked first one way, then the other, then turned his gaze back on Reggie. Even dying, the man's eyes glinted with their cold, blue light.

'I'm lying,' the killer said, his voice hardening and taking on a flat tone. 'If I live, I'll come back someday and hunt you down. Even if you move to another town, I'll find you. Even if you change your name, I'll find you.'

The killer rose shakily to his feet. His ruinous leg, the meat and flesh hanging from it, the white bone peeking out from it, straightened and bore his weight.

There was a squelching noise as he stepped in something wet beneath him.

'The deputy was right that day,' the killer said. 'He was telling you the truth. The day I escaped from the police, I also raped and killed a woman. If I live, I'll find you and your mother, and I'll rape her before I kill you.'

Reggie's gun-bearing hand – his entire body – was calm. He felt as if all the world had silenced and stilled itself for his benefit. His eyes seemed to filter the night even better, so that the shapes about him grew sharper and more defined. The killer wasn't merely a shadow of a man anymore, but a man, whole and clear standing before him. He could make out the contours of the killer's clothing, the features of his face.

And the eyes, formed as if by arctic ice.

'I'll make you watch,' the killer said. 'I'll make you watch as I rape her. Then I'll make her watch as I kill you. It'll be slow. I'll make you watch each other suffer.'

Somehow, Reggie knew the killer was lying. He hadn't raped anyone the day he'd escaped. That wasn't how the killer did things. That wasn't the business he was in. Yet, Reggie was surprised to find that it didn't matter. He didn't care.

Lie or not, rape or murder, the threat was true enough. The man's very life was the threat. Every breath he drew, every day he lived, was a day of potential terror for someone else.

There was movement at the top of the arroyo wall. Without turning his attention away from the killer, Reggie watched in his periphery as a low shape stepped up to the edge of the drop.

The mangy dog sat and stared down at the scene. The killer heard the movement and saw the dog, giving it a cursory glance before turning his attention back to Reggie.

'Kill me,' the killer said. 'Or I'll kill you.'

He blinked once, like an invalid giving a signal, an affirmation, and Reggie obliged and pulled the trigger. The loud crack echoed through the night, and the killer slumped over, dead. From his face a new hole spilled forth a red, soupy gruel.

The dog watched from her perch above, and Reggie, dropping the pistol, climbed up to meet her. They headed across the dark desert together back towards the border, silent companions on a grim journey.

4.

They entered their own country through the hole in the fence without trouble. No border patrol or police waited to arrest him. The boy wondered about this, and then he remembered all that had happened in the past week, and

314

wondered about it no more. The world was the way it was, and there was no sense, no rhyme or reason to it.

He followed the highway home rather than trek through the woods. Some sign of civilization – be it as simple as a road – seemed important to him at that time, and it calmed him, the way it stretched over the gentle roll of the desert into the horizon.

The dog walked beside him on the long, harsh road, and there was a cursory comfort that he again had a friend in this wide and desolate world. Yet even this weak hope was heavy laden by the knowledge that it wouldn't last.

Nothing in this world does, and that was okay. Save the memories of fleeting, better times, and the anticipation of more to come, there was nothing worth preserving.

And no matter what he did in the years to come until the end, it was the blood he remembered most, pouring into the desert sand. The red dirt, the red earth; life in its unbecoming.

Undone, forever gone.

Chapter Fourteen

1.

The stain upon the asphalt was still discernible from the surface around it even after all this time. That seemed fitting to Reggie. Blood shouldn't be so easily scrubbed away, as if nothing had happened.

His mom stood beside him over the dark spot, giving his hand a squeeze before letting go. The mangy mutt sat in the space between them, having given the dark blot a single perfunctory sniff before shying away from it.

The FOR LEASE sign hanging in the church's window was new. Everything else looked the same, if a little run-down. Paint along the adobe walls flaked away in places. Along the roof's gutters the occasional tile hung askew, blown or battered by desert winds and rains.

Surprisingly, the place was worse in Reggie's mind, where thoughts and fears mingled into nightmares creating realities that had never existed, than it was in person. The church was neither a place of God, where the Almighty dwelt among his children, as he'd been raised to believe, nor a house of death, where his father's wake had been held and Reggie had spied the waxen corpse in the casket that had haunted him the past year.

It was just a building, weather-worn and slightly dilapidated.

'You okay?' his mom asked, and Reggie nodded.

He knew that simple question referred not simply to what they were doing now, standing at the site of his dad's murder. It also signified everything that had happened in the past few days.

Returning home after the shoot-out with the border patrol, Reggie had arrived to find his mom waiting for him on the porch. The glow from the porch light revealed the note from his desk in her hands, clutched fiercely like an heirloom.

He'd told her everything. Finding Ivan in the woods. Nursing the man's injuries as best he could. Deputy Collins coming to the house and the struggle that followed. How Reggie and the killer had disposed of the man. The false trails laid through the woods to put the police off of Ivan's track. The excursion into the woods and crossing the border.

And, finally, the killer's death.

'We don't have to do this now,' his mom said as they stood over the old stain, even though it had been Reggie's idea. 'We've got all the time in the world.'

But that was exactly it: they didn't. Time was catching up to all of them, and no one got away. He had to do this now, today, because there was no telling what tomorrow would bring.

'I'm fine,' Reggie said, startled to realize that this was actually the case. Or, if he wasn't exactly fine, he was getting there.

He knelt, touched the darker spot on the asphalt. It was warm under the Arizona sun, and he kept his fingers there for a few moments, letting that warmth chase away the prior coldness that had been inside him for awhile.

After listening to the whole story that night on the porch, his mom had rejected Reggie's suggestion to call the police. It would make no difference, she said. The killer was dead across the border. The things the man had done were over, and there was no way to undo them.

What about the things I did? Reggie had asked.

You've got your whole life to make up for them, she'd said. *You can't do that from juvenile hall or some halfway house.*

This wasn't an evasion or an excuse. Reggie could see that in the stern set of her face and the firm gaze with which she considered him. His days of wallowing in self-pity were over. She would expect many things from him in the coming days, months, and years. And he would expect them from himself.

Together, the three of them – mother, son, and dog – turned away from the old building, crossed the parking lot back to the car, and got in. As they turned out onto the highway, Reggie cast one last glance in the rear-view mirror, watched as the church shrank in the distance.

Summer heat was baking the street, wafting up in distortion ripples. For a moment the colourless currents seemed to take a vaguely human form, and it seemed to nod or wave in their general direction. As if in parting or farewell or approval. Deciding this was something worth believing in, Reggie smiled, closed his eyes, and allowed himself to be carried forward into whatever tomorrow would bring.

Keep Reading ...

If you enjoyed *Are You Afraid of the Dark?*, make sure
you've read Seth C. Adams's previous novel ...

We were so young when it all happened. Just 13-years-
old, making the most of the long, hot, lazy days of
summer, thinking we had the world at our feet. That
was us – me, Fat Bobby, Jim and Tara – the four
members of the Outsiders' Club.

The day we found a burnt-out car in the woods was the
day everything changed. Cold, hard cash in the front
seat and a body in the trunk ... it started out as a
mystery we were desperate to solve.

Then, the Collector arrived. He knew we had found his secret. And suddenly, our summer of innocence turned into the stuff of nightmares.

Nothing would ever be the same again ...

Acknowledgements

Thank you to Tamara Thorne and Dean Koontz for impressing upon a young writer the importance of the technical side of writing (syntax, grammar, etc.). Though not the sexiest part of the job, it's at least equal to the creative aspects in the pursuit of delivering to the reader a quality story. And thank you to Kathryn Cheshire and Janette Currie, editors extraordinaire, for their eagle-eyed attentiveness to early versions of the manuscript. Everything right with this novel is in large part due to these four individuals. Any shortcomings are solely on the shoulders of the author.